Praise ... the Blood Coven V...

"Dark, delicious, and full of surpr... series is like vampire candy. Readers will devour every bite!"

—Heather Brewer, *New York Times* bestselling author

Bad Blood

"A vampire book so worth reading, with dark humor, distinctive voice, and a protagonist clever enough to get herself out of trouble . . . A great ride."

—Ellen Hopkins, *New York Times* bestselling author

Girls That Growl

"An amusing teenage vampire tale starring a fascinating high school student . . . Young adults will enjoy growling alongside of this vampire slayer who has no time left for homework."

—*Midwest Book Review*

"A fast-paced and entertaining read." —*LoveVampires*

"A refreshing new vampire story, *Girls That Growl* is different from all of those other vampire stories . . . a very original plot." —*Flamingnet*

continued . . .

Stake That

"A fast-paced story line . . . both humorous and hip . . . A top read!"
—*Love Vampires*

"Rayne is a fascinating protagonist . . . readers will want to stake out Mari Mancusi's fun homage to Buffy."
—*The Best Reviews*

Boys That Bite

"A wonderfully original blend of vampire/love/adventure drama which teens will find refreshingly different."
—*Midwest Book Review*

"Liberal doses of humor keep things interesting . . . and the surprise ending will leave readers bloodthirsty for the next installment of the twins' misadventures with the undead. A ghoulishly fun read."
—*School Library Journal*

"A tongue-in-cheek young teen tale starring two distinct, likable twins, the vampire between them, and a coven of terrific support characters who bring humor and suspense to the mix . . . Filled with humor and action . . . insightfully fun."
—*The Best Reviews*

Berkley titles by Mari Mancusi

NIGHT SCHOOL

BAD BLOOD

GIRLS THAT GROWL

STAKE THAT

BOYS THAT BITE

Night School

Mari Mancusi

BERKLEY BOOKS, NEW YORK

THE BERKLEY PUBLISHING GROUP
Published by the Penguin Group
Penguin Group (USA) Inc.
375 Hudson Street, New York, New York 10014, USA
Penguin Group (Canada), 90 Eglinton Avenue East, Suite 700, Toronto, Ontario M4P 2Y3, Canada
(a division of Pearson Penguin Canada Inc.)
Penguin Books Ltd., 80 Strand, London WC2R 0RL, England
Penguin Group Ireland, 25 St. Stephen's Green, Dublin 2, Ireland (a division of Penguin Books Ltd.)
Penguin Group (Australia), 250 Camberwell Road, Camberwell, Victoria 3124, Australia
(a division of Pearson Australia Group Pty. Ltd.)
Penguin Books India Pvt. Ltd., 11 Community Centre, Panchsheel Park, New Delhi—110 017, India
Penguin Group (NZ), 67 Apollo Drive, Rosedale, North Shore 0632, New Zealand
(a division of Pearson New Zealand Ltd.)
Penguin Books (South Africa) (Pty.) Ltd., 24 Sturdee Avenue, Rosebank, Johannesburg 2196,
South Africa

Penguin Books Ltd., Registered Offices: 80 Strand, London WC2R 0RL, England

This book is an original publication of The Berkley Publishing Group.

Cover design by Springer Design Concepts.
Interior text design by Tiffany Estreicher.

PRINTING HISTORY
Berkley trade paperback edition / January 2011

Library of Congress Cataloging-in-Publication Data

Mancusi, Marianne.
Night school / Mari Mancusi.
p. cm.
Summary: After learning that their ex-hippie parents are actually fairies, vampire Rayne and her twin sister Sunny are forced to hide out in a secluded Swiss boarding school for vampire slayers that, the twins discover, is hiding some secrets of its own.
ISBN 978-0-425-24042-7
[1. Fairies—Fiction. 2. Vampires—Fiction. 3. Twins—Fiction. 4. Sisters—Fiction. 5. Boarding schools—Fiction. 6. Schools—Fiction. 7. War—Fiction. 8. Switzerland—Fiction.] I. Title.
PZ7.M312178Ni 2011
[Fic]—dc22 2010029806

PRINTED IN THE UNITED STATES OF AMERICA

10 9 8 7 6 5 4 3 2 1

To my Blood Coven Vampires in Training

Hugs, kisses, and vampire blood!

www.bloodcovenvampires.com

My Story Thus Far . . .

~~My name is Rayne McDonald and I am a fairy princess.~~

Argh! I can't even say that without feeling sick to my stomach! I can't be a fairy princess—I'm the antithesis of a fairy princess. Fairy princesses—in their pink, gossamer gowns and filmy, ethereal (and probably pink) wings—should fear me as a deadly creature of the night. A vampire. Not to mention a vampire slayer. (Long story, don't ask.) My clothes are black, my hair is black, hell, my soul might even be black at this point.

Not pink, for God's sake. Never pink!

But I'm getting ahead of myself here. For those of you just joining us, it's been a long, strange trip so far. Starting with the day, last spring, when I was still just your typical high school Goth girl with a thing for vampires. Team Edward and all that, LOLz. Except I took it one step further—I met up with a real vampire coven and signed up to become one of them. (It's really easier than you might expect, as long as you don't mind all the homework.) The certification takes three months of classroom time and then they do a bunch of background checks—sampling your DNA and running your blood. It's all very high-tech and sophisticated these days. After all, no one wants to give a diseased mass-murderer, who can't spell, e-t-e-r-n-a-l l-i-f-e, right?

Needless to say, I was approved. But on the night of my selected undead birthday—the dumb-ass vamp, Magnus, who was chosen to become my immortal beloved accidentally bit my identical twin sister, Sunny, instead! (Yes, yes, we're Sunshine and Rayne. Hippie parents—or so we'd always thought.) Of course my oh-so-innocent, field-hockey playing, drama-loving, (up until this point) normal-as-can-be twin sister had no idea vampires even existed. And let's just say she was so not pleased about being told she'd be turning into one of them by the end of the week. So she and my intended had to go on this big adventure to England to find the Holy Grail and reverse the transformation all before prom. During the process, go figure, they fell in love. (Which was fine by me. Magnus is a bit of a tool and so not the type I want to spend eternity with. I need someone way more dark and brooding.)

Six months later, they're still together—though recently things have become a little dicey after Magnus, who's now master of the Blood Coven, almost found himself a new blood mate to help him rule. Fortunately for Sunny, that didn't work out so well for him in the end. And now he swears the two of them will be together forever and no other vampire or mortal will come between them. (I'll believe that when I see it.)

But anyway, back to me. At this point, I'm still human, still blood-mate-less and if that weren't enough, one day our drama teacher calls me in to tell me that I'm the next vampire slayer.

(Yes, just like on that *Buffy* show.) Can you believe it? The girl voted most likely to go vamp—finds out she's destined to kill them for a living? And I couldn't even say no—seeing as they oh-so-sweetly informed me that I was injected with some kind of nano-virus when I was born that they can activate at any second if I decide to go AWOL.

Luckily, the gig involves slaying baddie vamps only. And certainly not anyone from the upstanding Blood Coven itself. Which is a total relief, considering staking your twin sister's BF in cold blood is a good way to get you blacklisted from any and all future family reunions.

In any case, during my first mission as slayer, I hooked up with Jareth, the Blood Coven General and Magnus's right-hand vamp. At first he was kind of a pain in the neck, if you excuse the pun, but in the end, I discovered he was simply misunderstood. Kind of like me. He saved my life, too; the evil vampire I was commissioned to slay managed to inject me with a deadly blood virus (yes, everyone and their mother is out to poison me these days) and I was fading fast. Until Jareth bit me, that is. The good news? I'm finally the vampire I always wanted to be. The bad news? Because of the blood virus, I'm powerless as a little lamb. Sigh. At least I got one benefit the other vamps don't have—I can go out in the sun. Which totally helps me when I'm on slayer missions like saving our town from werewolf cheerleaders . . .

But forget about them. We've got bigger problems now. Like our estranged parents telling us they're actually not ex-hippies who escaped from a commune to live a more yuppified life, but magical fairies who escaped from a mystical Irish island, to live a more . . . mortal one. And now, it seems, the other fairies back home have tracked Sunny and me down. And want us to return to them.

We never saw it coming.

1

It's Friday night, Las Vegas, Nevada, and Sunny and I are feeling pretty darn awesome. After all, together we just saved the Blood Coven (yet again) and have been proclaimed heroes of the free vampire world. In other words, life is good.

Okay, fine, technically Sunny did most of the actual saving of the coven. I was, um, well, let's just say I have been a bit preoccupied. (I mean, Vegas, baby! Those penny slots don't just go and play themselves, you know!) But hey, I swung by at the pinnacle moment and saved the day, so that has to count for something, right?

In any case, evil's been vanquished, Magnus and Sunny are back together, and hell has frozen over (aka my mother and father are in the same room together, actually speaking like civilized adults.) We've returned to stepmom Heather and Dad's luxury condo after watching this *Dracula* revue Sunny is starring in. (She did a good job, I have to admit, though the play's dialogue was more than a little cringe-worthy.)

So here we are, hanging out in the contemporary-styled living room, sipping mugs of steaming green tea, assuming soon we'll go to bed and wake up in the morning and head home to Massachusetts, Vegas adventure over for good.

We couldn't be more wrong.

"So guys," Mom says, settling down in a small, white leather chair. It must kill her vegetarian butt to sit on a dead, skinned animal like that, but she's too polite to call Heather out on her barbarian ways. "You're probably surprised to see me here in Vegas."

"Uh, yeah," I say. I mean, understatement much? "What's the deal? Did you miss us too much? I mean, really, Mom, we've only been gone a couple of days. But I know how you can be about your daughters." I pause then add, "Unlike *some* relatives I know," while shooting Dad a glare. He squirms in his seat, obviously uncomfortable, which is fine by me. Any guy who's perfectly willing to abandon his daughters for years on end should, by right, feel a little prickly about it.

Mom shakes her head, as if she wants to defend him but knows as well as I do the guy isn't exactly up for *Dad of the Year* any time soon. "I wish that were it, Rayne."

Her pale face suddenly has me worried. Right before we left for Vegas, my Slayer Inc. guardian, aka David, Mom's boyfriend, told me that his company had word of a new threat sweeping into town. A threat that might be against our mother.

There's more to your mom than you know, David had told me.

I shiver.

"Mom, what are you trying to say?" Sunny asks, before I can find my voice. "What's going on here? Are you in some kind of trouble?"

I catch Mom and Dad exchanging glances. He nods at her, urging her to continue. "Look, let's just say things aren't exactly . . . safe . . . for us in Massachusetts anymore," she says, seeming to choose each word with care. "That's partially why I was so willing to have you two come out here this week. I figured it'd keep you out of harm's way until I figured out our best move."

"Mom, you're scaring us," Sunny says, her face white as a ghost. "What's not safe?"

Mom swallows hard. "You have to believe me—the last thing I ever wanted was to involve you two in any of this. In fact, that's why your dad and I moved to Massachusetts to begin with. I didn't want you to grow up in the world we did. I wanted us to be a happy, normal, everyday family. And they left us alone for so long, I'd really begun to think that we'd actually escaped them for good." She bites her lower lip nervously. "But now, war has broken out between two families and they're demanding we return to aid them in their fight. And if we don't, they have promised to make things very difficult for us."

I raise an eyebrow. Is she going to tell us we're like part of the mafia, or something? Do they even have Scottish mafia?

"I don't understand," Sunny cries in that high-pitched Minnie Mouse voice she gets when she's freaking out. "Some family feud? Why do they need us for that?"

"Dear, you're speaking to them in riddles," Dad chides our mother gently. "It's best if you just tell them the whole story, no matter how hard it will be to believe at first." He turns to us. "Look, guys, we've always told you that you come from Irish and Scottish ancestors, right? Well, there's a little more to it than that. Our families are actually descended from a people living on a small island off the coast of Ireland, known as Tír na nÓg." He pauses, then adds, "Some know us as the Sidhe."

I stare at him, horrified. Sidhe? Does he mean like . . . ?

"What the hell is a Sidhe?" Sunny demands.

But I know what Dad's going to say before the words leave his mouth. "The term you might be more familiar with," he tells Sunny gently, "is fairy."

WTF?

"So let me get this straight," I interject, my mind whirling to make sense of it all. "You're trying to tell me that we're descended from fairies? Actual fairies?"

"We're not just descended," Mom clarifies. "We're full-blooded fairies. And now the royal court is demanding we return to fairyland immediately."

"Or else," Dad adds, "they have promised to kill us all."

The room is silent. You could hear a pin drop. Mom wrings her hands together worriedly. Dad bites his lower lip. Sunny looks as if she's going to pass out. Poor girl—she just went through a life-or-death supernatural situation and now we're back there all over again.

I shake my head in disbelief. Fairies. Actual fairies. It's hard to wrap my head around. I mean, sure, I always figured since vampires and werewolves are real there's got to be other things out there going bump in the night, but I never thought they'd turn out to be close relatives.

"Look," Dad says, breaking the silence. "You don't have to worry. It's not going to come to that. We'll figure out a diplomatic solution to all of this. You'll see."

"And it won't involve us moving back to fairyland," Mom adds, taking a sip of her now-cold tea. "I can promise you that. No daughters of mine are going to grow up to be fairy princesses, that's for sure."

I raise an eyebrow. "Princesses?"

"Oh." She blushes. "I guess I didn't mention that part. Before I ran away, I was technically a fairy princess. Heir to the Light Court throne. Your dad was my bodyguard. We fell in love, but my parents disapproved. They wanted me to marry Apple Blossom, general of the royal fairy army."

"Apple Blossom?" I snort. "He sounds, um, real masculine."

Mom shrugs. "Fairy names are all like that. I mean, your dad's real name is—"

"ANYWAY!" Dad interjects, effectively cutting her off. "I wasn't about to let your mother go off with that slimy Rotten Apple. So we eloped and left fairyland behind forever. We had our wings surgically removed and your mother soon became pregnant with the two of you. We thought we'd live happily ever after."

"Except you left," I remind him pointedly. "Before, you know, the *ever after* part."

Dad hangs his head. "Yes," he says. "As it turns out, fairytale romances aren't always able to survive the harshness of the real world."

I open my mouth to retort, but Mom effectively cuts me off. "You have to understand," she continues, "we'd never been outside fairyland before. And we definitely weren't prepared for what we found there. With no money, no skills, no education—heck, we didn't even have social security numbers—we soon found ourselves in dire straits. Like any other illegal immigrant, we struggled to find work and put food on the table for you two. It was a tough time and our relationship suffered because of it."

"We were so young and stupid," Dad says, shaking his head. "It's hard to believe we thought we could make it on our own with no help."

"But you did," Sunny reminds him. "I mean, obviously you must have worked it out somehow. We live pretty well."

My two parents look at one another and smile. "Thanks to Heather," they say in unison.

Sunny and I glance over at our stepmom, who up until now has been quiet. She nods. "Guilty as charged," she quips, raising her right hand. "I was able to relocate them."

"Heather works for Slayer Inc.," Dad explains, shooting me a knowing look. "In their fairy division. They help out fairy refugees trying to make it in the real world."

I stare at my stepmom, pretty sure my jaw has dropped to the floor at this point. Heather works for Slayer Inc.? And here I thought she was a stripper or something. Also—they have a fairy division?

"Heather was able to secure us our first apartment in Massachusetts, new jobs, social security numbers—the works," Mom says, looking over at the woman formerly known as Home Wrecking Bitch with grateful eyes. "She saved all our lives. We wouldn't be here right now if it weren't for her kindness."

"And so you went and made a baby with her to show your gratitude?" I query sarcastically.

Dad's face turns bright red. He glances over at our mother who is also blushing furiously.

"Back then even though we were living as humans, we were still thinking like fairies," she confesses. "And fairies—quite simply—believe in the free expression of love. We'd both grown really close to Heather after she literally saved our lives and so, at the time, it just . . . seemed natural, I guess."

I stare at her in disbelief. Here I thought Mom was going to be torn apart if she knew of Stormy's existence. But it turns out she not only knew—she approved of it, too!

Seriously, fairies are worse than hippies!

"Of course then I made the mistake of telling one of the PTA mothers about the whole thing," Mom remembers with a sheepish cringe. "You should have seen the look on her face. I started to worry that we'd done something wrong. Something that would make us stand out as different—maybe even give away our whereabouts to the Light Court. So I told your father he had to stop seeing Heather altogether. And that we could never tell you two the truth about your half sister."

"And that's why Dad ended up leaving with Heather in the end?" I conclude. "He couldn't deal with being apart from her?"

But Dad surprises me with a shake of his head. "Not exactly," he says, reaching into his pocket and pulling out a piece of paper. After unfolding it, he hands it over to Sunny and me. I scan through it, my eyes widening at its contents.

"A contract?" I ask, looking up.

"About four years ago, our cover was blown and the fairies found us," he explains. "Your grandmother was still furious at me—a commoner—for taking her daughter away. I begged them to leave us alone and finally she agreed, with one stipulation. I had to step out of the picture." He hangs his head. "I knew your mother would try to stop me if I told her the situation. And I loved her too much to let her put her own life—and yours—in danger because of me. So I packed up my things and moved to Vegas—with Heather serving once again as my Relocator." He shook his head. "It was the hardest thing I've ever had to do in my entire life."

I stare at him in disbelief, my heart in my throat. All these years I'd assumed he'd taken the easy way out. Ditched his family for a younger woman, living the life of luxury while we struggled to move on in a fatherless existence.

Was it all true? Had he really done it all to protect us?

Had I been hating my dad all these years for no good reason?

"I know I missed a lot of birthdays," Dad adds, his voice thick with regret. "But I didn't know how much contact they'd allow me without getting angry again. And I didn't want to inadvertently destroy the wonderful lives your mom had built for you. So I watched from afar and tried to move on, best I could." His voice chokes on the last sentence. "But I missed you guys so much," he adds. "Not a day has gone by when I didn't want to call you or visit . . ." He trails off and both Mom and Heather lean over to console him.

I look over at Sunny, who's about as wide-eyed as me right about now. In fact, I don't know which is more surprising: that we're really descended from fairies or that Dad isn't quite the bastard we've always believed him to be. It's truly a toss-up, to be honest.

I decide to concentrate on the fairy part. I need more time to digest the rest. "So Sunny and I are princesses," I interject. "Then why don't we have wings? Or, I don't know, magical powers or something?"

"Because you've never been through the ritual," Mom explains. "Once a fairy hits puberty, they're supposed to go through a magical ceremony to kick-start their transformation. It involves a lot of nonsense, like kissing your elbow."

"Is that even possible?" Sunny asks, trying to maneuver her arm into elbow-kissing position. Mom's eyes widen and she roughly grabs my sister by the hand.

"Sunny, this isn't something to play around with!" she scolds. "If you become a fairy, there's no turning back." She glances at Dad. "Even without our wings, we still retain our powers. Though, of course, we never use them."

"Never?" Heather teases, looking straight at our father.

"Well, just once in a while," Dad adds, a little sheepishly. "When I can't find my keys . . ."

Sigh. Does *everyone* in this freaking world have "powers" except for me?

"So let me get this straight," Sunny says, pulling her hand back. "Dad did what they said and now they *still* want us back?"

Our father nods.

"But why do they care? Is there a fairy shortage or something?"

"In a sense, yes," Mom replies. "A couple weeks ago, we're told that Dark Court agents invaded and killed your grandmother, the Light Court queen."

Oh my God. "Grandma's dead?" I cry. "And . . . wait . . . she was a fairy?"

Dad and Mom exchange glances. "Actually, the woman who lives down in Florida isn't your real grandmother," Dad confesses. "When you two were young, we . . . well, we wanted you to still have some sense of extended family. So we hired a few actors to play the parts. Grandma, Aunt Edna . . ."

I swallow hard, feeling my world crash down all around me. Everything I thought I was, everywhere I thought I knew, has all been a lie. My stomach swims and I'm this close to throwing up.

"In any case," Dad continues, "the throne of the Light Court is now empty. And they need to crown the next in line."

Sunny turns to Mom. "So . . . you're supposed to be the new fairy queen?" she asks, eyes wide.

"No, Sunny," Mom replies gently. "*You* are."

2

"This is so not good. So not good!" Sunny moans as she hits disconnect and sets down her cell phone after leaving her gazillionth message for Magnus to *please, please call her*. After attending the play, her vampire boyfriend had hopped on his private plane back to New England, where the Blood Coven's headquarters are. He'd be incommunicado, he'd told her, for at least five hours. At the time, it hadn't seemed like a big deal; Sunny had assumed she'd spend a peaceful night with Mom and Dad—a rare treat—and then jump on a plane herself the next morning to join him back home.

Now everything has changed. Our lives have been flipped upside down. And not being able to share the news with Magnus is tearing Sunny apart. My own boyfriend, Jareth, is also traversing the world somewhere without cell phone service, but, to be honest, I am in no great hurry to mention the skeleton wings in our family closet. I mean, fairy princess? Could there be anything more embarrassing for a self-respecting vampire? After all, everyone knows real vampires don't sparkle.

After hearing the news, we somehow convinced Mom and Dad to let us out of the condo for a few precious moments of decompression. We'd found a local diner and gotten a booth, each ordering a cup of coffee to keep the waitress Nazi at bay. I'd have preferred a vodka straight up but unfortunately my fake ID was confiscated last night at the Excalibur and also as a vampire I can't get drunk, so the spirits would be worthless anyway.

"Sunny, relax," I tell my twin as she bangs her head against the table in frustration. I look around and catch the waitress eyeing us suspiciously from across the room. "It's going to be okay."

Sunny looks up, tears streaming down her cheeks. "In what freaking universe do you live that any of this could possibly be okay?" she demands.

"Uh," I look down at my mug and notice a faint stain of pink lipstick on the rim. Good point.

"Why does this keep happening to me?" Sunny wails. "First I get turned into a freaking vampire. Now I find out I'm an effing fairy princess!"

"At least you'll probably find the fairy wardrobe preferable," I mutter, wishing she'd keep her voice down. "Lots of pink?"

Sunny shoots me a glare.

"All I want to be is a human." She sniffs. "A normal, everyday human who grows up and goes to college, gets married, has babies, and lives in a four-bedroom two-and-a-half-baths house with an open kitchen, granite countertops, and a pool out back. Is that so wrong?"

"It's pretty specific, but I guess it's not wrong," I say, reaching out to her, squeezing her hand. "But you know, Sun, we can't always get what we want."

"Please don't start quoting Rolling Stones songs. Seriously, I will stake you."

I let go of her hand. "Look. You gotta have faith. And no—" I hold up a hand "—I'm not quoting George Michael, so don't even start. Dad's working on it and he's assured us that everything will be okay."

"Like how he assured us he'd be there for our birthday last spring?" Sunny asks pointedly. She picks up her cell phone. "I'm going to try Magnus again. Maybe he had a stopover . . ."

I give up, pushing away from the table and throwing a handful of change down for my un-drunk, lipstick-stained mug of coffee. "You know you're not even supposed to be telling anyone any of this, remember? Dad and Mom were both pretty clear on that. They said it could be dangerous."

"It's not *anyone,*" Sunny says, phone to ear. "It's Magnus. If anyone can help, he can."

"Of course. All while simultaneously achieving world peace and solving the nation's financial crisis, I'm sure," I mutter. To my sister, Magnus is not only coven master, but Superman, Batman, and the Incredible Hulk all rolled into one. "I'm going home."

I can hear her scrambling after me as I stalk out of the diner, and another stab of pity bites into my gut. I don't mean to be short with her—she has every right to be upset about the situation. But I hate that she won't let me help her. I'm her twin—I'm supposed to be there for her. Yet all she cares about is her stupid boyfriend. Sigh.

She catches up, but still has the damn phone glued to her ear so I ignore her and cross the street, taking a right into Dad's condo building. I hear her leave yet another codependent message as she steps into the elevator behind me.

"I hope he didn't get in a plane accident," she comments worriedly as the doors slide close. Argh. If I didn't love my hair so much, I'd be pulling it out until I was bald right about now.

As the doors slide open on the seventeenth floor, I grab her by the shoulder and turn her to face me. "Look, I know you're upset," I say, my voice as stern as I can make it. "But try to suck it up in front of Mom and Dad, okay? They're doing all they can and Mom's clearly freaking out. So don't go and make her feel even worse."

Sunny scowls. "I won't. Geez. Give me a little credit here."

Shaking my head, I push open the apartment door. Dad and Heather are sitting together on the couch with Mom in a nearby chair, eating a big bowl of popcorn and watching that eighties movie *Ferris Beuller's Day Off*. Mom bursts out laughing.

"Oh that Ferris!" she says, giggling. "He's such a scamp."

"Clearly freaking out, huh?" Sunny mutters in my ear.

"So, uh, what's the plan anyway?" I ask. Dad grabs the remote and pauses the movie and the three of them look over at us, surprised.

"Your mother and I are going back to fairyland tomorrow," Dad says, "to plead our case. You guys are going to stay here with Heather."

"What about school?" Sunny asks. "We're supposed to go back Monday."

"Consider it a bonus vacation. I'll talk to your teachers," Mom replies.

"But I've got a field hockey game on Tuesday!"

"Then you'll have to miss it," Dad butts in firmly. "I'm sorry, but you can't go back. It's not safe."

"The court knows where you live," Heather adds. "Their soldiers have been watching the house. If you hadn't had that super security system installed, I'm not sure your mom would have gotten out so easily."

David. I've had my squabbles with Mom's new boyfriend, but thank goodness he was there for Mom while we were away. I should have never come to Vegas in the first place after he told me she might be in danger. What kind of slayer/daughter does that?

"Then when can we go home?" Sunny cries, sinking into a nearby chair, her face ashen. I realize she's back to thinking about Magnus again.

Mom rises to her feet and goes over to give her a hug. "I don't know, honey," she says, smoothing her hair. "But we're together and that's the important part. And there's no way the fairies know we're here."

Suddenly, as if on cue, a weird thundering noise assaults the apartment. Like the buzzing of a thousand bees. I look over to the window and my jaw drops as I see a shirtless man hovering outside, peering in . . .

Beating his wings.

"Um," I say, pointing. "Are you sure about that?"

3

The window shatters before anyone can answer me. Though to be fair, it was kind of a rhetorical question anyway. I duck, hands over my head, to avoid the raining shards of glass, as six tall winged men float into my stepfamily's living room, sinking down into the plush white carpet. Each, I might add, armed with flaming swords, unlike any I've seen outside an RPG video game.

The fairies have landed.

And just FYI, if you're thinking "fairy" means the kind of lithe, lispy, glittery creature you might find at a David Bowie tribute night, let me set you straight: These guys are built to the max. Broad shoulders, expansive chests, six-pack abs, and muscular legs. At the same time, each one of them is oddly . . . pretty, I'd guess you'd say . . . with chiseled cheekbones, wide eyes with long lashes, and blindingly white teeth. Like Disney animated princes sporting wings.

Delicious but deadly.

A black-haired fairy—the spitting image of Cinderella's Prince Charming, though a lot more pissed off—steps forward, his flashing dark eyes bearing down on my mother.

Mom stands her ground, shoulders back, a fierce mama-bear expression taking hold of her usually serene, hippie-chick face. A trill of pride spins down my spine as I watch her stare the big, bad invaders down, ready to protect her cubs at all costs.

Yeah, take that, fairy man. My *mom's no shrinking violet.*

"Princess Shrinking Violet?" the fairy addresses her.

Uh . . . Well, you know what I mean.

"Sir Apple Blossom?" Mom replies, through clenched teeth.

My eyes widen. This is the hottie Mom was supposed to marry back in the day? And she chose *Dad* over him? I mean, sure, I'm glad she did, seeing as we'd never have been born otherwise, but *damn* . . .

Apple Blossom continues, "We have come for the girls."

I hear a squeak of fear to my left and turn to find a white-faced Sunny hunched up beside me, literally shaking with fright. I grab her by the arm, pulling her close to me.

No one steals my Sunshine. At least not without getting through me first.

Or my dad, it seems, for that matter. We watch as our father steps protectively in front of us. "I am their father," he says in a voice that leaves no room for argument. "And you will take them only over my dead body."

Wow. For a guy who never remembers to send a birthday card, Dad can really turn up the parental protection vibe to eleven when he feels like it. I glance over at Sunny, who's staring at our father like she's never seen him before.

"Over your dead body?" Apple Crisp smirks. "I think that can be arranged!"

On cue, his friends unsheathe their flaming swords. Seriously, how is the sprinkler system not going off at this point? If we survive all this, I'm so complaining to building management . . .

"Violet—catch!" Seemingly out of nowhere, my dad somehow manages to produce a pair of swords of his own (though sadly, neither one appears to be on fire) and throws one to my mother, while wielding the other himself. Hippie, dippy Mom—who is always lambasting Mario Brothers as too violent a video game—catches the blade with ease, like she's freaking Lara Croft or something. Behind her stands Heather, who has also somehow managed to commandeer a sharp-looking sword. Where do they get these wonderful toys?

"Sunny! Rayne! Run!" Mom cries, without turning around.

What?! I can't run. After all, I'm a slayer. Not to mention a vampire. And I guess, if you want to be technical, a fairy to boot. There's no way I'm bowing out of this fight.

I consider searching the evidently well-stocked luxury condo/ armory for another secret sword, but then get a better idea. As Mom, Dad, and Heather engage the fairies, I dive across the room to my purse. Digging in, I toss away Caesar's Palace poker chips, orange gum, and a really cool Living Dead Doll I found at a small Goth shop way off the Strip, looking for the pièce de résistance.

My stake.

My fingers wrap around the smooth wood, just as Apple Pie and Ice Cream manages to plow through Heather and lunges at me. I whirl around, stabbing with all my might, stake straight to the chest.

Okay. Good news and bad news.

BAD NEWS: Fairies don't "poof" into an easy-to-sweep-up pile of ashes when pierced through the heart by a wooden stake like vampires do.

GOOD NEWS: With enough force, wooden stake to the heart = hurts like hell, even without the whole handy-dandy poofing side benefit.

The fairy bellows in a mixture of rage and pain, clutching his heart as he falls to the ground, blood gushing from his chest. After a moment of convulsing, his eyes roll up into his head and he lies still. Nausea sweeps over me—killing fairies is a lot messier than killing vampires—but I swallow it down. No time for puking when my family's still in mortal danger.

It's then that I realize everyone's stopped fighting and is staring at me. "She killed Apple Blossom!" cries the smallest of the fairies.

"Oh God, Rayne! What have you done?" Mom whispers hoarsely.

I look at the fairy, then at my parents, confusion warring inside of me. "What have I done?" I reply. "I . . . saved . . . I mean, I protected . . ." What's going on here? Weren't we fighting to the death?

"Get her!" the fairy cries. The five remaining creatures take flight, swarming in my direction, swords blazing. I suck in a breath, hold up my stake, wondering how the hell I'm going to kill all of them at once.

"No!" Mom suddenly cries, leaping in front of me, just as the fairies start dive-bombing me. They slam into her instead and her thin body crumples like tissue paper as she falls to the ground.

"Mom!" Sunny screams from behind me. It takes me a moment to realize I'm screaming, too. In fact, I can't stop. And I can't look away, either. Mom. White as a ghost, not moving at all. Is she . . . Could she be . . .

I can feel Dad grabbing me and dragging me away from the action. "We're going to Plan B," he shouts at Heather, who's busy facing off with the remaining fairies.

"Plan B?" I whirl around. "What's Plan B?"

But Dad doesn't answer. Instead, he reaches into a bag and blows some sparkly dust in our direction.

What the—

I accidentally inhale some of the dust and my lungs seize up. I start choking, my vision fading fast and my muscles atrophying at an alarming rate. "Don't fight it," I hear Heather say, as blackness races toward me at top speed. "I'll see you on the other side."

"Mom!" I cry one last time before succumbing to the encroaching night.

There's no reply.

4

I wake to the sound of birds, cheerfully chirping to one another in a nearby tree. Probably gossiping about some worm one of them managed to procure, just by getting out of bed early. So annoying. I try to pull the pillow over my head to drown them out, but then remember I'm supposed to be in Vegas, a place where even birds see the merits of sleeping in.

Birds . . . feathers . . . fairies . . . It all comes racing back to me. Flashes of wings, flaming swords, and screams of pain. My mother, jumping in front of me to shield me from the fairies' blades . . .

I sit up with a jolt. "Mom!" I cry.

"Shh," Heather says in a soothing voice. I look over to find her sitting in a small folding chair, by the side of my bed. "You're safe."

Heart in my throat, I glance worriedly around the room, not recognizing anything I see. Where am I? Not Heather and Dad's apartment, that's for sure. My stepmom would never approve of such Spartan decor. Plain white walls, two twin beds—one on which I'm lying—a pile of boxes in the corner, and a small window. Outside I can see the tops of what appear to be large pine trees, blowing in the wind.

Definitely not Vegas.

"Where are we?" I demand. The place smells like bleach, like a hospital ward. But I don't appear to be injured in any way. "Where's Mom? Where's Dad? What happened to the fairies?" The questions spill from my lips, fast and furious, and I realize I need to stop asking and allow Heather a chance to answer.

Heather swallows before replying, her eyes betraying her concern. "Those were messengers of the Light Court," she explains. "Evidently the prime minister has grown short on patience, waiting for your parents to turn you over to the court to begin your training. He decided to take matters into his own hands."

My mind flashes back to the dive-bombing fairies, with flaming swords, slamming into my mother, hitting her square in the chest. She crumples to the ground, writhing in pain.

"Is Mom . . ." I trail off, not being able to vocalize my greatest fear. A large lump wells up in my throat and tears blur my vision. "I mean, is she . . . ?"

Heather reaches out and touches my arm. "She's alive," she assures me. "It's very hard to kill a fairy, unless you wield weapons of iron. Something other fairies can't touch."

Relief washes over me like a tidal wave. My mother and I have had our moments, that's for sure, but at the end of the day, she's like my best friend and I love her to death. If anything were to happen to her . . .

I shake my head. I can't even think that way. "So where is she then?" I demand. "I need to talk to her!"

"That won't be possible. She and your dad surrendered to the fairies and were escorted back to fairyland."

Horror slams into my gut and I feel like I've had the wind knocked out of me. "Wh-why would they do that?" I cry.

Heather gives me a steely look. "To buy me enough time to scurry you two away." She glances over at the other bed and I suddenly realize the lump under the blankets must be my sister.

On cue, Sunny sits up with a start. "Where am I?" she cries, looking around, her tear-stained face white with fear.

Heather gestures for her to cross the room over to my bed. "They call this place Riverdale," she explains. "Hidden deep in a remote valley, nestled within a large mountain range in the Alps, only a handful of people know of its existence."

I stare at her, shocked beyond belief. Not only are we not in Vegas anymore, we're not even in the United States? That pixie dust crap must have knocked me the hell out.

"It's a type of boarding school," Heather continues as Sunny joins us on the bed. "Run by an international affiliate of Slayer Inc. Here, they prepare teenagers to become slayers. Assassins who police otherworld creatures who don't follow the rules." She looks over at me pointedly. "But you know all about that, right, Rayne?"

Well, that answers the question on whether she knows I'm a slayer. But does she know about my other . . . condition . . . as well? I mean, Slayer Inc. vice president Teifert does, but he swore to secrecy. (Seeing as not everyone in the organization would be pleased about having a vampire–vampire slayer on the payroll.)

I decide it's best not to ask, just in case.

"A school for slayers?" Sunny pipes in. "What about that whole 'once a generation is born a girl destined to slay vampires' thingie?"

"Yeah, that would make for a pretty small graduating class," I add.

Heather chuckles. "The 'once a generation' thing was a pretty idea, but a totally outdated methodology for all practical purposes," she explains. "The otherworld has grown exponentially over the years—with new vampires, werewolves, fairies, and other creatures that fall under Slayer Inc.'s policing jurisdiction. Obviously it's not realistic to rely on only one slayer for all that. So they introduced slayer charter schools to train multiple potentials."

"Hang on," I interrupt. "I never went to any sort of school."

"We do things a little bit differently in America," Heather explains. "Our VP of operations, Charles Teifert, prefers to train his slayers one-on-one."

"So then why did you bring us here?" Sunny demands. "Why are we at a school for slayers now?"

Heather looks surprised at her question. "Because it's the best place to hide you from the fairies," she explains. "Until your parents are able to work things out."

I open my mouth to object, but at that moment a knock sounds on the door. "Come in," Heather invites and a moment later a big, burly guy with arms full of boxes enters the room.

"These are the last," he informs our stepmom in a heavy German accent. "Where would you like them?"

Heather gestures to the pile of boxes in the corner. "Right there is fine," she says. "The girls can unpack at their leisure."

My eyes widen as my stuffed Skelanimals bat, Diego, falls out of the top box as the mover sets his load down. "Our stuff?" I cry, realization hitting me with the force of a ten-ton truck. "You brought our stuff? How long do you think we'll be stuck here for anyway?"

Heather shrugs. "I can't really say. A few weeks? A few months?

Hopefully less than a year." She shoots me a sympathetic look. "Unfortunately there's a lot of bureaucracy in the Seelie courts. Sometimes conflicts can really drag on."

"Where's the phone?" Sunny interjects in an urgent voice. "I need to make a call."

"Sorry," Heather says. "No phones. We're miles away from any cell towers and there are no landlines on the premises either."

Sunny stares at her, horrified. "What?"

"It's for the best," our stepmom adds. "It's vital that no one knows you're here. Even those you think you can trust. If word got out to the court, they'd come and take you away immediately. And all your parents' negotiations would be for nothing."

"But Magnus . . . My boyfriend . . ."

"I'm sorry, Sunny. But it's for the best. Really," Heather soothes. Then she rises to her feet. "I need to get going," she tells us. "The helicopter is waiting. We'll send word when we can." She reaches out to hug me and Sunny. My sister pulls away angrily, staring down at her hands. Heather sighs. "I know you're upset," she says. "But you have to trust me. This really is all for the best." And with that, she turns and walks out of the room, leaving Sunny and me alone with our boxes.

My sister flings herself at her bed, collapsing in tears. I feel her pain. This situation sucks big time. I can't believe they locked us away in some kind of weirdo slayer boarding school with no telephone and I'm sure no Internet access either.

And worse—no blood substitute.

I swallow hard. I've been surviving on Blood Synthetic since Jareth turned me into a vampire back in the spring. (Yes, real blood is just too "ew" for this vegetarian.) But there's no way on Earth they're going to have some kind of *True Blood*–type thing in stock at a school for slayers, right? And any regular food will just make me puke.

Which basically means I'll either end up starving to death within the first week of being here or have to resort to switching to real blood. And let's just say snacking on one's schoolmates probably isn't the best way to make homecoming queen . . .

In fact, it might even get me staked.

5

My troubled thoughts are interrupted by a loud cry of anguish from across the room. I'm on my sister's bed in two seconds flat, pouncing on her with my best twin sister hug. "Are you okay?" I murmur, squeezing her tight.

"Of course I'm not okay!" she sobs into my shoulder. I pet her back, trying not to think about her runny nose seeping onto my delicate spider web sweater. "I had just gotten him away from Jane finally. And I gave up Jayden for him. We were supposed to go home and live happily ever after. It's so not fair."

Oh geez. I push her away. I should have known. While I'm busy suffering snot stains and worrying about the fact that my very existence on the planet may soon be coming to an extremely violent (or at least hungry) end, my dear sister is, once again, only concerned with her love life.

I guess I shouldn't be surprised. I saw how freaked out she

was when she was trying to reach Magnus last night. The girl couldn't even bear being incommunicado for a five-hour plane ride. Now she's faced with the very real possibility that she may not hear Maggy Waggy's *sweet wittle* voice or see his *zomg so beautiful* face for nearly a year.

I realize she's glaring at me—I must have pushed her a little harder than I meant to. After all, while I may not have vampire super-strength, I *have* been working out a lot at the Oakridge High gym since becoming a cheerleader. "Sorry, Sun," I say with a shrug. "I know it sucks. But what can we do?"

She flails back onto the bed, staring up at the ceiling miserably. "The worst thing is he won't even know where I am. Or why I didn't come home. What if he thinks I've changed my mind? That I ended up running away with Jayden or something?" She swallows hard. "And what will Jayden think, for that matter? I told him we'd still be friends. He's going to think that was just a line to get rid of him."

I bite my lower lip. While I'm not a fan of the angsty love-triangle melodrama she's spouting, I have to admit she does have a point. After all, technically Slayer Inc.'s the only one with the GPS coordinates on our whereabouts right now. And it's not like they're going to send out the secret location of their vampire-killing school to the local coven, even if we asked nicely.

Which brings me to my own immortal beloved. What's Jareth going to think when he comes home from his international coven relations trip next week to find out my whole family's disappeared without a trace? He's got to know something's not right; he's the Blood Coven General, after all. Will he send out the troops for a worldwide hunt? Put my face on a blood carton? What if he gets lonely waiting for me to come back and decides to find himself another blood mate or just a human girl on the side?

I shake my head, not wanting to think of that, and reluctantly turn my attention back to my sister. "How can I survive a year without Magnus?" She's wailing. "I might as well be dead."

Sigh. Seriously, if she were narrating this story, you'd probably start seeing the same blank pages that *New Moon* had after Edward left Bella. (Which, I might add, was a terrific waste of trees, especially considering how many of those books there are.)

"May I remind you, sister dear," I say, rising from her bed, "that two days ago you were ready to break up with your little vampire boyfriend 'cause he was all blood mating with another chick? And now, suddenly, you're telling me life is meaningless and empty without him by your side?" I shake my head. "Come on, Sun, even you've got more spine than that!"

Sunny opens her mouth to retort—or maybe start crying again, who knows—but a knock on the door cuts her off. I glance over nervously. Who could it be? Evil fairies bent on our destruction? Or just more movers?

The knock sounds again. "Sunshine? Rayne?"

I grab a box of Kleenex off the dresser and toss it in Sunny's direction. No need for whoever it is to see her so tear-stained. Then I turn back to the door. "Come in," I say.

The heavy door creaks open and a curly orange–haired girl who looks a lot like Little Orphan Annie peeks her head inside. I squint my eyes at her. I swear she looks vaguely familiar, though I'm positive I would have remembered if I'd seen that haircut before.

"Hi guys!" she cries with a chirpiness that does indeed make me think she may, at some point in the future, be belting out a rousing rendition of "Tomorrow." Not exactly the type of girl you'd expect for a Slayer in Training. But then again, these guys hand-picked super-size Bertha, so their selection process has always been a bit suspect, if you ask me.

"I'm Lilli! Welcome to Riverdale! Or as we like to call it, Slay School! It's so great to have you! We don't have any twins here! You're the first!"

(Yes, in case you're wondering, she really does speak entirely in exclamation marks. Which, I can tell, isn't doing much for my dearly depressed sister's nerves. Or mine, for that matter.)

"Wow, besides your hair color, you're, like, totally identical, huh?! That's so neat! Do you ever play switcheroo?! Like when you're on dates with your boyfriends!?"

On cue, Sunny breaks into a fresh set of tears, pulling a pillow over her head. I cringe. Oh great. She had to say the "B" word.

"Is she okay?!" Lilli asks me, wide eyed and concerned as she glances over at my mopey sister. "Did I say something wrong?!"

"She's *fine.*" I kick the lump under the covers in the vicinity of my sister's butt. "*Right*, Sunny?" The last thing we need is to get a reputation of being whiny little emo bitches our first day here. "She's just a little cuckoo for cocoa puffs right now."

"Oh my God, I totally understand!" Lilli replies, shooting the Sunny "lump" a sympathetic look. "I was soooo homesick when I transferred here six months ago. Did you guys transfer, too?!"

"Actually," I say, "until now I've been personally trained by the vice president of Slayer Inc. himself." I look at her smugly. There. That ought to be worth some kind of street cred, right?

"Oh, right. You're part of *that* Slayer Inc. group," Lilli says knowingly.

I cock my head in question. "Is there more than one Slayer Inc.?" I had no idea.

"Well, technically they're all under the same parent company," Lilli replies. "But each franchise has its own rules. Like your group, for example. People here call them vampire sympathizers."

I stare at her. "Vampire sympathizers?" What is she talking about?

"Yeah, I mean, you have to be a pretty evil vampire doing some pretty evil things to get yourself slain by one of Teifert's slayers," she explains. "Here at Riverdale, they're not so forgiving. They believe the only good vamp is a dead vamp. And they teach their slayers to stake first and ask questions later."

She gives me such a knowing look I have to suppress a shiver. This is not good. Now I'm not only stuck in a school with no blood substitute, but I'm in danger of getting staked by the student body at a moment's notice. I really need to keep my immortality on the down-low here.

Lilli shrugs. "Well, um, anyway, I'm here to escort you to the main office! Headmistress Roberta has summoned you and you do NOT want to keep the headmistress waiting!"

I'm not sure this is entirely true for either myself or my sister. After all, we're just witness protection fairies here, not slayer students worried about tardy slips. But I guess for our cover's sake it's best to go with the flow. Besides, to be honest, I'm curious to see what's behind Dorm Room Door #1. Not to mention get a reprieve from Sunny sobbing.

So I drag my sister out of bed, force her to wash her tear-stained face, then follow Lilli out of the room. We step out into a richly decorated corridor, with textured plush carpet of a shadowy, crimson shade. The walls are paneled with dark, oily wood and golden-framed portraits of teenage girls brandishing stakes hang on every surface.

"These are our sisters of the stake," Lilli explains, catching my curious glance at the paintings. "Slayers from ages past. Some of them have truly amazing histories. Like this girl Abigail Williams. She took out an entire nest of evil vampires waiting to pounce on her Puritan village in Salem, Massachusetts in 1692. Of course the stupid townspeople called her protection wards the devil's work and burned her at the stake as a witch. Dumb assses."

She shrugs. "Of course that was before Slayer Inc. was officially formed and sanctioned as a vampire protection agency. Back then, it was every slayer for herself." She turns to the next portrait. "Like with Amelia Earhart here. She staked vampires all around the world, but got drained dry on her last mission—a renegade coven setting up shop on a small island in the Pacific." She gives Amelia a pitying look. "The cannibal vampires ate every bite of her and her co-pilot. Their bodies were never found."

"Are all famous women throughout history actually slayers?" I ask curiously.

Lilli laughs. "Of course not," she says. "Some of them were vampires. But don't bring that up to the professors. They get a little touchy about that kind of thing."

I'm about to ask who, but she changes the subject as we head down a set of sweeping *Gone With the Wind*–type stairs and into a large, chandeliered foyer below, relating in way too much detail how the school was founded a hundred years ago and has trained some of the top slayers in the world, including Sally Ride, first slayer to tackle vamps in space.

Our guide pushes open the heavy double front doors and we step outside onto the grounds. The air is fresh but crisp, and I notice Sunny wrapping her arms around herself. As a vampire, neither heat nor cold bothers me much, but I mimic her actions just the same. Don't want Slayer Lilli, as sweet as she seems, to develop any suspicions as to my mortal state.

"Sorry," she says, glancing over at us. "I forgot to warn you. It gets really cold here. Especially at night." She shoots us a sympathetic look, then launches back into the tour. "There are two dorms on campus," she continues. "The one we just left houses all the girls, and the one over there is home to all the male slayers." She points to a nearly identical Gothic structure across the road. "Obvs, they want to keep the co-ed hooking up to a minimum. Which is too bad, 'cause some of the boys are completely hot."

I look at her questioningly. "There are male slayers?" I ask, surprised. I thought this gig was girls only.

Lilli laughs. "Of course!" she cries. "Why, some of our most talented slayers through history have been of the male persuasion. Have you ever heard of Wyatt Earp? He slayed a couple of pretty hardcore vampires at the OK Corral back in his day. Then there was Jack Ruby, who managed to take out Lee Harvey Oswald, a vampire from the Grassy Knoll Coven, with a wooden bullet . . ."

Lilli gestures for us to follow her along a narrow, winding cobblestone road that slopes gently downhill. We pass ancient-looking stone-faced mansions featuring elegant cornices and grand arches. Thick tendrils of dark ivy climb marble columns and grand carved doors bearing golden knockers mark every entrance. I can't help but stare as we walk by, impressed by it all. This place is like freaking Hogwarts for Vampire Slayers. I wonder if I'll get assigned an owl.

I turn my attention back to our escort. "These are the classroom buildings," Lilli is explaining. "Though we do a lot of hands-on stuff down at the bottom of the hill." She points to a football field–size grassy area below, nestled in a copse of pine. The wind picks up for a moment and I inhale the sweet scent of the needles. Delish. After a week in Vegas, the fresh air is more than a bit wonderful and, I realize, I'm looking forward to getting down there and working out. (Yes, this cheerleader stuff has ruined my Goth/vampire lazy sensibilities. Sue me.)

We continue down the hill, which gradually starts getting steeper as we go. "Cafeteria, nurse's station, chapel." She gestures to a beautiful Gothic cathedral to our right—stained glass and flying buttresses galore. "We're not a religious school," she adds. "But we do meet there once a week for announcements from the administration." She shrugs. "Plus it's a great hideaway if we're ever under siege from an angry coven of vampires."

I take an experimental step toward the cathedral, wondering if the force of God will push me away or something, but nothing happens. Hm. Their protective vault may not be as protective as they might like. Not that I'm going to share that little fact with them. Low-profile vamp all the way.

"What's that?" I ask, squinting at the next building we pass, across from the chapel. Weird. While every other building on campus resembles a Victorian mansion, this one looks more like an abandoned factory. Built entirely of brick, it's got boarded-up windows and barbed wire fencing. The whole thing screams "horror movie waiting to happen" and is totally out of place in this otherwise elegant, Gothic setting.

"Oh!" Lilli replies after taking a furtive look at the building, then turning away with a small shudder. "That's . . . Night School."

Oh-kay. I wait for her long-winded explanation. The kind she's given for every building, tree, and overturned rock we've passed on the property. But instead, bubbly exclamation girl seems to have suddenly turned mime. And while the momentary quiet should be somewhat of a relief, instead it makes me slightly nervous. I glance back at the building, a shiver crawling down my back. What is that place? And why is it here, an ugly wound on the otherwise beautiful Swiss mountainside campus?

"Here we are!" Lilli cries, interrupting my troubled thoughts. Her voice is all cheery chipmunk/exclamation points again. "The headmistress's office and teacher quarters!"

I reluctantly turn away from the mysterious Night School and follow Lilli and Sunny into an impressive-looking two-story brick mansion at the bottom of the hill. Inside we find ourselves in a marble-floored lobby with sweeping staircase and majestic chandelier. I whistle, impressed. Seriously, this whole school is beyond opulent. Slaying vamps must command some serious coin. I'm so demanding a raise—or, let's face it, a paycheck to begin with—when I see Teifert again.

A bored-looking receptionist reading, of all things, *Vampire Academy* waves us through and we step into a large office with dark crimson walls and mahogany furniture. Behind a massive desk sits an older woman, probably in her sixties, with watery blue eyes shielded by bifocals and a firm-set mouth, set off by thick frown lines. She wears a severe black suit with a high collar and a pristine set of pearls rests at her throat. If you looked up *headmistress* in the dictionary, you'd so find this woman's picture. Cross-referenced with evil stepmother and fourth-grade math teacher.

"Here they are!" Lilli announces cheerfully. "I brought them, just like you asked me to. I even gave them a little tour along the way. Did you know they had no idea who—"

"That will be all, Lilith," the headmistress interrupts in a haughty English voice that leaves no room for argument.

Our tour guide's face falls, but she nods quickly and skitters out of the room. Feeling the headmistress's hard stare, I can't help but wish we could join her. I'd even put up with the exclamation marks.

"Sit," the headmistress demands in a commanding voice most save for talking to dogs or small children. Compelled, Sunny and I scramble for nearby seats. I cross my ankles and fold my hands, my skin prickling with nervousness. *We're not in trouble*, I remind myself. *We did nothing wrong. Hell, it's not like we asked to come to this stupid school in the first place.*

"Sunshine and Rayne," the headmistress reads off a piece of paper. She looks up at us with skeptical eyes. "Rather unusual names, don't you think?"

"Yeah, well, we have . . . rather unusual parents," I say with a shrug. In fact, now that I know just *how* unusual, I'm only thankful neither of us ended up being called Petunia Bottom.

She sniffs. "So I am told," she says—rather snottily, if you want my opinion. "Well, I suppose I have no choice, but to welcome you to Riverdale Academy," she adds with a deep sigh, as if our presence is causing her great inconvenience. "As your Relocator probably told you, we're a school for vampire slayers. Children come here on their twelfth birthdays to train for six years with our specialists. When they turn eighteen, each potential is evaluated to determine whether they're fit for field assignments or should be placed elsewhere in the agency." She looks over her thick, black-rimmed glasses, giving me a hard stare. I'm guessing this old biddy never saw a day out in the field. "I understand you were trained one-on-one by vice president Charles Teifert of the American division," she says, a grudging degree of respect creeping into her voice. "So I expect you will have no problem keeping up with the slayers in your own age bracket while you're here."

I shrug. Teifert might not agree with that. After all, he's always saying I'm the worst slayer ever. Not to mention I started my training just a few months ago, at seventeen. Unlike these child prodigy slayers they've evidently got here at Riverdale.

Still, I remind myself, I've taken down two big-bads at this point, not to mention a pack of cheerleading werewolves. I'd like to see these preppy prep school brats take on something like that!

"I understand you, on the other hand," the headmistress continues, glaring at my sister as if she were a smooshed turd she'd just discovered on the bottom of her shoe, "have had no training whatsoever."

"Yeah, weird, that," I pipe up, feeling the annoying need to defend my twin, who is just sitting there looking ill and tortured. "Since, you know, she's NOT A SLAYER."

"Believe me," Headmistress Roberta sniffs, "I am quite aware of that fact." Her eyes bore through Sunny, who looks *this close* to bursting into tears again. Then she sighs deeply. "I guess we can put you in the beginner class."

"I have to . . . ? But I can't . . . ? I mean—" Sunny, to her credit, tries to croak out.

"Um, can't she just lay low, hang in the library or something? Take some electives?" I interject on her behalf. "You guys got to have basket-weaving here, right? Stake carving 101?"

"Look"—the headmistress's once-watery eyes are blazing now—"I didn't ask to have you here. In fact, I was very against the idea from the start. After all, your very presence here puts my students at risk and that's not something I tolerate lightly." She scowls. "But now that you're here, you are under my rule. And you will not treat this fine institution like summer camp. You will participate as full-time students, taking all required classes and following each and every rule. You will keep a low profile and not cause any disturbance. If I find that you so much as get a tardy slip, I have every right to punish you."

"And expel us?" I ask hopefully. Maybe misbehaving is the key to getting sprung from this place.

"Unfortunately no. But I can make life very miserable. After all, you have the nano-virus lying dormant in you, do you not? I'm pretty sure Teifert still does this to his potentials . . ."

I make a face. Of course I do. Wooden nano-capsules, swimming through my bloodstream, ready to cause serious bodily harm, should I displease the bigwigs at Slayer Inc. "But Sunny—"

"Doesn't," Headmistress Roberta finishes for me. "Right. Well, then, I guess you, Rayne, will have to take the punishment for the both of you," she says with a smirk. "Should, you know, you decide to . . . get out of line."

I can hear my sister's soft whimper next to me. I reach over and squeeze her hand. I don't know why she's freaking out though. I'm the one at risk of getting staked from the inside out here.

"Look," the headmistress says, her face softening a bit. "I don't mean to sound harsh. But this is for your own good. You must act like regular slayer students in every way or someone may take notice and report you." She sighs. "Remember, even the tightest-run organizations can have foxes in their henhouses. And I'm afraid Riverdale is no exception."

Man, this is the best place Heather could find to keep us safe from the fairies? Some Relocator she is. I mean, why not send a vampire to a beach hideaway in the sunny Caribbean while she's at it?

"I see. Well, never fear, we'll be model pupils. Phi Beta Kappa, perfect attendance. Do you have a cheerleading squad by chance? I'm all about the after-school activities these days." I rise from my seat, pulling Sunny up with me. "And uh, thank you for letting us stay here," I grudgingly add, forcing myself to swallow the bitter taste in my mouth.

Headmistress Roberta sniffs again. I'm beginning to think she should have that nose of hers checked out. "You're welcome," she manages to spit out at last. Though I'm pretty sure she doesn't mean it.

But in any case, we're dismissed and we walk out of the office and back onto the grounds. "Do you want to explore a little?" I ask my sister. "Or go grab some food?" As a vampire I can't eat . . . food . . . but judging from the current state of bloodlust I'm in, I'm betting Sunny must be starving.

"No," she says sulkily. "I just want to go back to our room and fall asleep. Maybe I'll wake up and find out this was all just a crazy nightmare and I'm not hiding out from evil fairies at a school for vampire slayers with my beautiful boyfriend on the other side of the world."

Oh man. Is she going to be like this the whole time we're here? I should have asked Headmistress Roberta if I could switch to a single . . .

"Fine," I reply, starting the trudge up the hill. Maybe I'll walk her to the room and then go out exploring myself.

We make it about halfway to the dorm when the cathedral bells start to chime. Suddenly our path is flooded with children of all ages and teens, pouring out of the classroom buildings and down the hill toward the cafeteria. We do our best to push through them, feeling like salmon swimming upstream, but it's pretty tough with the sheer number of students they got here. I mean, really, how many slayers does Slayer Inc. need to train?

Eventually, the crowds start to thin and we're able to make more headway. But before we can get to the dorm, our path is obstructed again, as a group of five teens—two guys and three girls—purposely step into our path. They're dressed like something out of one of those secret society–type movies—long red cloaks, dark sunglasses, haughty expressions on their faces. They look very out of place among the otherwise very normally attired Riverdale student body.

"Well, well, well," says the tallest boy in the group, surveying me with a critical once-over. "What have we here?"

6

I square my shoulders and narrow my eyes preemptively as the group forms a semi-circle around us, effectively blocking any chance of escape. I can see behind them other students giving us a wide berth as they pass, throwing nervous glances in our direction. Whoever these kids are, I'm guessing they're not from the Riverdale welcoming committee, here to invite Sunny and I to popcorn and movie night back at the dorm.

Luckily I don't like popcorn. "Do you mind?" I demand, taking a step forward, facing off with the tall boy who's standing directly in my path. He's got messy brown hair, a strong chin, and cheekbones that could cut glass. Kind of hot, if you like the jerk-off, a-hole type—which, of course, I usually do. I mean, before I met Jareth anyway. "We're trying to get back to the dorm."

Jerk-off surveys me calmly, not stepping out of the way. "I take it you're the new girls," he observes. "I heard you were coming."

"Glad you got cc'ed on the e-mail," I retort. "Oh wait, I forgot. You don't have e-mail at this godforsaken place."

His mouth quirks in a small smile. "And you're supposed to be . . . slayers of some sort?" he asks, giving Sunny a skeptical look.

"I swear they're letting anyone in these days," mutters the blonde to Jerk-off's right. She shrugs her cloak over her shoulder, revealing a perfect hourglass figure accented by a brown leather corset and a long, midnight blue, Victorianesque skirt that falls to her feet. Suddenly I feel super underdressed in my black sweater accented only by Sunny's dried-up snot.

But cool outfit or no, she's so not getting the best of me. "They let *you* in, didn't they, Little Red Riding Hood?" I sneer. I can feel Sunny poking me hard in the ribs, but I ignore her.

"Now, now, Little Slayer," Jerk-off scolds. "Take care. Here at Riverdale, we're taught to speak to our superiors only when spoken to."

"I'll have to keep that in mind if I run into anyone superior here."

Jerk-off chuckles. "What school did you transfer from?" he asks, his voice filled with amused curiosity.

"School? Please." I roll my eyes. "I, Rayne McDonald, was trained personally, one-on-one by Slayer Inc.'s vice president, Mr. Teifert, himself." There, that ought to give me some street cred with these losers.

Instead, to my surprise, the group looks at one another, then bursts out laughing. "So you were home-schooled?" The red-headed girl standing next to the blonde chuckles. She's wearing a short gold dress with black tights and platform heels and is the spitting image of Miley Cyrus. "That's so ADORABLE."

Argh! Of all the . . . I mean . . . ARGH! I squeeze my hands into fists, fury pumping through my veins. That bitch. I swear if I wasn't a vegetarian vampire trying to keep a low profile in a school full of slayers, I'd so bite the crap out of her.

Instead, I raise my fists. "I'll show you *adorable.* Right up your effing—"

"Rayne! Stop it!" Sunny hisses, this time stamping on my foot to get my attention. I look over angrily and she wags her finger at me. "Remember what Headmistress Roberta said," she warns.

"Yeah, Rayne," mocks the shorter boy, who's stocky and wearing a tool belt lined with wooden stakes. "Remember what Headmistress Roberta said."

I swallow hard, forcing my hands down to my sides. "Fine," I manage to spit out. "But I'll have you know, I'm no babe in the slayer woods just because I didn't go to your stupid boarding school. I've taken down two big-bads through this so-called home-schooled program. And that doesn't even count all the werewolves. All while you have been stuck reading, writing and 'rithmatic'ing here at Riverdale I'll bet."

Jerk-off smiles nastily at me, then turns to the Miley Cyrus girl and nods. "Varuka, do you want to break it down for Home School?"

Varuka pulls out a small pad of paper from her Betsey Johnson purse and flips through it. "Peter has staked seventeen vampires in total," she reads. "Mara has eight under her belt—but she just transferred last year. Leanna"—she nods in the direction of corset girl—"has killed twenty-seven, though some of them were during the burning lair assignment. You tend to rack up kills pretty quickly that way. I just hit sixteen yesterday . . ."

"And I, Corbin Billingsworth the Third," interrupts Jerk-off, "have slain sixty-three since arriving at Slay School." He pulls off his sunglasses and stares me down with flashing, cat-like green eyes. "All stakes, Little Slayer," he adds, mockingly. "And all vampires."

I swallow hard. Oh-kay then. Evidently they're quite . . . progressive . . . here at Slay School. I'm suddenly really, really glad they can't tell I'm a real-live vampire.

"Well, well," I manage to say at last. "I stand corrected. And while I'd love to stay and pop the celebratory champagne for your oh-so-amazing feats of wonder and awe, my sister and I have to get back to the dorm. So if you lovely slayers will excuse us . . ."

I attempt to elbow past them, but before I can break through, Corbin nods to Peter and the tool with the tool belt grabs me by the arms, whirling me around and effectively pinning me against his chest.

"Let me go!" I growl, struggling to free myself. But Peter just twists my arm, causing me to involuntarily squeal in pain.

"I'm sorry, Little Slayer," Corbin says smoothly. "But you didn't say 'please.' "

Ooh, that does it. I'm so ready to kick some serious Slay School ass. Seriously, it'd be almost worth getting nano'ed just to get one good punch in . . .

But no. For Sunny's sake, I need to suck it up. "Fine," I say, through gritted teeth. "May we, my good sir, PLEASE have permission to step away from your glorious presence for a short time?"

Corbin smirks and for a moment I think he's actually going to deny me still, but then he nods his head at Peter. "Let her go," he commands.

Peter does and I accidentally-on-purpose stomp on his foot as I stumble away. He howls in protest and Corbin's cat eyes lock onto mine. "You're a feisty one, Little Slayer," he purrs. "I like that." Giving me a mocking bow, he adds, "I'll be keeping my eye on you." Then he turns to his little minions and gestures for them to follow him down the hill, thankfully leaving Sunny and I alone at last.

"What a jerk!" I growl as I watch them go.

"You weren't exactly Miss Congeniality yourself," Sunny reminds me.

"What was I supposed to do?" I ask her. "Get down on the ground and let them walk all over us? Kiss their skinny slayer asses? Not in this lifetime, sister."

Sunny opens her mouth, probably to say something super annoying about turning the other cheek, but luckily is interrupted by an anxious Lilli, who's standing a few feet away, wringing her hands together, her face white and anxious.

"Are you guys okay?!"

"Yeah, we're fine. Just a little wounded pride." I glare down the road at the retreating gang. The others students scurry to keep their distance as they pass by like they're God's gift to vampire slayers. "What's up with those losers?"

Lilli rolls her eyes. "They're Alphas," she explains. "The best of the best, here at Slay School and they know it, too. Total bullies to anyone who doesn't live up to their skill or coolness standards—which is just about everyone besides the five of them. Trust me, you're best off avoiding them as much as possible."

"Don't worry," I say, shaking my head and turning away from the group. "I have absolutely no interest in becoming friends." With them or anyone else at this godforsaken school at this point.

"Anyway, I swear not everyone here at Slay School is like that. In fact, most people are really nice," Lilli insists. "Why don't you come down to the cafeteria with me and I'll introduce you around? We could get you some food or a . . . drink of some kind." She looks at me like she can tell I'm starved.

Her offer makes my stomach growl, but sadly not for what

the Slay School cafeteria will provide. This growing bloodlust is going to be a serious problem. I wonder how long I can go without drinking . . .

I realize Lilli is waiting for an answer.

"Sun? You want to eat?" I ask my sister for the second time today.

But predictably, Lady Lovelorn shakes her head. "I just . . . I just want to go back to our room," she says sadly. "I'll catch you later." And with that, she turns and continues to trudge up the hill toward the dorm without even a good-bye.

"Sorry," I say to Lilli. "I'd better go check on her. She's really homesick."

Lilli watches Sunny go. "I understand," she says. "I can grab some extra food and drinks and bring them back for you."

I guess I should be grateful there's at least one decent person at this ridiculous school, even if she is a bit annoying. After thanking her, I say my good-byes and head back to the room to find my sister.

I find her, not surprisingly, I suppose, curled up in a ball, cradling her useless cell phone in her arms. The speakerphone is on and I can hear Magnus's voice over the airwaves. One of the last messages he'd left her yesterday, before any of this happened. It's all she has, I guess.

Hearing me, she sits up with a start, her face flushed with embarrassment as she clicks off the phone.

"You okay?" I ask, sitting down beside her on the bed, reaching over to stroke her hair. She's growing it super long these days. Probably to further differentiate herself from me. The thought makes me a little sad.

"Not really," she replies, staring at the blank wall in front of her. "This is pretty much the worst day of my life."

"I know it sucks," I soothe. "But we can get through this. It's only temporary."

"You don't know that!" she cries angrily. "What if, after all this, Mom and Dad can't convince the fairies to leave us alone? Then one of us will be stuck becoming a fairy queen!"

"Yeah, but . . . well, that's not the end of the world, is it?" I ask. "I mean, there's probably a lot of great perks that come with being a fairy queen. Think about it: riches beyond belief, magical powers, all the nectar you can drink, limitless glitter." I pause, then giggle. "Not to mention a hot prince named Dew Drip . . ."

"Stop it!" Sunny cries, rolling over to face me. Her eyes are stormy and bloodshot from all the crying. "Don't you get it? It's not a joke! It's my freaking life here!"

I hold my hands up in surrender. "Okay, okay. I just thought—"

She scrambles up and starts pacing the distance between beds. "Sure, it's not big deal to you. You're already supernatural six ways from Sunday anyway. And you like it that way, for some unfathomable reason."

"Well, yeah." I shrug. "Though I'd like it better if I had some kind of powers . . ."

She turns to me, staring me down, fury clear on her face. "Well, I don't. I *don't* want to be a vampire. I *don't* want to be a slayer. I certainly *don't* want to be a fairy queen. I just want to be a human girl and I just want to be left alone." She shakes her head. "I mean, what's left, Rayne? Are we going to find out our long-lost cousin was a freaking leprechaun?"

"Ooh, that'd be cool. Maybe he'd share his pot of gold with us. Or at least his Lucky Charms."

Sunny glares at me.

"Come on, Sun," I cajole. "You gotta look on the bright side.

Glass half full and all that. I mean, what's the worst that can happen? You become fairy queen?"

"I will *never* become a fairy queen," Sunny mutters. "I'll kill myself first."

"Well, you're already a *drama queen*." I shake my head, rising from her bed, defeated. Obviously she's in no mood to listen to reason. I head over to my own bed and plop down, staring up at the ceiling, annoyed as all hell. From across the room, I hear Sunny pressing keys on her phone, to listen to Magnus's messages again—this time, sans speakerphone.

What am I going to do? I know she won't make good on her threat to kill herself, but at the same time, I feel terrible that she's so upset. She's my twin. And as the oldest by seven minutes, I'm supposed to be the one taking care of her. And yet I know, at the end of the day, if the fairies want her as their queen, there's very little I can do about it.

I crawl into bed and pull the covers over my head, hugging a pillow to my chest, feeling the tears spring to my eyes. I've been working overtime all day to be strong and optimistic for my sister's sake, but now, alone in bed, reality is starting to sink in big time. If only Jareth were here; he'd know what to do. And even if he didn't, he'd still take me into his arms and infuse me with the strength to face whatever was coming our way. With him, I feel invincible. Now I just feel kind of defeated.

Part of me hates admitting this. After all, a kick-ass chick like me shouldn't be all weepy over a guy. I'm not like my sister. But at the same time, Jareth and I are such a good team. I feel like half of me is missing without him by my side. When did I get all codependent girl? Ugh.

I wish I wasn't so messed up when it comes to relationships.

I usually blame my dad, but now even that excuse has gone all cloudy on me. Did he really leave to protect us? Did he really miss my last birthday to save my life? Was the birth of Stormy really not that big a deal? I've been furious at him for so long it's hard to accept the fact that I may have misjudged him. If we ever get out of this, we're so going to have to spend some time together to figure things out.

I hope he and Mom are okay in fairyland. As conflicted as my feelings are for my dad, I'd clearly die if anything happened to Mom. My best friend. The one who loves me unconditionally no matter how screwed up I am. I can't lose her. Not to the fairies, not to anyone.

I hear a muffled noise and peek out from under the covers. Sunny's tossing and turning, trying to get comfortable in the rickety twin bed. Poor girl. I feel bad for grumping at her a few minutes ago. She has every right to express her unhappiness, and it's probably a lot healthier than stuffing it deep down inside like I tend to do. But, at the same time, I hate seeing her appear so vulnerable. So scared. If only there was a way to ensure I became the fairy queen and not her. Not that I want that, per se—hell, I look freaking awful in pink—but I'd do it in a heartbeat if it meant allowing her to forever live in the human world as she so deeply desires.

I lift my arm in the air and study my elbow. Could it really be as easy as a quick kiss, as Mom said? A simple kiss to save my sister's life and ensure she never has to become something she doesn't want to be? Tentatively, I lift my head, pressing my lips to the wrinkly elbow skin, my entire body buzzing in anticipation. Here goes nothing.

7

I wake up the next morning with the worst backache ever. For being a posh private school, Riverdale's beds are lumpy as all hell. I glance over at Sunny, who's still in bed with the covers pulled over her head, then at the clock, which reads ten to seven. Ugh. We've got ten minutes to get dressed and get to class—or incur the wrath of Headmistress Roberta.

"Sunny, wake up!" I leap out of bed and cross the room to shake my sister. She moans in protest. "Get up and get ready."

"Five more minutes," she pleads.

"How about five more seconds? One, two . . ."

"Okay, okay!" My twin sits up, rubbing her bloodshot eyes. Has she been up all night crying? "Geez, you ever think of a career as an alarm clock? You're totally overqualified in annoyingness."

"It's for your own good, Sun," I say, rummaging through my tiny dorm-room closet for something suitable to wear. "You don't want that evil headmistress coming down on you. Or, you know, me, for that matter." According to my schedule, which was dropped off by Lilli when she came by with lunch yesterday—grilled cheese sandwiches and a huge jug of strawberry Kool-Aid, all of which I ended up tossing in the trash since Sunny wouldn't eat and I can't. I've got combat training most of the day so I'm thinking sweats are probably more practical than my normal lacy black dresses.

I have to forgo makeup, but I manage to get us both dressed and down to the field, where classes are held, with thirty seconds to spare. The morning air is crisp and cool and the other students are huddled around one another for warmth. I look around for our one friend, but Lilli's nowhere to be found. Must be in a different class.

A man in his forties, carrying a clipboard and sporting a porn mustache and muscle mass that would make Mr. Universe extremely jealous, walks over to us and looks down at his list. "Which one of you is Rayne?" he asks.

I raise my hand.

"Okay, great. You're in my class. Sunshine?" He turns to my sister. "They've put you with the beginners. They meet inside the gym." He points to one of the one-story outbuildings down at the end of the field. Sunny shoots me a worried glance—I know she doesn't want to be separated from me—but I give her a comforting squeeze on the shoulder.

"It'll be okay," I whisper in her ear. "You'll be in with a bunch of twelve-year-olds. How bad could it be?"

She nods, reaching over to hug me, holding on a second too long. Professor Pornstar clears his throat impatiently. Reluctantly, Sunny lets go and shuffles down the field at a snail's pace. I let out a frustrated breath. I gotta figure out a way to get her to snap out of this funk or she's going to get us both in serious trouble.

"Well, well, if it isn't Little Slayer."

Speaking of trouble. I whirl around, not surprised to see Corbin standing behind me, a smug smile on his face and his arms crossed over his chest. He's forgone his red robe for today's training and is wearing black sweatpants and a tight white T-shirt, which annoyingly accentuates his abs. I mean, yeah, the guy's a total a-hole, but that doesn't mean he's not ripped. In fact, he looks just like freaking Jason Stackhouse on that *True Blood* show. If only he were just as dumb, too.

"Well, well, if it isn't *Big Dick*," I mimic in my sweetest voice. "Are you in my class?"

"I'm way above you in *class*," he replies with a sneer. "But yes, I will be your partner today."

Wait, what? I try to mask my surprise. "Excuse me?"

"Mr. Klaus assigned me to show you the ropes," he explains. "So we'll be sparring partners." He grins. "In other words, you're about to get your ass kicked, Little Slayer."

"By you and what army?"

A few of his friends step up behind him, looking down at me with scornful expressions on their faces. Oh, right. *That* army.

He laughs. "Actually, I don't need an army to take you," he assures me. "In case you didn't know, I'm an Alpha here at Riverdale."

"Alpha?" There was that term again.

"Alphas are the best of the best," Leanna says haughtily. "First-tier slayers on the front lines, after they graduate Night School."

Night School? A vision of that creepy building across from the admin office flashes into my brain. "Wait. You guys go to Night School?" I ask.

"Um, well, not yet," Corbin replies, looking a tad sheepish for the first time since I've met him. "But we will," he adds. "Hopefully very soon. We're just waiting for our official invitation."

Interesting. I open my mouth to ask more, but Professor Pornstar, aka Mr. Klaus, blows the whistle. Guess it's time for fight club. I suck in a breath and turn to our teacher, who's passing out wooden stakes from a red velvet bag.

"Okay," he says. "You guys know the drill. One of you is the slayer, the other the vamp. Slayers try to slay your opponent by touching the tip of your stake to your vampire's chest. Don't forget to dip them in red paint first, so we'll be able to judge your accuracy. Vampires, try to bite your slayer. If you get neck contact first, you win. Get a red mark anywhere near your heart, that means you're dead and need to leave the field."

Okay then. We're playing vampire paintball. Or paint-stake, I guess.

He looks around "Any questions?" he asks, throwing me a stake. "Now, on the count of three . . ."

I turn to Corbin, who, as it turns out, must be counting challenged. Before Mr. Klaus even gets to one, he grabs me, pinning my arms behind me, his hot lips searing my neck.

"You're dead!" he crows. His little lackeys cheer.

"Wait a second!" I cry. "I wasn't ready. Mr. Klaus didn't even blow his whistle yet," I protest, slapping at him to get him off of me. God, what an ass.

"I've got news for you, chickie." Corbin laughs, shoving me unceremoniously to the ground. I land on my knees and pain reverberates up my spine. Jerk. "In real life, vampires don't wait for any whistle." He pauses, then adds, "Guess they didn't teach you that in *home school*."

He holds out a hand and I stupidly reach for it, assuming he's trying to help me up. He laughs. "Your stake," he clarifies.

Oh. I can feel my face burning as I hand him the weapon and scramble to my feet unaided. I watch him dip his stake in the bucket of paint, not feeling all that great about having my new mortal enemy casually wielding in his hand the one thing that can kill me.

Not that I'm going to let him win so easily this time.

"Are you ready, Little Slayer?" he asks patronizingly. "I wouldn't want to dare begin before you were completely ready. Should I count to three? Maybe a hundred?"

I roll my eyes. "Bring it, Slayer Boy," I snarl. "If you think you can."

"Oh, I *know* I can."

He charges forward, so quick I have no choice but to duck his strike. Once down on the ground, I throw my arms around his shins and yank them forward with all my might. His momentum interrupted, he lurches backward, slamming down on the field, butt first. He lets out a cry of surprise—guess he figured he'd have it as easy as he did before. But I'm ready for him now.

He rolls over and leaps easily to his feet. His eyes are dancing with laughter. "Oh, you're more fun than I thought, Little Slayer," he purrs, circling me with the stake clutched firmly in his hand. "I am going to enjoy taking you down."

"Enjoy this," I reply saucily, giving him the bird, feeling better already. This is kind of fun.

I follow his moves, studying carefully, watching and waiting for weaknesses, as Teifert taught me to do. All the recent cheerleading has made me limber and strong, and I know I can take him. I just need to wait for the right—

Corbin strikes again, jabbing the stake in my direction. I respond with a roundhouse kick, slamming my foot into his extended arm. He howls and the stake goes flying down the field. He dives after it, but I'm too quick, cartwheeling toward the stake (and yes, showing off a little!) and grabbing it mid-second-cartwheel. When I flip back to a standing position, he's right in front of me. Without even a pause, I shove him squarely in the chest, pushing him back. Then I throw myself on top of him, using my entire body weight to bring him down.

A moment later, I'm straddling him, my hands pinning his shoulders to the grass, my mouth at his neck for the mock vampire bite. I've won!

Or have I? As my lips graze his neck, I freeze. He's so warm. And he smells really good. Like vanilla, mixed with sandalwood. I pull back a bit, watching the artery in his neck pulse, circulating blood through his body. My stomach groans in protest and I feel my fangs slide into position. God, I'm so hungry. If only I could take a small nibble. I lean in, opening my mouth wide . . .

Corbin moans.

I sit up with a start, my face on fire and my breathing labored. What the hell am I doing? I don't drink real blood—especially not directly from a human. Especially not from a human Slayer in Training attending a school run by Slayer Inc. One bite and I'd be dusted before I could even swallow down the sweet stuff.

"Rayne . . ."

I realize, suddenly, that Corbin's staring up at me, his eyes glazed and his breathing as heavy as mine. His arrogance has faded away, replaced by some kind of deep admiration, mixed with desire. Is he okay? Oh no, did I accidentally vampire scent him when I was daydreaming about his blood? Vampires have very enticing pheromones, you see, designed to bewitch hapless mortals if they're not careful.

And I, wrapped up in my bloodlust, was so not careful just then.

Embarrassed and horrified, I roll off of Corbin and scramble to my feet. "I . . . um . . . I win!" I say, while waving a hand around my body, trying to fan away any residual scent, praying my teeth will retract before anyone sees them.

Corbin just stares up at me, totally bewitched.

Suddenly I find myself surrounded by the other Alphas. "Wow, that was rockin'," Varuka cries.

"Yeah, we've never seen anyone take down Corbin before," Mara agrees.

"You're one tough slayer chick."

"Maybe you'll be our next Alpha."

I smile helplessly, not able to speak and hide my fangs at the same time. I steal another worried glance down at Corbin. Is he okay?

"Hey Corbin," Peter says, nudging him with his foot. "You got beat by Home School."

The spell seems to break and Corbin scrambles to his feet. He glares at me with vile hatred deep in his emerald eyes. Guess the vampire scent has worn off. And he's so not looking pleased about the new girl kicking his ass in front of his friends.

"Good job, Little Slayer," he manages to grind out, while brushing himself off. "But I'm afraid next time you won't be so lucky." He gathers his friends and together they head down the field.

I watch them go, feeling my fangs finally retract. Lucky? He doesn't know how lucky he just was. And as for next time? Well, the hunger is growing. And I don't know how I'm going to be able to stop myself.

8

"Oh my God, everything in my entire body hurts," Sunny moans as she limps down the cafeteria aisle, tray of food in hand. She sits down across from me and Lilli, who has invited us to her table to eat with her and her friends.

"I thought you were in a class with twelve-year-olds," I remark, pushing my food around my plate to make it look like I'm eating. I ordered a burger extra, extra rare and tried to suck the blood out of it before the others showed up, but it just made me puke. If I don't find Blood Synthetic soon, I'm in big trouble.

"Yeah. Try huge, strong, ridiculously well-trained twelve-year-olds," she moans, holding out an arm so I can see all the blue-and-black bruises already starting to form. "Who don't have a drop of respect for their elders." She sighs.

"How did you get to be a slayer?" one of the girls at the table asks curiously. "If you're totally not into the fighting thing?"

"Long story. Don't ask," Sunny mutters, shoveling a big spoonful of mashed potatoes into her mouth.

"Hey Rayne, do you want to come grab some more Kool-Aid with me?" Lilli asks, after slurping down the last of her drink. Man, the girl's addicted to the stuff. "You must be *really* thirsty after all that practice out on the field."

"No thanks, I'm good," I reply, pretending to take a sip of my water, not wanting to hurt her feelings. Even as a mortal, Kool-Aid was never my thing.

Lilli shrugs and jumps up from her seat. "Suit yourself," she says as she skips down the aisle.

"Don't look now," hisses her friend Evelyn to my right, "but Corbin's looking over here."

Of course, she said *don't look*, which always makes me automatically turn around to do just that. I see Corbin and his friends sitting a few tables away, their table piled high with food. Sure enough, the Alpha slayer has turned away from the group and is watching me intently with longing green eyes. When he catches me looking, he scowls and turns away.

I shiver involuntarily. What have I done to him? And is there a way to undo it? If only Jareth were here. He'd know what to do.

"I heard you took him down this morning," Evelyn says, forcing my attention back to my new friends. "No one's ever done that before."

"Yeah, everyone at school is talking about it," adds Amber, another one of the lunchtime gang. "You're, like, famous already."

Great. And here I was supposed to be keeping a low profile. What was I thinking, taking down the big bad Alpha slayer? Seriously, forget slaying—finding trouble should be my full-time job. I'm certainly good at it.

* * *

We spend the afternoon inside, listening to lectures on vampire history, vampire politics, vampires in literature, etc. By the two P.M. study hall break, I'm already all vamped out. I mean, I don't even think actual vampires know as much about their kind as these monotone Slay School teachers do. Or maybe it's just that vamps prefer to learn at their leisure, seeing as they've got more than a couple lifetimes to soak it all in. Mortal slay students are the ones who have to cram.

In any case, study hall is held in a beautiful, musty old library with stained-glass windows, well-worn wooden desks, and walls lined floor to ceiling with ancient books. There are a few computers scattered here and there, but since none of them connect to the Internet, I don't bother checking them out.

Instead, I spend the hour wandering through the stacks, running my hands over the rows of hardcover tomes, breathing in that delicious old book scent. Nothing here has been written after the 1900s and I kind of like that. I pull out a crumbling first edition of *Wuthering Heights* and flip through it, sighing contentedly. I've always found the story of Heathcliff and Catherine so romantic.

After a few minutes, I put back the book and continue exploring. The next aisle is filled with "Otherworld Nonfiction," according to a metal plaque at the end of the row. My interest piqued, I step into the row, surrounding myself with large, thick hardcovers depicting vampires, werewolves, angels, and . . .

Fairies.

Ooh. Talk about required reading. I start grabbing fairy books off the shelves until my arms are weighted down and I can barely see over the stack. Then I drag them off to a quiet corner, where I find a small, moth-eaten armchair next to a tiny table and Tiffany lamp. I set the books down and curl up in the chair, pulling my feet up and under me. Then I grab the first book and start paging through.

Time to get a little family history.

The Sidhe (pronounced *Shee*) are also known as the "People of the Mounds," and they evidently go way back in Irish and Scottish history. They live in fairyland, a dimension beyond our own world, under a monarchial system; kings and queens living in the lap of luxury in beautiful otherworldly palaces. There are several different courts and none of them can ever seem to get along.

Besides their wings, they look just like regular people, as opposed to the pint-size pixies that make up a lot of the old fairy tales. But their powers go way beyond those of men. Besides being able to fly, some of them can also change shape at will. Pretty cool, if you ask me.

What's not so cool is how petty some of them seem to be. Like, for centuries Irish families have attempted to appease mischievous sprites by leaving little bowls of milk out for them at night. (Evidently, fairies are big on dairy as well as nectar.) If they forget—or the cat gets to the milk first—the thirsty fairy will get so mad they'll actually go and steal the family's baby and replace it with a green-tinged, vicious changeling child instead.

Like I said, so not cool.

The text goes on. Some fairies are unable to tell a lie, others can chat with animals and turn invisible. And most of them are deathly allergic to iron. I turn the page, my eyes widening as I find the section of text I've been looking for: "How to start your fairy transformation." Evidently, in addition to the elbow kissing thing, teen fairies take part in this big, fancy ceremony when they turn sixteen to kick-start the process. (Talk about a *sweet* sixteen!) But in extreme cases, the text seems to indicate, you can start the transformation by yourself, as long as you know the right invocation to accompany the elbow kissing part. And luckily for me, they've got it all transcribed in the book.

I look around the library: No one's nearby. I wonder if I should actually go through with this. After all, there's no turning back, as Mom said. And do I really want to be a fairy for the rest of my life? I mean, I'm already a vampire. And a slayer. That's a lot in and of itself.

Then I think back to Sunny's anguished face. Her desperate wish to remain mortal. She's my sister, as much of a pain in the ass as she can be sometimes. And it's my job to protect her.

So really, what choice do I have?

I look back down at the book, whispering the incantation to myself, while repeatedly kissing each elbow and praying no one walks by—as, let's face it, I must look freaking ridiculous to say the least. But luckily the place remains empty and I finish the ritual, uninterrupted, with a little twirl, as per the book.

I plop down on my chair, feeling more than a little bit embarrassed. Did I really just do a jig in the middle of the library, thinking it would turn me into a fairy? *Seriously, Rayne, you're losing it, definitely losing it.*

But just as I'm about to close my book and go home, the room starts to spin. I grab on to the sides of my chair, my heart in my throat. Is something happening? Did the ritual work? I try to look down at the book, but the text seems to waver in and out of focus. I try to stand, but my legs are too weak to hold my weight. My heart pounds in my chest and my breath comes in short gasps. What's going on? Am I becoming a fairy at last?

Before I can know for sure, I find myself succumbing to the blackness.

"Excuse me? Miss?"

Feeling a rough hand on my shoulder, I wake with a start. A beady-eyed man with a big nose and an even bigger potbelly peers down at me. He's dressed in light blue coveralls and is holding a broom.

"Sorry, miss," he says. "Library's closed. And it's well past curfew. You'd better get back to the dorm before Johan catches you."

Wow, how long was I out for? I scramble to my feet, forgetting I have a pile of books still on my lap, and they all go crashing to the floor. The janitor looks down, his eyes widening as he catches a glimpse of them.

"Fairies?" he asks, looking up at me suspiciously.

"Um, yeah. I have a . . . project," I reply, not knowing why I suddenly feel so nervous. What do I care what some janitor sees me reading? "An essay about the history of the Sidhe."

The janitor gives me a hard stare—like he doesn't believe me—and I squirm under his gaze. Am I in trouble here? Did I just give myself away? I try to surreptitiously glance over my shoulder to see if I've suddenly sprouted wings. I don't see anything, but still . . .

The janitor shrugs and starts picking up the books. "I'll reshelve them for you," he tells me. "You'd better get back to your dorm."

I nod and grab my coat, hurrying toward the library entrance, completely creeped out. I look back at the janitor, who has taken a seat in the armchair and is paging through my books. I shake my head. Seriously, paranoid much, Rayne? I mean, who cares if the janitor knows what I'm reading? Or anyone else, for that matter? It's not like someone's going to be all "Hey she's reading a book about fairies—I bet she actually is one!"

Still, I can't shake the nervousness as I slip out of the library and start heading up the cobblestone path toward the door. The campus is quiet and dark, all good slayers have long since gone to bed.

Except for one building where the lights are blazing and I can see shadows moving through cracks of boarded-up windows. A strange hum of electricity dances in the air, igniting my vampire senses. Little hairs prickle my arms and a chill crawls down my back as I study the building curiously, wondering what on Earth could be going on in there. Are there really Alpha slayers training for secret ops inside? And if so, why are they doing it late at night? Do they have some sort of secret they don't want the rest of the slayers to see?

I take a step closer, curiosity overwhelming me. Suddenly the front door creaks open and a solitary figure steps out, dragging a large bag. I leap aside, trying to retreat to the shadows, but the figure's eyes are already locked on me. Crap. I've been spotted.

"Rayne McDonald?" it demands. "What are you doing out here?"

Oh great. It's Headmistress Roberta, of all people. The last person on Earth I wanted to run into after curfew. After all, she's practically looking for an excuse to nano me anyway and here I go, handing her one on a silver platter.

"Um, sorry, I just fell asleep in the library," I stammer. "I didn't mean . . . I'm . . . I'm heading back to the dorm now."

The headmistress narrows her eyes at me, pursing her lips together in a deep frown. At first I think she's going to say something, but then she seems to change her mind. She shakes her head and points up the hill.

"Very well," she says. "But get inside immediately. And don't let me catch you out after dark again." She pauses, then adds in a menacing voice, "Or else."

I don't try to argue and head up the hill double time. As I go, I can feel her hard stare behind me. In fact, if eyes could really burn holes in someone's back I'm pretty sure I'd be Swiss cheese right about now.

I pull open the dorm room door and slip inside, not able to resist the urge to take one last peek down the hill before I close it again, even though I'm pretty sure it'll turn me into a pillar of salt if the headmistress catches me doing so. Luckily, Roberta has evidently tired of watching my retreat and is back to dragging the large bag down the street toward the sanitation building at the very end of the road.

I squint at the bag. Is that what I think it is? And did it really just . . . move?

I bolt into the dorm, not caring as the door slams behind me, probably waking half of Slay School. Leaning against the wall, I suck in a shaky breath, my thoughts whirling like crazy in my head.

'Cause that bag she was carrying? It looked a lot like a body bag. And whatever was inside? It didn't seem all that dead.

What the hell is really going on at Night School?

9

Argh, my back! I wake up the next morning, feeling like two knives are simultaneously stabbing me between my shoulder blades. Seriously, I'm starting to think there's some kind of *Princess and the Pea* thing going on with my mattress. (Since I technically am a fairy princess, after all!) I mean, sure, I've worked out a lot lately on the training field, but I'm also in pretty good shape from being a cheerleader. There's no way I should be this sore.

I glance over and see Sunny is already awake, lying in bed, staring at her useless cell phone, probably flipping through old texts from Magnus. "Hey, Sun!" I call to her. "Will you take a look at my back for a second? Tell me if I have any weird bruises?" I climb out of bed and walk over to her side of the room, turning around and lifting my shirt over my head so she can get a good look.

"Oh my God!" she shrieks. I whirl around, just in time to see her stumble backward onto her bed, trembling hands covering her wide open mouth, her eyes as big as saucers.

"Come on, they can't be that bad," I say, trying to twist around to see for myself.

"They're . . . they're . . ." Sunny stumbles. I see her hard swallow. "Rayne, what did you do?" she asks finally, her voice barely a hoarse whisper.

"I just sparred a few times with Corbin. But I totally won. So I don't see—"

"I'm not talking about that," she interrupts. "I'm talking about . . ." She shakes her head, as if in disbelief.

"What?" I cry, fear starting to creep through me. "Just spit it out!"

"Did you go and kiss your elbow or something?"

I stare at her, suddenly remembering the ritual I performed in the library last night, horror slamming through my insides. Leaping from my bed, I dive for the full-length mirror I installed behind my closet door. Twisting around, I try to catch a glimpse of . . .

My wings.

Well, not wings exactly. Not yet. But there's definitely some kind of growth going on back there. Two large lumps, protruding from my shoulder blades . . .

Covered in white feathers.

My head spins and I force myself to return to my bed, sinking down onto the mattress, a combination of fear and excitement whirling through my brain.

It worked. It actually worked. I can't believe it.

"Rayne! Why would you do that?" Sunny cries in an anguished voice. "After all Mom and Dad have done, you just, willingly . . . UGH!" She buries her eyes in her pillow. "I can't even look. It's so grotesque."

"Nice, Sun," I snap, feeling a little offended. I turn my head to see the little feathered bumps. "Thanks for making me feel all self-conscious." They are kind of weird, yeah, but once they grow into full-fledged wings, I bet they'll look kind of cool. Though a little hard to keep under wraps . . .

"Why, Rayne? Why would you do this? I mean, of all the crazy things you've—"

"I did it for you, dummy," I interrupt grumpily. "So how about you lay off the whole judgmental thing for once?"

"Wait, what? For me?" she demands, looking over, her face full of confusion. "What do you mean, 'for me'?"

"Look, it's simple, really," I tell her. "Like you said, if Mom and Dad fail in their talks, one of us is going to have to take the fairy queen gig, right? So who're the fairies going to choose now—the reluctant mortal who can't stand the taste of nectar or the full-fledged fairy with amazing wingspan who's ready and willing to go?"

Sunny shakes her head in disbelief. "Rayne, I never wanted you to have to—"

"You're my sister, after all," I interrupt. "And I love you. Even if you are a total crybaby at times."

"Uh, thanks. I think."

I grin wickedly, then turn serious. "Sunny, I want you to be able to have the happily ever after you want for yourself. And I know this way you'll actually have a chance to have it."

Sunny crosses the room in two seconds flat and throws her arms around me, burying her face in my shoulder.

"Hey, hey! Watch the wings! I don't want to lose any feathers. After all, fairy pattern baldness is no joke. And I doubt Rogaine would work for something like that."

Sunny giggles and cautiously reaches out to pet the wings in question. As her hands make contact, she squeals and scampers back to her side of the room.

"I still think it's totally freaky," she says, rubbing her palm on her flannel PJ bottoms.

"I do, too," I admit. "Not to mention once they start growing, they're going to be a bit of a problem hiding from the student body."

"And here I thought you concealing the fact that you're a vampire was bad enough."

I let out a frustrated breath. "That's even worse. I'm so hungry for blood I'm going crazy. I had a nightmare that I broke into a blood bank and drained it dry."

Sunny looks concerned. "There's no place to get blood here?" she asks. "What about . . . from me?" I can tell it takes her effort to say this and I appreciate the grand gesture.

Luckily I can easily turn her down. "Holy Grail blood, remember?" I remind her. "Poisonous to vampires over a few months old."

"Oh yeah," she says, relief clear on her face. She's quiet for a moment, then adds, "So what are we going to do? You can't stay here and starve to death. And if those wings keep growing they're going to be a problem."

"Yeah," I say, glancing at the mirror at my little winglets. "I have no idea how fast these things are going to grow either." I shake my head, annoyed with my impulsiveness. Seriously, what was I thinking, going through the ritual like that? I guess it just seemed so ridiculous—I didn't think it would actually work . . .

"I think we have no choice," Sunny says, interrupting my self-rebuke. "One way or another, we have to get out of here." She looks over at me, setting her chin determinedly. "We're breaking out of Slay School tonight."

10

"Okay, I think the coast is clear," I hiss, after peering out the front door of our dorm room and looking left and right, taking special care to make sure Headmistress Roberta isn't out on her nightly body bag run. (I didn't mention that whole thing to Sunny 'cause I didn't want to freak her out too much.) But the campus appears dark and still, with only a crescent moon to light our path. I slip outside, careful to stay in the shadows. My sister steps out beside me, her backpack stuffed to the brim.

"I thought we agreed we'd travel light," I remark, raising an eyebrow at the nearly overflowing bag on her back.

"I need all this stuff," she protests. A moment later, a string bikini top falls out of the bag. She grabs it with a sheepish look. "It's designer," she explains. "And Magnus gave it to me, so it's sentimental."

I sigh and shake my head, then begin slinking around the side of the dorm, back up against the cold stone walls. The temperature has dropped at least twenty degrees and I'm hoping that, in addition to her Calvin Klein resort collection, Sunny has a big warm parka in her overstuffed escape luggage. After all, we have no way of knowing just how far we may have to travel tonight.

Earlier in the day, I hit the library, trying to do some research on exactly where in the world we are here at Riverdale Slay School. Lilli had said the only way out was by helicopter, but my guess is that's something they say to all the new students to encourage them to stay put. After all, they don't want them slipping out at night and heading to the nearby town tavern to get wasted and dance on tables. So not behavior becoming of a Slayer in Training.

And sure enough, after paging through a billion cryptic texts—no books in this library are less than a hundred years old, I swear—I was able to get a general idea of where the school resides and information about a small village probably located somewhere in the vicinity.

Sadly, "somewhere in the vicinity" isn't exactly GPS coordinates so we may be wandering for a bit. Still, it's better than staying put and having my fairy vampire status discovered by the student body and faculty. Because I'm guessing that's grounds for immediate expulsion. And not the kind where you're just sent home in shame, either.

We reach the back of the dorm and settle into complete darkness. I look over at my sister and nod. "Okay, now!" I cry, breaking out into a run. The cold air whips against my face as we dash for the nearby forest, crashing through the underbrush. Only after a few hundred feet of "dodge the big pine tree" do I dare stop and turn around to look, hands on my knees, panting to catch my breath. Sunny catches up to me a moment later. The forest behind us is silent and still. I grin at my sister. We did it.

"Piece of cake," I say. "We should have tried this our first day here."

"Yeah, but . . ." Sunny looks around the woods. "Now what? Do you have any idea where we're supposed to be going?"

"Well . . ." I tap my chin with my finger. "Look! There's a path. Let's follow it. It has to lead to somewhere, right?"

"Sure. Like to the gingerbread house where the evil witch waits to throw us in the oven."

"Please. That was totally Germany. We're in Switzerland. A whole 'nother country." I step over a rotting log and head for the path. "In fact, I bet this is the road they use to bring in weekly supplies. After all, they have to get the students' food from somewhere and helicoptering it all in isn't exactly economical."

Sunny looks at me doubtfully, but falls into step anyway. Reaching in my pocket, I pull out a small LED pocket light/lighter combo—all I could find at short notice. I flick it on and point it down toward the ground, keeping the light low. Don't want someone back at school to see it flickering and alert the guards.

As we walk down the windy path, the wind whistles through the trees and tall shadows, cast by my light, dance madly across the road. Sunny grips onto my shoulder, her fingernails digging into my flesh. "Should we be dropping bread crumbs or something?" she whispers, still on her little Hansel and Gretel kick, I guess.

I open my mouth to answer her, but a crashing noise behind us makes me shut it again. I whirl around, shakily shining my flashlight into the bushes. A wild animal? Or something more deadly? From beside me, Sunny whimpers in fear.

We wait, holding our breaths, but are greeted with nothing but silence. I shrug at Sunny and motion for us to continue. After all, it's too late to turn back now.

But a moment later, another noise erupts—a low growling sound, somewhere to our left. Sunny looks over at me with wild, frightened eyes. "What was that?" she hisses.

I shrug, hand in my bag, reaching for the stake they gave me with my Riverdale enrollment papers. Though what good a small hunk of carved wood is going to do against a big, snarly wolf or lumbering bear is anyone's guess. Fear pounds through my heart as I shine the flashlight into the woods. Maybe the light will scare the creature off . . .

Suddenly I'm grabbed from behind. I scream, but my voice is muffled by a smelly rag, stuffed into my mouth, and a black hood, pulled over my head. Two hands grab my shoulders, two more grab me by the ankles. I kick as hard as I can, but they're too strong.

I can hear my sister thrashing behind me. Oh God—whoever these people are, they've got her, too.

After what seems an eternity, our captors stop and I'm plopped unceremoniously onto the ground, my butt slamming against hard rock. I can smell something here. Something like . . . burning flesh. The hood is ripped from my eyes and the gag pulled from my mouth. I look up, catching sight of the glowing eyes of the . . .

Alphas.

More precisely, the laughing-their-asses-off Alphas.

"Oh man, we got you!" Varuka crows, high-fiving Mara. Leanna does a little dance around the bonfire while Peter works to untie my sister.

"You should have seen your faces!" Mara cries. "You were totally freaking out."

"Who did you think we were?" Leanna asks gleefully. "Vampires?"

But, to my ultimate annoyance, it's Corbin's face that glows with the most satisfaction. "Hmm," he observes. "Maybe you're not as brave as you thought you were, huh, Little Slayer?"

Now untied, my sister leaps to her feet, her eyes blazing with fury. "How dare you?" she screams at the group. "How could you—?" She breaks off and I realize she's this close to crying. I don't blame her. My whole body's still trembling, amped up with fear and adrenaline. I scramble to my feet and cross the campsite to be by her side, shooting Corbin my best Raynie Look of Death.

"Nice," I growl. "Real effing nice."

"What?" he protests, holding up his hands in mock innocence. "You're just lucky it was us and not the patrol. I mean, let's face it, you guys weren't exactly subtle, crashing through the forest like that. We heard you and saw your light a mile away. And if the guards caught you, there'd be hell to pay." He grins wickedly. "We saved you from a fate worse than death, if you want to know the truth. You should be thanking me."

I scowl. "Well, next time don't do us any favors, okay?"

"Aw, don't be like that!" Peter begs, evidently in a merry mood. He prances over to me, playfully hooking an arm around my shoulder. I shove it away. "Hang out for a while. We've got beer and burgers."

"Yeah, you should stay!" Mara pleads. "I've made way too much food—even taking into account the boys' appetites."

"You can't go back now anyway," Leanna interjects. "You'll get caught by the patrols for sure. We're far enough out not be noticed here, but go any closer and you're sitting ducks."

"Yeah," Peter adds. "You're stuck with us 'til at least two. That's when Johan takes his twenty-minute snooze."

I'm about to retort that Johan can stick his twenty-minute

snooze up his ass, but Sunny suddenly cuts in. "Fine. We'll stay," she says, breaking away from me and plopping down on one of the log stools. I stare after her. What is she doing?

Corbin flashes me another one of his annoyingly sexy grins. As if he's won somehow.

"Fine. I guess we're staying." I shrug. "But for the record? I'm still completely pissed off at you and I will get you back for this."

"Fair enough," Corbin replies with another smirk. He hands us each a can of beer and I take my seat next to Sunny at the fire. "I shall look forward to bearing the brunt of your revenge, Little Slayer."

I roll my eyes and turn my back to him to address my sister. "You okay?" I murmur.

"Yeah," she whispers back. "Just more . . . embarrassed than anything."

"Yeah. Imagine how I feel. I'm supposed to be the big bad vampire slayer here. And I got tricked by a bunch of amateurs." I sigh. "If only I thought I could take on all five at once . . ."

"Don't even think about it," she admonishes me. "Besides, as jerky as they might be, they aren't the bad guys here. They're your fellow slayers and you don't want to be all getting in trouble with Slayer Inc. on top of everything else. Besides," she adds, "we're going to have to postpone the escape plan anyway. Otherwise one of them might report us to the headmistress and we'll miss our head start."

She's right, I know. We can't trust these guys as far as we can throw them. (And without vampire powers, that's admittedly not very far at all.) Still, it sucks we're stuck at school for at least another day. Not to mention stuck out in the woods for the next two hours with the Alpha-bets.

"Who knows," Sunny adds. "Maybe they can help us in a way. You heard what they said about the guard Johan. They may know other useful stuff like that."

"Right." I sigh, reluctantly agreeing with her. "You see, this is why you're so much better at navigating the various high school circles of hell than me. You're way more diplomatic." I take a sip of slightly warm beer. As a vampire I can't eat, but I can drink my weight in alcohol and not get the slightest buzz from it.

The others settle around the fire and Mara starts placing uncooked burgers on a small grill plate. The sight and smell of bloody meat assaults my senses and it's all I can do not to beg her to put a drip tray underneath and let me drink all the greasy droplets that fall into it. Unfortunately, I recognize that kind of odd request would just make things awkward.

"So, um," Sunny says brightly, obviously straining to come up with conversation with our archenemies. "How did you guys all find out you were destined to become slayers?"

Five pairs of confused eyes look over in her direction. "Destined?" Mara repeats doubtfully. "No one's just destined. We all chose to become slayers." The others look at one another, nodding in agreement.

"Wait, what?" I interject. "I thought you had to be born into the whole thing. Once a generation there is a girl, etc., etc."

"You've obviously seen one too many *Buffy* episodes." Varuka sniffs haughtily. "In real life, no one's *born* to be a slayer. It's a choice they make when they turn twelve. You apply, take a test, go through boot camp, and if you make it, then you can come here and start your training."

They get to choose? Man, that's so unfair. Why can't it work that way in America? I mean, then at least they'd get slayers who really wanted the gig to begin with—instead of forcing unwilling girls like me to take the job and threatening to kill them if they refuse.

"Is something wrong, Little Slayer?" Corbin asks sweetly. "You look a little pale. I mean, more than usual."

I can feel Sunny staring at me, but I can't bring myself to meet her questioning eyes. Instead, I swallow hard and force myself to turn the questions back on the group. "So what made you decide to join up then?" I ask.

"Well, I got in some trouble at school," Peter confesses. "And my dad told me it was either Slay School or juvie." He grins. "And slaying vamps just sounded way cooler. Now I'm just like Blade!" he adds, launching into some sort of strange looking kung fu pose I'm positive the real Blade never used.

"Well, I'm a direct descendent of Van Helsing," Varuka snottily adds. "So vampire slaying is in my blood."

I don't have the heart to tell her that according to the Blood Coven files I've read, Van Helsing wasn't the great slayer that Bram Stoker made him out to be. In real life, he was secretly seeing Mina (when her fiancé, Jonathan, was overseas visiting Count Dracula) and when Dracula showed up and chose Mina to be his blood mate, Van Helsing got pissed off and vowed revenge.

Mara looks up from her book. "I've just always been Team Jacob." She shrugs. "It was so unfair that Bella chose that sparkly piece of stalker crap instead of him."

"But that's just a—" Sunny starts. I kick her. After all, we have no idea whether the *Twilight* saga is fictional or not. Why not a Cullen coven?

"And what about you?" I ask, turning to Corbin. "Are you Team Jacob as well?" I tease.

He scowls. "I'm Team Corbin and that's it," he snarls. Rising to his feet, he storms off into the woods.

I look at the rest of the Alphas, puzzled.

"It's a sore subject for him," Leanna whispers. "His parents were killed by vampires."

I raise my eyebrows. "How?"

"We're not sure," Mara says with a shrug. "He never talks about it. He was only a little kid when it happened though."

"Becoming a Slayer is his way of getting revenge against the vampire race," Leanna adds. "And he takes his role very seriously. That's why it was such a big deal that you got the best of him yesterday."

"His goal in life is to kill every vampire on the face of this Earth," adds Peter. "Whether they're good, evil, or totally Switzerland neutral."

Wow. I stare after Corbin, a mixture of pity and unease warring through my insides. Pity, because he's obviously had a rough life. I can't imagine how I'd feel if my parents were drained dry. Unease, because I'm thinking if he ever finds out what I truly am, stake practice may suddenly turn deadly. And I don't know if I can guarantee I'll beat him every time—especially once he has added motivation.

"Yeah, vamps, along with any other otherworld creature he manages to track down," adds Varuka helpfully. "Werewolf, leprechaun, Santa Claus. You name it: If it's supernatural, Corbin's ready to kick its ass."

"Um, awesome?" I mean, what else can I say to that? Sunny reaches over and squeezes my hand comfortingly. I give her a rueful smile, suddenly very glad she's here.

"So what are you two doing out here tonight, anyway?" Peter asks. "Trying to go AWOL from Slay School?"

"Of course not!" Sunny interjects, with far too much force to be believable. Once again the "actress" in the family is the worst liar ever. "We're just . . . um . . . exploring."

The Alphas laugh. "Sure you are," Varuka says patronizingly. "'Cause there's so much to see at midnight."

"Don't worry, we won't tell," adds Leanna. "We've all tried it once or twice."

"Yeah, I'd say most new recruits get the idea after a day or two of training," Peter agrees. "They suddenly aren't sure what they've gotten themselves into. But Riverdale hasn't lost a student yet. The outside world is just too far to get to on foot. The nearest village is probably a hundred and fifty miles away."

Sigh. So much for my great navigation skills. I swear, it looked so close on the map!

"The only way to get out is by helicopter," Leanna says. "And, unfortunately, they keep that locked away, up on the roof of Night School."

"What's the deal with Night School anyway?" Sunny interjects curiously. "We passed the building and it looks all creepy and stuff."

The Alphas glance uneasily at one another. "Um, well, we're not entirely sure," Mara says. "We just know that they only accept a small graduating class of the best and brightest slayers."

"When you graduate, you're given one of three assignments," adds Leanna. "A field job where you're commissioned to go slay vampires out and about, a desk job at Slayer Inc. headquarters in some kind of administration position . . ."

"Or," Varuka butts in, "if you're really lucky, you can go on to Night School. A continuing education program reserved for the top six slayers of each graduating class."

"And what happens to them?"

"We don't . . . know exactly," Mara says, after a pause. "But they're like top-secret ops. A Secret Slayer Service."

"I heard they even do plastic surgery on their faces," Peter adds. "So no one will recognize them. That's how big a deal it is."

"Really?" Sunny makes a face. "And people willingly sign up for this?"

"It's the greatest honor a student here can be awarded," Leanna says reverentially. "Everyone wants to sign up. But only six are chosen."

"And this year, it's definitely going to be us." Varuka smiles smugly. "They don't call us Alphas for nothing. We're the best this school has to offer."

"Hey, maybe you'll be our sixth!" Mara adds, excitedly, turning to me. "If you play your cards right. After all, you're amazing out in the field—"

I'm about to say no thank you, but my words are cut off as Corbin bursts through the forest into the clearing, his eyes wide with fright.

"Someone's coming!" he cries.

The Alphas are on their feet in an instant. "Is it Johan?" Peter asks.

Corbin shakes his head. "No," he says, his voice hoarse and scared. "Definitely not Johan. In fact . . . I don't even think it's human."

11

The camp erupts in a flurry of activity as the Alphas scurry to grab knives and stakes and other assorted weaponry they have lying around the fire. I had no idea they came out here packing so much heat. How dangerous are these woods anyway?

"Stay close," Corbin commands, motioning for everyone to stand on the far side of the fire. "Keep quiet."

We huddle together in silence. The only sound, the sizzling of now-overcooked burgers. So much for dinner. My stomach growls and Varuka shoots me a look. I shrug apologetically.

Then, suddenly, I hear it: a weirdly familiar buzzing sound. At first I can't place it. It's low-pitched and burning, almost like the beating of—

Oh my God. I look over at Sunny, who, I realize, is looking back at me with terrified eyes. *They've found us. Somehow, some way, they've found us.*

Corbin notices our exchange and shoots me a hard stare. "What?" he demands in a hoarse whisper.

"I think it's . . . Oh God." I swallow hard. This is so not good. "I think it might be . . . fairies."

The buzzing grows louder. How did they find us here? This can't be just some random attack. Did the janitor guy sell me out? Headmistress Roberta? Who else knows we're fairies? I reach for my stake, but Corbin stays my hand and offers me a razor-sharp knife instead.

"Go for their wings," he whispers. "That's the sweet spot."

Just the idea makes my own winglets ache a little, but I accept the knife gratefully. Beside me, Sunny's now gripping her own dagger and I can only hope she's far enough back from the action that she won't have to use it.

I open my mouth to tell her to stay behind me, but they're on us before I can speak, dive-bombing into the camp. Just like at Dad's condo, though there's at least ten of them this time. All, once again, looking just as handsome and plastic as a platoon of winged Ken dolls armed with swords. (Thankfully, these particular ones are not flaming or we'd have a serious forest fire on our hands.) They descend at high speed, releasing an ear-piercing shriek on approach. I ward the closest off best I can, slashing at his chest with my blade, then following up with a sound kick to his groin. He staggers backward, dropping his sword to clutch his privates.

I take advantage of his momentary weakness and throw myself forward, knocking him off balance. Together we crash to the ground. I stamp my foot down on his wings, so he can't get up, then reach down and slice one clean off. He howls in pain as blood fountains from the wound, splattering my legs. It's all I can do not to puke in his face.

"Behind you!" I hear Corbin shout and I whirl around, just

in time to dodge an arrow spinning in my direction. It misses me and pierces a nearby tree trunk. From a few feet away, I see Corbin take the archer down.

I glance around frantically for Sunny, but can't locate her in the fighting and confusion. I pray she's all right—that the other Alphas have protected her or led her to safety.

Suddenly I hear a fairy shriek. I look up and realize one of them has taken flight again, preparing to dive-bomb Corbin. The Alpha is busy helping Peter with another fairy and doesn't see him coming. Realizing I have to do something, I leap into the fray, tackling Corbin and throwing him off target. A moment later, the fairy slams into me instead, the force knocking the wind out of me. He rolls me over, his sword slicing at my stomach, and I scream in pain.

Corbin responds. On his feet already, he stabs his sword into the fairy's back. The fairy falls on top of me, his weight crushing my wounded stomach. Corbin kicks him off, and kneels to examine my wounds.

"You're bleeding badly," he says, his voice betraying his fear. "I need to get you out of here."

"No!" I protest weakly as he picks me up like a baby in his arms. "I can't . . . Sunny . . ." Pain stabs at my belly and I moan in agony.

"You won't do her any good in this state," Corbin scolds. "The other Alphas will guard her. Now stop struggling."

I give in. The pain's so fierce I can barely manage to take a breath, never mind start fighting again. Corbin runs through the bushes, carrying me as if I weigh nothing at all. A few moments later, we reach a small cave, tucked into the hillside and hidden by green, leafy vines. If you didn't know to look for it, you'd never find it in a million years. A perfect hideaway.

"Inside," he instructs as he lowers me gently to the ground. I manage to drag myself in and then collapse onto the cool dirt floor. He bites his lower lip. "I should stay . . ." he hedges.

"No! Please!" I beg. "Go back. Make sure my sister is safe!"

After a moment of indecision, he finally nods and disappears. I can hear his quick footsteps through the brush and pray he's not too late. If only Sunny and I had that telepathy thing twins always seem to have in the movies. Then I could know for sure that she was all right.

I won't die myself. After all, I'm a vampire. But let me tell you, that doesn't mean my stomach doesn't hurt like a freaking mother. I try to put pressure on the wound to stop it from bleeding, but it doesn't seem to help. I've already lost a ton of blood. And without any Blood Synthetic to replace what I've lost, it's going to take me a long time to heal.

I wait for what seems an eternity, my mind racing with worst case scenarios. I see Sunny's bloodied body lying twisted and broken by the burned-out fire. I see her tied up and taken away—dragged back to fairyland to become their captive queen. Oh God, why did I have to go and get hurt?

I freeze at the sudden rustling in the bushes outside. A moment later, Corbin pokes his head into the cave and I let out a sigh of relief. "It's just me," he says, crawling in alongside of me, having to duck from the low cave ceiling. He shines a flashlight over my body. "How's your stomach?" he asks, his voice laced with concern. Gone is the big, bad Alpha arrogance he displayed earlier. I guess a near-death-by-fairy experience will do that to a guy.

"Sunny . . . ?" I manage to question hoarsely.

"She's fine," he assures me. "They found her hiding in a nearby bush and are taking her back to school. She's got a few cuts and bruises but that's it. I think she's more scared than anything."

I let out a sigh of relief. Thank God. If anything had happened to my sister . . .

"So we beat the fairies?" I ask, realizing that the battle must be over.

"Oh yeah," Corbin says, his cocky grin returning. "Guess they weren't expecting us to kick so much ass. We wounded three of them and that was enough to send them running. Well, flying," he corrects. He shakes his head. "Man, I can't stop shaking. That was a lot more intense than the sims."

"Sims?"

"You know," he says. "The simulation rooms back at school. Where we practice our slaying."

I stare at him. "Hold on a second. Those vampire kills you were bragging about were glorified video games?" I cry. I start to laugh, but stop as my stomach protests.

"Well, of course," he says, looking offended. "How else would you . . . ?" He stops short, looking at me with wondering eyes. "Are you saying those two kills you made . . . those were real vampires?"

"Duh."

"Wow." He hangs his head. "I don't think any of us have even *seen* a real vampire, never mind slain one." Looking up, he adds, "I think I owe you an apology, Little Slayer."

I'm about to say no big deal, when pain stabs at my stomach again, forcing me to involuntarily cry out in agony.

"Are you okay?" Corbin asks worriedly. He looks down at my stomach, which has started bleeding again. "Oh God. Here I am going on and on and you're hurt. We need to get you back to the clinic." He makes an effort to move. "Can you walk? If not, I'll carry you."

"Wait," I cry. I can't have him take me to the clinic. They'll discover I'm a vampire. Not to mention a fairy. But I can't exactly just assure him that if I lie here long enough my body will heal itself either. At least not without arousing his suspicions.

I try to scramble to my feet, but there's no way. I'm too weak. I've lost too much blood. If only I had some . . .

My gaze falls to Corbin. Even in the low light, my vampire eyes can lock onto the small blue vein pulsing temptingly from his neck . . .

Suddenly I know exactly what I have to do.

"Corbin," I say, swallowing back my extreme unease. "Look at me."

He does. And instantly his piercing green eyes go soft, lost in my spell, just like on the practice field a day before. "Oh Rayne," he murmurs. "You're so beautiful."

I wince at the vampire scent–induced compliment. It kills me that I have to do this. Especially to him, of all people, whose parents were actually murdered by vampires. There's no way if he were in his right mind, he'd be cool with any of this.

But, of course, he's not in his right mind. He's thoroughly knocked out by my vampire seduction. And suddenly he's kissing me. His lips attacking me with a hunger I'm completely unprepared for. And as I open my mouth to protest, his tongue invades, taking me, claiming me, making me his own. He tastes sweet, like mint gum. He feels hot and heavy against my cool vampire skin. As he presses the length of his body against me, I can feel his heartbeat pounding, hard, fast, intense. And when he reaches for me, his touch is firm, with an underlying gentleness I never would have predicted, judging from his cocky outer facade. I breathe in, lost in his scent of vanilla mixed with sandalwood.

Jareth, forgive me, I think as I surrender to his passion, kissing him back with the same fervor he's using with me. I try to remind myself that this is just an appetizer, not foreplay. That it will lead to a meal, not sex. Still, it's more than a little weird to find myself making out with a guy who's definitely not my boyfriend. Even more so when my body responds so hungrily to his touch. But, of course, that's just the bloodlust.

I think.

He groans in pleasure as my lips leave his own to trail kisses down his face, nibbling at his jaw line, then dropping lower to his neck. The idea is to keep him seduced and not startle him out of his trance until I reach the sweet spot. That beautiful vein that will save my life. My body trembles as I lick his dewy skin, desperate for a taste.

This is it. The first time I will ever bite a human. There's no going back after this.

My fangs slide out eagerly, no hesitation at all. They slice through delicate skin as if it's softened butter, sinking in and piercing the vein and enabling sweet blood to start flowing into my desperate mouth. I suck hard, swallowing mouthful after mouthful of blood as Corbin moans in ecstasy, completely lost to the drug of the vampire scent.

This is old-school vampirism. Why we have that scent to begin with. While now we only use it to get out of parking tickets, back in the day before sanctioned donors, victims had to be seduced before being drained. They'd offer their bodies willingly, never imagining they were about to have their lives stolen by their hearts' greatest desires.

I drink and drink, Corbin's life force flowing through me in almost orgasmic waves. Why did I wait so long to try this? It feels so good. So powerful, rich, delicious. Nothing like that disgusting, vile substitute I've been drinking. There's no way I can go back to that, now that I've tasted the real thing . . .

My thoughts are interrupted by the desperate sound of Corbin's heart, pounding frantically in his chest, and I realize I need to stop—now—before I accidentally drain him dry. With major effort, I manage to retract my fangs.

The letdown is instant and the craving inside me nearly unbearable. My victim collapses beside me, passed out instantly in a dead faint. I press my shirt against his neck wound, putting pressure on it to stop the bleeding.

It's then that the fear finds me, hitting me hard and fast. What have I done? How am I going to explain this to him when he wakes up? Will he remember that I did this to him? Will he report me if he does? Or just kill me himself?

Panicked, I shake him roughly to awaken him from his slumber. He looks up at me with glazed eyes. "God, Rayne," he slurs. "You're amazing."

Amazingly awful and disgusting, I think to myself. Then I shake my head. After all, there will be plenty of time for the guilt hangover later. "Don't try to talk," I tell him. "You were bitten by a . . . fairy. A nasty, evil *fairy*. You have a mark on your neck from him," I add. "But you'll be okay."

"Mark . . . fairy . . . okay . . ." he murmurs. Then his eyes roll to the back of his head and he's passed out again. I let out a frustrated breath, praying that he'll remember my words when he wakes up.

It's then that I realize I'm breathing without pain. I look down at my stomach wound, which has completely healed over. The skin is smooth, as if it were never sliced at all.

I shake my head in disbelief. The blood did the trick. I'm completely healed.

Though . . . at what cost? I look over at Corbin's bruised,

swollen neck and feel sick to my stomach. So disgusting. So vile. So monstrous. Who could do such a thing to a person?

I could, I guess. And I just did.

But I swallow hard, forcing myself not to throw up. After all, there's real, genuine life-giving blood in my stomach. And who knows when I'll get the chance to feed again.

Why, anytime you like, a snickering little voice inside reminds me. *He's yours for the snacking now.*

12

I wake the next morning back in my dorm room bed, totally and utterly starving. You'd think all that protein I drank the night before would stay with me for a bit, but evidently no such luck. I want more blood and I want it bad.

And I don't know how the hell I'm going to get it.

Last night after . . . feeding . . . I left Corbin unconscious in the cave and went to find my sister and the other Alphas. Peter had run back to school to get the medics and when they all arrived at the clearing, about twenty minutes later, I brought them to the cave to help Corbin. I told them how a fairy had bitten him and he'd collapsed from blood loss. They accepted my story without much questioning and put him on a gurney to bring him back to the school infirmary. Guilt tore at my insides as I watched them pick up his limp, lifeless body and cart it away. What had

I done? And more important, would he remember, when he woke up, that I'd done it to him?

I dodged the medics' medical examination, insisting I was fine, and headed back to the dorm where I tossed and turned all night, wondering if Corbin would wake up and implicate me in his biting. I became convinced every sound outside my door was the headmistress coming to nano me for my sins. That I'd never again see the light of day.

But no one came and I eventually fell into a restless sleep, woken only by the birds' incessant chirping this morning.

I look over at my sister's bed and see that it's empty. She'd been sound asleep when I returned to the dorm last night and had refused to acknowledge even my most excessive poking. I was dying to talk to her about what happened—to figure out how the fairies had found us—but she was too worn out so I let her sleep.

And now she's gone. I'll have to find her at lunch.

I rise from my bed—feeling stronger than I've felt in days—and glance into the nearby mirror. My skin is flush, my eyes are shiny, my lips are full and red. Even my little winglets have fluffed out prettily. Wow—I look awesome. I guess that's no surprise, considering last night's dinner.

Memories start flooding my brain and guilt slashes at my insides. I remember Corbin's glazed eyes. His smooth neck. His lips on mine, kissing me without relent. What would Jareth think if he'd seen us together? I mean, he'd probably be happy in a way—that I'd finally given in and drunk real blood at long last. But the way it happened . . .

Okay, let's just come out and say it here. I cheated on my boyfriend. I made out with another guy. Even if he was just a midnight snack. That's not how good girlfriends—blood mates—behave.

I shake my head. No, no, I can't be thinking like a human here.

This wasn't some sexual thing. I didn't want to sleep with him. I just needed to drink. And if I hadn't seduced him first, he never would have let me do it. That's why vampires have pheromones to begin with. It's all very natural and normal and not something I should feel guilty about. If I hadn't drunk, I would have, quite simply, died. And Jareth, I'm sure, would prefer me kissing a random guy rather than dying.

It was a self-preservation kiss, that's all.

I touch a finger to my lips, still swollen from Corbin's mouth.

A really good self-preservation kiss . . .

I shake my head. It's over. It's done. Moving on. And Jareth never has to know. It'd just hurt him for no reason, right?

If only he were here . . .

I close my eyes and picture my beautiful vampire boyfriend in my mind. Then, once I've got the image locked, I send out a cry for help. Sometimes I can reach him this way—one of my few vampire powers.

Problem is, I don't know this thing's reach. And Jareth is probably on the other side of the world. Can he hear me when I call? Unfortunately, because the sending only goes in one direction, I have no way to confirm it.

After trying a few times, I give up and get changed into sweatpants and a T-shirt. Slay School classes don't stop just because of a near-death experience. This morning we have combat training, followed by afternoon classes on Slayer Inc. history and Vampire Slaying 201. I wonder if Corbin will be out there. I wonder how I'll face him if he is.

It's another cold day out on the training field. All the students huddling close together, blowing on their hands, desperate to get warm. Except the Alphas, of course, who hang out by their own personal space heater, a little ways down the field. As I approach,

Mara sees me and waves me over. Grateful, I head in her direction, feeling the envious stares of other students burn into my back. I guess this is what it feels like to be popular. Weird.

"Hey, Rayne!" Leanna greets, putting a mittened hand on my arm and pulling me into their circle. The others throw me wan smiles, still looking stressed and nervous from the events of the night before. Several of them have cuts and bruises on their faces and probably other spots as well, underneath their long red robes. "How you holding up?"

"I'm great!" I burst out. "Just a little hungry!"

Wait, what? I cover my hand with my mouth as the others look at me in confusion. I hadn't meant to say that at all. I'd meant to play hurt, confused, scared. Why would I tell them I was great? Not to mention . . . hungry . . .

"Um, and scared," I add quickly, because suddenly I am very scared. Scared of what these students would do if they knew the truth about what I really am and what I'd done to their friend. "How's Corbin?"

"Still in the clinic," Mara says sadly. "They say he lost a ton of blood from the fairy bite." She shudders. "So awful. I can't even imagine!"

Okay, so they bought the whole fairy bite thing. That's good.

"Yeah, that fairy really . . ." I start to say, then trail off, my words seeming to catch in my throat. I'm trying to say *that fairy really messed him up*. But for some reason, I can't spit out the lie. "That fairy . . ." I try again, ice suddenly swimming through my veins. Oh God, what's wrong with me now?

". . . completely effed him up," finishes Peter helpfully. "No kidding."

"Did you see it happen?" Varuka asks.

I swallow hard. "Y-yes," I manage to say, then shut my mouth, forcing myself to stop talking after that. Because what I want to say, for some crazy reason, is that *I not only saw it, but I did it myself.*

What the hell is wrong with me?

"I'm going to go visit him after practice," I blurt out, trying desperately to figure out a way to change the subject. "To see how he's doing."

Luckily, Mr. Klaus picks that moment to blow his whistle and start class. Relieved, I take my spot on the field. Since Corbin's out of service, Peter takes his place as my partner.

"So what really happened last night?" he asks, circling me, waving the stake dangerously in his hands. "Corbin told the powers that be that he got bit by a fairy and you dragged him off to safety."

I try to nod. I really, really, REALLY try to nod my head. But instead I find myself shaking it into a no. I suddenly remember my fairy research. How some of the Sidhe—including me, evidently—are completely unable to tell a lie. Oh God, this is going to make things tough.

"No?" Peter cocks his head in question. "That's not how it happened?" He jabs the stake in my direction, but I block it easily. He's not half as good as Corbin in technique, thank goodness.

"I . . . I . . ." *Oh God, I have to figure out a way to say this right.* "A fairy attacked me. Then I saved him from his attack. We were both . . . injured."

There. That was technically true. Even though his injuries were, like, completely minor compared to what he suffered later at my hands—er, fangs.

"And then he was bit?" Peter presses. Luckily he doesn't say "by a fairy" and I'm able to nod my head this time.

"I guess that's what's really bothering me," he adds, "the

whole fairy bite thing. After all, I'm minoring in fairy studies here at Riverdale. And I've never read anything about them drinking blood. They can have fangs, sure, but that's mostly to suck the juice out of nectar-producing fruits . . ."

"I . . . don't know," I manage to spit out. "I don't know too much about fairies." Though I seem to be learning a little more by the second. Like, for example, the fact that they seem to find it completely impossible to lie.

"Come on, girls!" Mr. Klaus shouts. "This is not home ec. Take down your partner already!"

Peter makes his move, his foot connecting with my chest. However, his technique is poor and he's not that strong. I manage to stay upright and grab his leg, pushing him backward . . .

. . . clear across the field!

Crap! I watch in horror as he sails through the air and lands on his butt, way, way too far down the field to rationally explain. *Did I do that?* I barely touched the guy. I glance around the field anxiously, but luckily no one seems to be paying too much attention.

No one except Peter, of course, who's trying to get back to his feet, holding his butt in agony. I rush over to help him.

"Ugh. Sorry about that!" I cry, helping him up. He looks at me, a shocked expression on his face.

"Damn," he says. "Corbin said you were good, but I had no idea . . ." He shakes his head in disbelief. "You're freaking Superwoman."

I wince. "Sometimes I don't know my own strength." *True!*

Peter reaches around to brush off his backside, then turns back to me. "I think I'm about done for today," he mumbles, then goes over to the coach. I can hear him, even from this far away, asking for a pass to the infirmary.

I can also hear the whispers of the other students as they sneak furtive glances in my direction. Great. In two days, I've sent two Alphas to the hospital. And this one I can't even be held responsible for. I mean, I'm good, but I'm not that good. That's like, vampire powers good. And you know I don't have—

A thought strikes me with the force of a ten-ton truck. Vampire powers. What if they're tied to drinking blood? What if, because I finally drank from a human, I'm able to tap into all the stuff I've been missing out on?

In fact, that makes perfect sense. Why Jareth was able to get his powers back shortly after he got the blood virus and I wasn't. Maybe the key is in the blood. By drinking synthetic, I've been keeping myself down.

And if I have vampire powers . . . and fairy powers, too . . . Maybe, just maybe, I can figure out a super supernatural way to get my sister and me the hell out of Slay School.

A smile slowly spreads over my face. I've got to find Sunny!

13

Lunchtime seems to take forever to come, but finally I hear the church bells chime and I make a mad dash for the cafeteria, excited to tell Sunny what I've discovered. I bet she's still freaking out about the night before. Scared, helpless, alone . . .

Or . . . talking animatedly to Lilli and Amber and Evelyn, a big smile on her face.

I cock my head in confusion. I expected to see shell-shocked, freaking out, maybe even a little comatose. Posttraumatic stressed to the max at the very least. After all, we did nearly lose our lives to evil fairies hell-bent on our abduction. But instead, my sister is beaming, looking as happy as if she'd just gotten crowned prom queen.

"Rayne!" she cries excitedly, patting the seat next to her. "Come sit with us!"

I walk over to their table, feeling completely confused, and take a seat. "How are you feeling, Sun?" I ask.

"I'm great!" she cries. "In fact, I just got promoted out of the kiddie class. No more twelve-year-olds for me! The teacher told me I'm so improved that I'll be placed into your class starting tomorrow. Isn't that awesome?"

"It's a little weird, to be honest," I say. Because I'm still feeling that no-lie thing hardcore. "How did you—"

"Oh my God! There's Peter! He's soooo cute!" Sunny interrupts excitedly. Everyone turns to look at the Alpha, who's limping over to the head table to join the girls. He shoots me a dirty look and I turn away.

Sunny turns back to her friends. "He totally saved my life last night from the evil fairies who were trying to kill us," she gushes. "Want to hear the story?"

Of course everyone does. And so I sit, completely baffled, as she starts recounting our night as if it were a really cool Michael Bay film.

What is wrong with her? She should have been scared out of her mind and yet she's making it out to be some big adventure. Does she have any idea I almost lost my life in the fray? That I had to pretty much sell my soul to the devil to survive the experience? I guess she doesn't, but still . . . something about this is just not right.

"So then Peter jumps in front of the creature and . . ."

And what's with this Peter thing? Why is she suddenly fixated on the Alpha? I mean, just yesterday the girl couldn't get out of bed because she missed her boyfriend so much. She can't now suddenly be crushing on another guy, can she?

God, if so, Hamlet was right about the whole frailty your name is woman thing. Poor Magnus.

"And look at him now, all injured and stuff. All because he was protecting me," Sunny says and her followers all sigh dreamily. "I'm going to go over there. Maybe a back massage will make him feel better."

And without further ado, my sister leaps from the table, bounding over to the Alphas. She reaches around to cover Peter's eyes in a "guess who" kind of way. He turns around, sees her, and starts laughing. Plopping herself down at the empty seat next to him, she starts rubbing his shoulders. I just shake my head in disbelief.

Who is this girl and what have they done with my sister?

My stomach growls, dragging my attention away from Sunny's flirtation and back to my own much more worrisome problem. I swallow hard, trying to ignore the gnawing emptiness inside, growing by the minute. If only I hadn't tried it once, I'm sure I could have staved it off a little longer. But now that I've had a taste—now that I know what I'm missing—I'm having a really hard time controlling my bloodlust.

Well, you're going to have to wait. It's not like there's just a bunch of donors hanging around the slay school—

"Rayne! There you are. I've been searching everywhere for you!"

I look up to see Corbin standing in front of me, dressed all in black, save a white bandage at his neck. His hooded emerald eyes lock onto mine with unshielded desire. My mind flashes back to last night in the cave—my lips at his throat, sucking down his sweet, syrupy blood as he moans in ecstasy. My face flushes and my stomach flip-flops in memory.

Oh God, this is not good. I need to get up and walk away. Now. Before it's too late.

Corbin holds out a hand. I find myself reaching out to take it.

His skin is warm, inviting. He wraps his fingers around mine and pulls me to my feet.

"Come with me, Little Slayer," he commands in a voice that leaves no room for argument.

And, against all my better judgment, I do as he says.

14

We leave the cafeteria and wander off the cobblestone path, hand in hand, around the buildings and into the woods. Corbin says nothing, just grips my hand, and my heart beats wildly in my chest as he pulls me along. I shouldn't be doing this—I know where it's going—where it has to go. Now that I've had my taste of forbidden fruit, I won't be able to stop myself from taking another bite, given the opportunity. And being alone with him in the woods? The guy might as well be wrapping up his neck in a ribbon and putting himself under the Christmas tree.

Just what I always wanted!

I know I should run screaming from the woods and never look back. I should tell him I never want to see him again and it's best we keep our distance from this point forward. But I can't. There's no way. Not when he's willing to offer me the one thing I need more than anything, even though I know it's the last thing I should take.

"So, um, how are you feeling?" I ask, trying to still the desire welling up inside of me with casual conversation.

He shrugs. "Better, I guess." Finding a fallen log in the middle of a small clearing, he sits down on it, gesturing for me to do the same. I sit, as far away as possible from him, but of course he closes the distance between us immediately. Sitting so close that our thighs are touching. I squirm in a mixture of hunger and desire. I hate how attracted I am to him. It makes me feel disloyal to Jareth. Of course, then again, I'm not looking to love Corbin. I just want what he can give me.

But he obviously feels a bit differently, reaching out and taking my chin in his hand and turning my head so our eyes meet, our lips only scarce inches away. "I wanted to thank you," he says earnestly. "For saving my life last night."

Oh God. I shake my head free, guilt assaulting me from every angle. He thinks I *saved* him! When, instead, I'm the one who accidentally almost ended his life altogether with my greediness.

"I . . . really didn't help much," I say. *True.*

"I'd lost so much blood," he continues, not listening to me. "If you hadn't dragged me away to that cave . . ." He shakes his head. "No matter," he says firmly. "I just wanted you to know that I'm sorry about tormenting you before. I'm an idiot sometimes. You're a better person than me and I'm now forever in your debt."

Cool. Then how about a sip of . . .

I shake my head. I feel like I'm going crazy here.

"The whole thing is so strange," he continues, reaching up to touch his bandaged neck. "Why were the fairies there? What did they want? And why would they take my blood? The guardians who interviewed me afterward told me that fairies rarely, if ever, take mortal blood. Most of them are sort of like otherworld vegetarians. Preferring nectar and other things found in nature."

I gnaw at my lower lip. "Well, maybe they suddenly had a Mac Attack?" I suggest, referring to the old McDonald's commercial. I guess I can get away with this "truth" because, honestly, I don't know what was going on in the other fairies' minds. Heck, maybe one of them WAS craving Big Macs while they were bearing down on us. You never know.

Corbin chuckles. "Well, anyway, the scientists swabbed my neck and are evaluating the saliva. Hopefully they can come up with a DNA match since most fairies are cataloged through the Slayer Inc. databases after the Fairyland Revolt in 2002. Maybe this way we can at least come up with which kingdom is responsible for the attack."

I stare at him in horror. Fairy DNA testing? That's so not good. I mean, sure, it's not like they're going to find my fairy DNA in their little database. But what if they figure out during testing that this particular fairy is also a vampire? That's going to put the whole place on red alert.

It had seemed like such a good idea at the time. Drink from Corbin, heal myself, erase his memory so he'd never know what bit him. But I should have known they'd never just let it go like that. Not at a school full of Slayer Inc. operatives.

And with a developing bloodlust, not to mention an expanding pair of wings and the sudden inability to tell a lie, I'm not going to be able to keep much of a low profile either.

"Don't worry," Corbin says, evidently catching a hint of major freak-out on my face. He reaches out to stroke my hand. "I'm sure it's no big deal." He brings my hand to his face and nuzzles my palm against his unshaven cheek, causing my stomach to start doing major flip-flops. "I'm fine, you're fine—that's what's important here."

His skin is so warm. So . . . alive . . . So human . . . "I'm really not that fine, to be honest!" I blurt out, my trembling voice taking on a slightly hysterical screechy tone that makes me sound like my sister. I need to get up and walk away. Now. Before it's too late. I start to stand, but Corbin grips my hand tighter.

"Please." He grins wickedly, capturing my eyes with his own flashing green ones. "You're *damn* fine, girl. In fact, you're downright beautiful. Have I ever told you how beautiful I think you are?"

Sure. Right before I bit you and nearly drained you of half your blood. A moment I'm probably going to be forced to repeat if you don't let me walk away right this very second.

But I can't say that. And I can't lie. So I sit there, helplessly silent, suffering miserably as I stare at his neck. Corbin, of course, takes this as a hint, leaning in, closing his eyes, parting his lips . . .

I shove him back, nearly knocking him off the log in the process. Oops. Damn vampire strength.

His eyes flutter open, annoyance mixed with hurt confusion. "What?" he asks. "Don't you like me kissing you?"

Tell him no! Everything inside me screams. *Tell him you'd rather just be friends.*

"Yes," I say out loud. Because, unfortunately, that's the truth. Now if he asked whether I *wanted* him to kiss me or if he *should* be kissing me or if I *wished* he wouldn't kiss me ever again, I might have had a chance. But did I like his kissing? God, yeah.

He smiles lazily and leans forward again. The electricity between us crackles and I scoot back a few more inches on the log. Any more and I'm going to fall off completely.

"So tell me about your parents," I blurt out, desperate for a topic change. "The other Alphas told me a vampire killed them?"

He groans, leaning backward on the log. "Wow. Okay, buzz-kill."

I grimace like that wasn't exactly what I meant to happen. "Sorry."

"It's okay." He rakes a hand through his black hair. "My parents were young. They had me when they were only eighteen. Obviously not on purpose." He throws me a rueful smile and shrugs his shoulders. "Anyway, it was tough on them. Mom had to drop out of college and they both ended up moving in with her mom—my grandmother. Dad worked two jobs just to make ends meet. Basically they had to grow up fast. Too fast, I guess.

"When they would get a night off, Grandma would volunteer to babysit. And they'd . . . well, try to make up for lost time, you might say. They started going to all these Goth bars and fetish clubs looking for an adult thrill that would make them forget dirty diapers and late-night feedings. And one day they discovered the Blood Bars."

I swallow hard. Oh God, I can see where this is going and it doesn't sound pretty.

"Mind you, I knew none of this at the time," Corbin adds. "I was just a kid, mostly being raised by my grandma, who was wonderful and kind and loving. In fact, I didn't find out what really happened to my parents until Grandma died a few years ago. I was hiding up in the attic during her funeral—I couldn't stand all those fake people standing around, pretending to be sad while stuffing their faces with food. I found my mother's diary hidden above a rafter."

I think about my diary and imagine my daughter stumbling

across it someday. What would she think about all my adventures? Then again, I realize, I'm a vampire. I'm not even sure I can procreate. The thought makes me a bit sad.

I force my attention back to Corbin's story. "I don't know if you learned about Blood Bars in your home school lessons," he continues. "But they're basically a type of fetish club, where humans sign up willingly to go to get sucked by vampires." He scowls. "They go into these . . . rooms and wait for the vampire to come and . . ." He trails off, shuddering. "It's so disgusting, Rayne. I don't know why anyone would volunteer for something like that, never mind get off on it, like these people do."

The indignant look on his face makes me feel like the lowest person in the world. God, what have I done? My stomach swims with nausea.

"Anyway, once I got to Riverdale, I was able to do some more research. Slayer Inc. actually has a file on the case. According to them, one night a Blood Bar vampire got too hungry and wasn't able to stop feeding on my mother. Drained the life right out of her as my father watched helplessly in a corner. When he realized what was happening, he tried to attack the vampire." Corbin laughs bitterly. "Which went about as well as you might expect. The vampire in question killed him and ran away, never to be heard of again." He shakes his head. "Slayer Inc. raided the Blood Bar and shut it down, but besides the surveillance tape they found, which documented the murders, there was no other evidence. It's still an open case. Unsolved."

"So you decided to join Slayer Inc.," I conclude.

"My grandmother died when I was twelve. Six years after my parents had been killed. Slayer Inc. showed up at the cemetery and invited me to train. I was more than willing." He squeezes his hands into fists. "I can't wait to graduate and track down that vampire who killed my parents. He's going to wish he had never been born."

His anger is so fierce, so raw, that suddenly I'm scared. I try to get up off the log, but he grabs my arm again, pulling me back down to him. "Don't go," he pleads. "Not after I've shared this with you. You're the only person I've told and . . ." He trails off, looking at me helplessly. "Now I'm feeling a little freaked out, to be honest."

"Oh, Corbin," I say, my heart going out to him. He acts so hard and cocky on the outside, but he's hiding so much pain. I reach out to give him a comforting hug.

It's all the invitation he needs. He takes my head in his hands and draws me to him, claiming my mouth as his own. There's frantic sadness in his crushing kiss. A need to escape the memories he's long buried deep inside.

But I can't do this. No matter how much I want to help him. I'm not that girl anymore. The one who would lie and cheat and betray. I belong to Jareth now. And that means something to me.

So I struggle to free myself, but his grip is strong and desperate and even my vampire strength is not helping here. His hands fumble with my blouse and I try to swat him away. All I can picture is Jareth, stepping into the clearing, disappointment and horror written on his face as he sees me and misunderstands.

I need to end this. Now.

"Corbin, stop!" I beg. But he doesn't stop. He's lost in his world of pain and anger and I hear a tear as he manages to rip my shirt.

I swallow hard. There's only one way to stop him now.

Pushing away my guilt, my hands fumble for the bandage, ripping it from his neck. My fangs slide out of my mouth and sink into his flesh . . .

And then it comes. The head rush of sweet metallic that nearly knocks me over from its ecstasy. Blood floods my eager mouth and I gulp mouthful after mouthful, as fast as I can. I'm warm, I'm fulfilled. I'm everything I ever wanted to be in my entire life.

"Oh God," he groans from underneath me. "Oh . . ."

He's enjoying this as much as me—maybe even more so. The same guy who, just minutes before, declared his parents to be sick monsters is enjoying the very thing he condemned them for. This is so not good.

I feel his life force pounding inside of me. So strong and stubborn and powerful, just like Corbin himself. No wonder the vampires of old used to drain their victims dry. To drink in someone's entire being—there couldn't be anything more delicious.

A moment later, I force myself to withdraw my fangs, though I'm still desperate for more. Between yesterday and today, Corbin's lost a huge amount of blood and another sip will likely kill him. And then I'll be just as guilty as the vampire who killed his parents.

And I'm not like that. I don't even drink human blood. I'm a vegetarian vampire.

Or, at least, I was.

Suddenly, I realize I'll never go back to synthetic again. Not now that I've had a taste of the real thing. In fact, all I can think of, even now as I'm buzzing with blood, is when I'll be able to get my next drink.

I feel a little sick to my stomach.

Corbin collapses onto the forest floor, panting and shivering. Guilt washes over me as I look down at his quivering frame. Gone is the power and arrogance and anger—I've sucked it all out of him—leaving him a shadow of his former self.

But he'll soon recover, I assure myself, and he won't have any recollection that anything ever happened. And he can go on with his life with the same self-righteous indignation, graduate from Slay School, become a full-fledged slayer, and go exact his revenge against vampire kind.

And I'll take his secret to the grave.

15

I'm up most of the night, high on blood and feeling as guilty as all hell, totally unable to sleep. I keep thinking about Corbin and hoping he's okay. After my little . . . snack, I managed to replace the bandage right as he was regaining consciousness. He groggily stumbled back toward school, saying he didn't feel that well and needed a little nap. I followed him at a distance, making sure he got back okay, though not sure what I'd do if he suddenly collapsed in front of me. Drag him back to the infirmary? They'd only ask what happened and, with my current inability to tell a lie, that interview could very well be my death sentence.

Luckily he managed to get home and I headed back to my own room as well, feeling disgusted with myself. I never, in a million years, when I signed up to become a vampire considered things ending up like this. I'd envisioned myself becoming an all-powerful princess of the night, living in the lap of luxury with a hot blood mate by my side. Not a disgusting monster who robbed innocent people of their blood and then used magic to cover it up. It all seemed so perfect back then—so innocuous: modern vampires, living civilly in peaceable covens, drinking donated blood like so much fine wine.

But what they don't teach you in vamp school is underneath that oh-so-placid surface lies something a lot darker. No matter what the PR firms try to tell you, vampires are not "just like us." And regardless of the strict rules put into place by organizations like Slayer Inc., the monster inside is still lurking, ready to rear its ugly head at a moment's notice.

I remember not understanding Sunny's distress when Magnus first turned her by mistake. After all, what could be so horrible about the gift of eternal life? But now I wonder if perhaps she was the smart one all along. Had I been so seduced by the glory and glamour that I ignored the evil lurking underneath it all?

And now it's too late. I'm a vampire. A bloodsucking beast. For eternity. And there's nothing I can do about it. I so wish Jareth were here. He'd know what to do. Not that I'm some helpless damsel in distress who's dependent on a guy, mind you. But sometimes it's nice to have backup.

Speaking of Sunny, where the hell is she? It's nearly dawn and it doesn't look like her bed's been slept in. God, I hope she didn't run into any trouble with curfew. My mind flashes to Headmistress Roberta dragging the squirming body bag down the road and I shudder.

Just as I've decided to head out and look for her (not like I'm getting any sleep anyway) the dorm room door creaks open and Sunny slips into the room on tiptoes.

"Where the hell have you been?" I demand, pointing at the glowing alarm clock, which currently reads 4:45. "I was worried!"

Startled, she gives a little shriek. Then she starts laughing. "You scared me!" she says, laughing and plopping down on the bed. I wrinkle my nose. She smells more than a bit ripe. Has she really been up all night?

"Yeah, well *you* scared *me*. It's nearly five A.M. I was about to send out a search party." I notice she's still wearing the same clothes she had on the day before. If it were anyone else, I'd totally be calling "walk of shame." But this is Sunny we're talking about. My sister. Innocent with a capital—

"I hooked up with Aiden," she announces excitedly. "Oh my God, he is *so* hot."

I lurch up in bed. "You what?" I cry. "You don't mean you actually . . . ? And I thought it was Peter that you were . . . ?" I trail off, confusion and horror whirling in my gut, not knowing which question I want answered first. "What about Magnus, Sunny? Are you saying you . . . cheated on him?"

I feel the walls of reality crashing down on me. Could it be true? Could my sister, after all this time of waiting, actually have thrown away her virginity to some random guy at Slay School? No way. No effing way. This has to be some kind of joke.

Silhouetted in the light streaming in from our window, Sunny gives me an amused shrug. "Magnus? Magnus who?" she says with a giggle.

"Are you effing kidding me right now?" I demand. "You've been sitting here for days, practically comatose 'cause you can't get in touch with the guy. Going on and on about how you're going to die without him. And now you're telling me you're just hooking up with random classmates and pretending he doesn't exist?" I shake my head in disbelief.

"Look, I'm bored. And a girl has needs, you know," she replies sulkily.

"Sunny, I've known you since you dropped out of the freaking womb. And you've never once had 'needs,'" I remind her. "Not to mention you told me a billion times you wanted your first experience to be special." I snort. "So was it special, Sun? Was hooking up with Aiden all you wanted it to be and more?"

Sunny looks a little taken aback. But she rallies. "It was great," she retorts. "Absolutely fantastic. I can't wait to do it again."

I can feel tears coming to my eyes and I'm not even sure why. After all, I've been trying to get her to give it up for years. I should be happy she finally got it over with, for goodness' sake. But instead all I can think of is Magnus's sad eyes. If he knew about this it would crush him. Absolutely crush him.

Sunny looks over at me and scowls. "Oh you're so self-righteous, aren't you?" she says scornfully. "What, do you think you're the only one allowed to have fun here?"

"Excuse me?"

"Don't act all innocent with me. I've heard all about your little rendezvous with Corbin in the woods," she says. "It's all over campus. Don't you have a boyfriend that you're not supposed to be cheating on, too?"

Oh God. Fears slams through my heart. People saw us? That is so not good. What if they put two and two together and—

"Yeah, I thought so," Sunny adds smugly, taking my silence as an admission of guilt.

I decide I need to come clean. After all, I have no one else to tell. I swallow hard and prop myself up in bed. "Sunny, I've wanted to tell you. I'm in the worst situation ever," I blurt out, feeling the tears welling up in my eyes. Bleh. I hate crying. Especially since vampires cry blood.

In a flash, my sister is on my side of the bed, peering at me with concerned eyes. "What's wrong, sweetie?" she asks. I breathe a sigh of relief. For all her sudden boy weirdness, she's still kind, caring Sunny underneath it all.

"I . . . I . . . drank his blood," I manage to say in a rush. The need to admit it out loud has built up inside like volcano, desperate to erupt. "I drank so much I think I almost killed him."

Sunny stares at me, a horrified look on her face.

"What? Why would you—?"

"I know, I know," I moan, collapsing back on my bed and staring up at the ceiling. "But I'm a vampire, Sun. And I've been starving to death this entire time, not having any blood substitute on campus. I was wounded during the fairy attack and I needed something to help me heal quickly before someone took me to the infirmary and they found out I wasn't human." I squeeze my eyes shut and then open them again. "It was supposed to only be a one-time thing. But then Corbin brought me out into the woods and . . ." I choke on my tears. "I couldn't help myself."

Sunny reaches over and smoothes my hair, gazing at me with worried eyes. "Poor girl," she says. "That must have been horrible for you."

"Please. I wish it were. I wish it were disgusting and horrible and nasty and I never wanted to do it again. But instead, it was amazing. Better than sex. It was all I could do not to drain the guy dry." I grip my sheets in my fists, making a face. "I don't know what's wrong with me."

"Well, it sounds like you're a vampire," Sunny says simply. "And that's what vampires do: They drink blood from people. It's in your nature. How can you fight it?"

I let out a frustrated breath. "It's so ridiculous. Now I'm a vampire, vampire slayer, and turning into a fairy to boot. I found out today that I can't lie anymore. Literally can't spit out anything but the truth. Isn't that crazy?"

Sunny stares at me, horror written on her face.

"Yeah," I admit. "The fairy thing is still happening. I should have never gone and kissed my elbow like that. I'm such an idiot."

Sunny opens her mouth to say something, but at that moment, the church bells start ringing outside. I glance over at her and she shrugs. A moment later, we hear scuffling outside our door. I get out of bed and peek out the window to see students, en masse, rushing toward the chapel.

"It's a little early for church," I remark.

Sunny joins me at the window. "Not to mention it's not Sunday."

A sudden knock at the door startles us both. We whirl around. Lilli peeks her head in, carrying her requisite squeeze bottle of Kool-Aid. "Mandatory meeting in the chapel," she informs us. "Get dressed and get over there quick."

Ten minutes later, we're seated in one of the back pews. The place is packed with students, all whispering to one another, trying to figure out why they've been called together at the crack of dawn. My heart pounds in my chest and my hands are shaking as I stare up at the still-empty pulpit. As a vampire, setting foot in a church already gives me flu-like symptoms. Add those to my growing trepidation about the meeting's topic and I'm pretty much a mess.

I feel movement and turn to see Corbin slipping into the pew beside me. The other Alphas take seats a row back. Corbin's freshly bandaged and looking anemic. But at least he's alive.

"Hey, baby," he murmurs, folding his hand into mine. Sunny

gives me a knowing look, but I turn away. What am I supposed to do? Reject him in front of his friends? Besides, holding hands isn't that big of a deal. It's not like . . . kissing. Or, you know, ripping his neck open and sucking out his blood.

"Do you know what this meeting's about?" I whisper as we watch the headmistress walk down the aisle and to the podium.

Corbin bites his lower lip, looking nervous. "Well, I blacked out yesterday. And so I went back to the nurse for a follow-up appointment." He swallows. "They think I've been bitten a second time."

I stare at him, horrified. Oh God, why hadn't I thought about him going back to the infirmary? Now they're going to know it wasn't part of some random fairy attack.

"I know!" he says, completely mistaking my look. "It's awful. I don't know what's happening to me."

I can feel Sunny's hard stare at my back, but refuse to acknowledge it. I already know what she's thinking: that I'm a disgusting, horrible monster. And she's right. To do this to a fellow human being . . .

I need to get out of this place and fast. Get back to the coven, get back on synthetic. Or hire a donor even. Whatever it takes to stop this horrible transformation. This horrible hunger.

Corbin smiles at me, completely clueless. "Do you want to grab breakfast after this?" he asks. "I'm starving from all the blood loss and I'd love to spend some time with you."

What have I done to this guy? Stolen everything. His blood, his dignity. And yet he still comes back for more. I'm so disgusted with myself I can't even see straight.

"Please?" he adds and the hopefulness in his voice makes me want to stake myself in the heart.

Luckily the headmistress starts talking before I can answer him. We turn our attention to the pulpit.

"Students of Riverdale, thank you for gathering so early this morning for this unannounced assembly," she says into the microphone. "I know rumors have been flying and I wanted to take this time to address them and also inform you of what's really going on."

Murmurs break out, but she silences everyone with a stern gaze.

"As you may have heard, two nights ago, some of our students were illegally partying off campus." She throws a disapproving look over in the direction of the Alphas, who squirm in their seats. "While outside of school grounds, away from the guards, they were attacked by some winged humanoid creatures that we first believed to be members of the Sidhe. Otherwise known as fairies."

I stare up at her in confusion. First believed? What does she mean "first believed?" Of course they were fairies. What else could they possibly be?

"However, we analyzed the bite mark one of the students received from these alleged fairies," she continues and a drip of fear splashes into my empty stomach. "And while it does contain a strain of fairy DNA, it also contains DNA . . ." She pauses dramatically and everyone sits with bated breath. "Of a vampire."

The whole chapel erupts into excited conversation, but the headmistress hushes them with a commanding wave. "I am not finished," she says and the room falls silent again.

"We originally assumed that it was a random attack. But last night, the bitten student came back for a follow-up examination. He'd blacked out and lost more blood. We believe he may have been bitten a second time by this vampiric Sidhe. Which means the creature is likely still at large and may be hiding around campus."

This time, the students aren't so easy to quiet down and the din of conversation reaches an almost deafening level.

"I promise you we're taking this very seriously," the headmistress says, her voice commanding over the chaos. "We've informed all your parents of the incident and they've agreed, for the time being, it's best to go into lockdown until we flush the monster out. No classes for the rest of the week and you will all stay in your dorms, under the watchful eyes of our best guardians."

This elicits initial cheers, quickly followed by disappointed groans. No classes—good. Stuck in the dorms? Definitely not.

The headmistress isn't done, either. "In addition to scouring the campus, we will be interviewing each and every one of you," she adds. "To learn if any of you has any information on this predator. If you can think of anything unusual, please come and see me at any time."

"Ow!" Corbin cries beside me. I look over and am embarrassed to realize that I've been squeezing his hand way too tight.

"Sorry," I whisper. "It's just . . . scary."

But scary isn't even the half of it. I'm stuck here now, under lock and key, making the possibility of escape even more difficult. And when they bring me in for questioning and I find myself unable to tell a lie?

Well, it's good-bye Rayne.

16

We're dismissed by the headmistress and black-clad guardians armed with stakes and other assorted weaponry escort us over to the library. They tell us we're to spend the day here and the night back in our rooms. As if anyone's interested in studying at this point.

The Alphas invite Sunny and I to the private back room. There, among expensive collections and dusty tomes, they've set up camp. It should feel like a sanctuary—dressed in fine, soft leather and rich, elegant wood. Instead it feels like a prison. Not to mention it's stuffy as hell and making me sneeze.

"I'm freaking out here!" Mara says, as she closes the door behind us and turns the key. "I mean, basically what they're saying is there's a murderer out there!"

"Well, not a *murderer* per se," I point out, before realizing I should just sit and keep my mouth shut.

Too late. All the Alphas turn to look at me.

"I mean, no one's actually dead," I finish lamely. If only they knew they'd just locked the monster in with them, instead of out.

"Yeah, for now," Peter butts in. "But how do we know this vampire-fairy mutant thing won't strike again? And what if this time he drains his victim dry?"

"I was pretty close to death," Corbin adds wearily and another pang of guilt stabs in my gut. He's plopped himself down in a nearby armchair, leaning his head back and closing his eyes. "That's what they told me in the infirmary anyway."

"Are you sure you don't remember *anything*, Corbin?" Varuka asks, peering at him with anxious eyes.

"No," he says, shaking his head, eyes still closed. "It's all a complete and utter blank."

The others let out frustrated sighs. "It's so maddening," Leanna complains. "To sit here and do nothing. Maybe we could research or something?" She grabs an ancient-looking book from a nearby shelf and starts thumbing through.

"It's not going to do any good," Sunny interjects. I can feel her looking directly at me and wish she wouldn't. "As the headmistress said, this creature is a totally new thing no one's ever heard of or seen before."

"It sounds so horrible!" Mara says, making a disgusted face. "Some disgusting vile monster putting its claws in poor Corbin and sucking his—"

I can't take it anymore. I burst up from my seat. "I've got to . . . go . . . check out a book," I mutter as I head for the door. I meant to say go to the bathroom, but unfortunately as a vampire, I no longer have the need to pee. And as a fairy I can't lie about it. What a winning combination.

I can feel the stares at my back as I unlock and push open the door, then head out into the library hallway, bloody tears welling up in my eyes. What am I going to do? How am I going to get out of here? I catch a guardian watching me from across the room with suspicious eyes so I swipe my tears away and turn the corner.

I'm trapped. A sitting duck. It's only a matter of time before they discover who I really am. *What* I really am.

I make a mad dash for the front door, but it's locked and the windows are all barred. And, I soon realize, even if I could just walk out, it wouldn't do me any good. There are slayer operatives everywhere, milling about outside, heavily armed with crossbows and stakes and scary-looking medieval axes. I wouldn't make it ten feet before being cut down.

I lean against the wall, feeling defeated. I'm going to die here. I'll never see my parents again. Never see Jareth again . . .

"Rayne!"

Oh God, what now? I turn to see Corbin, rushing down the hall toward me, his emerald eyes full of worry. "Are you okay?" he asks.

I try to nod, but that would be a lie. So instead I resign myself to shaking my head.

Corbin reaches out and brushes a lock of hair from my eyes with tender fingers. I know it's meant to be a comforting gesture, but it only serves to make me feel worse. If only he knew the truth about me. He'd be repulsed. Disgusted. He'd want nothing more than to strike me down then and there with his own bare hands. And, since we're all about the truth here in fairyland, I probably deserve all that and more.

Because even now, standing here with him in all my distress, I still can't stop thinking about his blood.

But he doesn't know. He has no clue. "Don't worry," he says

in a low, soothing voice. "I'll protect you. No matter what. You don't have to be scared."

"Thanks," I say, staring down at my feet. "I don't deserve you." So very true.

He leads me over to an empty corner and pulls me down to the floor. Pressing my back against the hard stone wall, I stare up at the ceiling. He reaches over and takes my cold hand in his own warm one and starts stroking my palm while whispering comforting nothings in my ear.

I know I shouldn't be doing this. I know I should be staying as far away from him as possible. But yet I find I can't pull away. Instead, I snuggle up against his shoulder, breathing in his warm, woodsy scent, trying to block out everything except this one moment of peace. Maybe the last one I'll be able to enjoy for a very long time. Maybe the last one forever.

Suddenly a squeal interrupts us. My eyes fly open, fear striking my heart. A moment later, my sister whirls through the hall, followed by a boy I don't recognize. They're laughing and screeching and ignoring the librarians' shushing.

"Your sister is a piece of work," Corbin remarks dryly.

I watch Sunny disappear around the corner. "She's not usually like this," I say. In fact, she's never like this. Has she just totally snapped because of all the stress we've been under? Or is something else going on here? "I'm going to talk to her tonight," I add.

"Actually, I was sort of hoping you'd come to my room tonight," Corbin says, looking over at me shyly. "We could sneak you in, past the guards . . ."

Oh God. I swallow hard. I've got to stop this. Now. It's gone way too far as it is. Because as much as I'd love to go to his room tonight, it's not for the reasons he thinks. And there's no way I can put myself in that situation again. Because I know what will happen. I'm not strong enough to resist once I get that close.

"Look Corbin," I manage to say. "I know we've been hanging out a lot lately and it's been really nice. I like you. A lot. But . . ." I scrunch up my face. It's going to be hard to break this to him gently when I can only tell the truth. "I have a pretty serious boyfriend back home and I don't think we should cross that line."

His face falls and he looks crushed at my words. My heart aches at the pain I've stupidly caused him by my weakness. I should have never let him kiss me. I should have died of starvation before taking his blood. "I know I should have told you earlier," I say sadly. "It's just . . . I don't know. You're great. And I've been having a great time with you. But . . . we can't . . . you know, let things . . . I mean, I've already let things go too far."

It's killing me to say all this. To see the tears well up in his eyes and know I'm the reason they fall. 'Cause I do like him. A lot. And I don't think it's only for his blood, either. He's a good person, under his arrogant exterior. Strong, caring, smart. A great catch for the right girl. But I'm not the right girl. And if I don't prove that now, I may end up killing him the next time we're together. And I couldn't live with myself after that.

He starts rising to his feet, anger overtaking his sadness. Scrambling up myself, I grab him by the arm. But he shakes off my grasp. "I'm sorry!" I say, desperately searching his face for some hint of forgiveness. "I know I should have told you from the beginning."

He waves me off. "You don't have to explain," he says. "I get it."

"Please, Corbin. I really like you. I want us to be friends."

He looks at me, his eyes a battleground between hate and love. Finally, he sighs, his shoulders slumping. "Come here," he says, beckoning me closer. "Give me a hug and we'll figure this out together."

I collapse in his arms, pressing my body against his sturdy frame. I can feel his heart beating wildly in his chest as he pulls me close to him. Burying his face in my hair, he runs his hands up and down my back and . . .

. . . suddenly freezes.

I watch in horror as he stumbles backward, fear clear in his beautiful green eyes. And suddenly I realize he's felt them. My little wings, which I've been trying to hide under loose clothing. Lost in the moment, I totally forgot they were there.

And now he knows what I am. Who I am.

And what I've done to him.

Slowly, he shakes his head, then turns and walks down the hall, leaving me standing there by myself, wondering what on Earth he's going to do.

I have to get out of here. Now.

17

I search the library for what seems like hours, looking for my sister. I finally find her—hidden behind the stacks, making out with some random, icky-looking boy with major zits on his face. Ew. What is she doing? So gross.

"We've got to talk," I say, tapping her on the arm when she comes up for air. She looks over, annoyed.

"Can't it wait? I'm busy."

I grab the boy by his shirt and shove him away. "Get lost."

He scowls at me. I raise my fist. He slinks off down the stacks, off to find another bored Slayer in Training to suck face with probably. This time preferably one without an overprotective twin. I grab my sister and drag her down the hall until we find a small, unoccupied office. I push her in, then step in myself, closing the door behind us.

"What's your problem?" Sunny snarls, propping herself up

on an empty desk. She's wearing a short skirt I've never seen before and doesn't even have the decency to cross her legs. "I was just getting to know Carl there." Her face is flushed and I notice she has hickeys up and down her neck. "Or . . . was it Chris?" she ponders to herself. "I'm so bad at names."

"I don't care if his name was Santa Claus," I growl. "Sunny, I need you to be serious for a second." I cross the room, stopping a few feet in front of her. "We have a major problem. Corbin felt my wings. And I'm positive he's figured out that I'm the one who bit him. We have to get out of here. Now. Before he rats me out. Or comes back and kills me himself, for that matter."

"But I don't want to leave," Sunny whines, actually sticking out her lower lip in a pout. "I like it here."

"Have you been smoking pixie dust?" I cry. "You were dying to leave just a few days ago. And now you're all big girl on campus?" I shake my head in disbelief. "Don't you want to find Mom and Dad and make sure they're okay? Not to mention Magnus, who I still can't believe you're cheating on with that disgusting dork in the stacks." I slump in my chair. "It's so not like you. These past couple of days—it's like you've turned into this whole other person. Like you've been body snatched or some—"

I stop short, suddenly remembering something I read that afternoon in the library.

Oh God. But that's impossible, right?

Then again, she did start acting weird the day after the fairy attack . . .

Without warning, I lunge at her, grabbing her in a headlock before she can leap away. She squeals in protest, squirming like crazy. But I'm stronger. "Who are you?" I demand.

"Duh! I'm your sister. Sunny. Let me go!"

I tighten my grip. "Don't effing lie to me!"

"Rayne, stop, you're hurting me."

"What's Mom's favorite meat to cook with?"

"Um . . . I don't know . . . chicken?"

"Yeah, right. Try tofu. What's your best friend's name?"

"You're my best friend!"

"Very flattering, but also wrong," I look down at her. She's gasping for breath. "Who did Magnus catch you kissing in Vegas?"

She glares up at me, her face suddenly defiant. "Mother effing Elvis, bitch."

Startled, I let go and she falls to the ground with a thump. I take a wary step back, pressing my back against the door as Sunny—or, more accurately, the fairy changeling pretending to be Sunny—slowly climbs to her feet, a menacing look on her scarred, twisted, green-tinged face. The glamour has shattered and she no longer looks anything like my poor sister.

The changeling starts to laugh, an evil cackle that sends chills through my bones. "You figured it out," she crows excitedly. "Took you long enough, by the way."

"Why are you doing this?" I manage to ask with effort. "And where did you take my sister?" I feel like such an idiot. How could I have not known? My twin sister—the one person I'm closest to in the entire world—and I couldn't even recognize the difference between her and an evil changeling. Wasting all this time, thinking nothing was wrong while poor, sweet Sunny has been floundering captive in fairyland, probably desperately wondering when someone would come rescue her.

"Your fool of a father thought he could hide you away and keep you safe." The changeling snorts. "But we have spies everywhere. With the right . . . donation . . . even Slayer Inc. operatives can be bought." She grins, as if proud. Hell, she probably is. She played me like a freaking fool. "Then it was just a matter of time.

You idiots made it easy, actually, by running away into the woods in the middle of the night, away from the protection of the guards. All we had to do was launch an attack, steal Sunny away, and have me step into her place instead."

"So where's Sunny now?" I demand. "God help you if you touched a hair on her head!"

The changeling yawns. "Puh-leeze." She snorts. "You've been listening to your parents too long. We're not uncivilized beasts, you know. Your sister will be treated like the royal princess she is. Transformed into a fairy and crowned queen. I can promise you, no harm will come to her."

"Right. Just like no harm came to the former queen, my grandmother, when you had her under your protection."

A flash of guilt crosses the changeling's face but then she waves a hand dismissively. "In any case," she continues. "None of this is your concern. Now that Slayer Inc. has delivered us a queen, we must pay what we owe to them in turn." She gives me a knowing look.

I shudder, guessing Slayer Inc. doesn't exactly take Amex for this kind of thing. "And that payment is . . . ?"

The changeling smiles. "Why, you, of course. You're very valuable, you know. The first-ever vampiric Sidhe. They're completely thrilled."

I stare at her, horror slamming into my gut. "You told them," I whisper hoarsely, suddenly realizing that anything Corbin might have figured out is nothing compared to what my sister's changeling has already done.

The changeling opens her mouth, but a sudden, commanding knock on the door is really all the answer I need.

"Sorry to *Rayne* on your parade." The changeling smirks. She blows me a kiss as the guardians push the door open, sending me flying to the floor. My palms skid against the hardwood, giving me one hell of a splinter. But I'm pretty sure that's going to be the least of my problems soon.

"Bye-bye," the changeling chirps, heading for the door. "I'll give your sister your regards back at fairyland."

I turn to the guardians, ready to fight. But before I can even scramble to my feet, they throw a silver net over my head. I know it's real silver, too, since the metal fillings singe my skin—making it sizzle and smoke. Helpless, I fall to the ground, writhing in pain, knowing there's nothing I can do. They've got me and they've got me good. And a moment later, I find myself swimming into blackness.

18

When I wake, I'm in four-points restraints—lying on my back with wrists and ankles cuffed to some sort of rollaway bed. Lifting my head, I strain to take in the room, desperate to figure out where the hell they've taken me. It appears to be some kind of mad scientist laboratory, complete with beakers and test tubes—their yellow and green concoctions boiling madly over red-flamed Bunsen burners, threatening to bubble over at any second.

Definitely not a part of Riverdale I've seen before. If I'm still at Riverdale at all.

After a brief scan of the room, my straining neck pangs in protest and reluctantly I settle my head back down on the bed, my gaze reverting to the dark, high-beamed ceiling draped in cobwebs. Large spiders seem to grin wickedly at me as they go about their work, as if laughing at my current predicament.

I suck in a breath, hoping to calm my jangled nerves. Questions come, fast and furious, with no answers naturally following their query. Where am I? Why am I here? To be honest, I figured I'd be taken to some sort of Riverdale jail to await trial. Or that they'd simply stake me in the heart and be done with it.

The changeling's words suddenly ring through my ears. *You're very valuable, you know,* she'd said. But valuable for what? That, as Hamlet would say, is the question.

"Awake, are we?"

A man with wild salt-and-pepper hair and thick bifocals steps into view. He's wearing the traditional white coat, probably acquired from some mad scientist uniform shop, and has the requisite crazy-man look on his face to boot.

I swallow hard. I've seen enough movies to know this is so not good.

"Hello, Rayne," he says in a screechy voice. "It's great to finally meet you. I'm Dr. Franken."

I grimace. Dr. Franken? As in Franken*stein*? Man, this place gets more cliché by the second. I mean, come on. If I'm going to die anyway, is it so much to ask for a little originality?

Dr. Franken holds out a hand, as if to shake mine in greeting, then seems to remember that I'm tied up at the moment. He cackles. Mad scientist humor. Awesomeness.

"Where am I?" I manage to choke out, trying to sound fierce, but succeeding only in sounding scared and helpless. "Release me at once!" I try again, without much more success.

He chuckles. "All in good time, my dear," he says, wheeling over a small metal table to the side of my bed. He picks up a syringe the size of a freaking turkey baster and connects it to a clear plastic tube. "But first I'm going to need a sample of your blood, if you don't mind."

"Actually, I do mind. I appreciate you asking."

"Your objection is duly noted," he replies. Taking a length of rubber off the table, he proceeds to tie it around my forearm. "It makes me wonder, though. Do you think Corbin minded when you took all that blood from him without asking?"

Corbin's name stabs like a dagger to my heart and my mind proceeds to treat me to a disturbing flashback of his glazed eyes, torn neck—blood spilling down and soaking his shirt collar. I wonder wildly what an interesting laundry detergent commercial something like that would make.

New Tide with bleaching action! Perfect for getting rid of those pesky bloodstains!

I shake my head, my stomach rolling with nausea. Maybe I deserve all of this. Hell, maybe I deserve worse. 'Cause let's be honest here; I haven't exactly been a class act recently.

"What do you plan to do with my blood?" I ask weakly, wondering if he plans to take only a little or completely drain me dry. I know in some TV shows vampire blood becomes a powerful black market drug, but I don't think it works that way in real life.

In real life, the only use for vampire blood is to make more vampires. But why would Slayer Inc. want MORE vampires? Isn't their whole mission in life to get rid of them?

"Why, I wish to study it, of course," he says brightly as he jabs the needle into my arm. I wince and force myself to watch as the thick, dark liquid drains from my body, down the tube, and into a plastic blood bag. "And hopefully someday make more of you."

Wait, what? My eyes fly from the syringe to his face. "Make more of me?" I repeat. "I mean, I know I'm awesome and all. But isn't one Rayne McDonald enough?"

"Oh, you yourself are much more than enough," Dr. Franken

replies, thankfully removing the needle and placing a cotton swab over the wound, binding it with white tape. "But your blood, on the other hand . . ."

"My blood?"

"But of course. The blood of the very first vamshee." He grins. "It's practically priceless."

I do a double take. "*Vam*shee? Are you kidding me?"

"Do you like that?" he asks. "I came up with the term myself. It's a combination of vampire and Sidhe. Kind of like banshee, which is loosely translated to mean female fairy. So thusly, *vamshee* means vampire fairy."

I roll my eyes. "No offense or anything," I say, "but that's pretty lame."

He stops laughing and sets his face to a scowl. *Way to piss off the mad scientist, Rayne.* "In any case, the name really doesn't matter," he says, waving a hand dismissively. "What matters is what we can make of it. A creature with the powers of a vampire and the powers of the fey folk, all mashed together in one delicious chain of brand-new DNA. A hybrid creature with unimaginable potential."

"But . . ." I struggle to understand. "Why would Slayer Inc. need a . . . fairy vampire?" (I'm so not using his stupid term.)

He looks down at me in surprise. "Why, my dear, they don't need *a* fairy vampire. They need an *army* of them."

An army? "But why . . . ?"

"Ah, there she is. Our little vamshee! Captured at last."

With effort, I twist my head to see Headmistress Roberta step into the room. She closes the heavy metal door behind her and walks over to my bed, looking down at me with a self-satisfied smirk on her face. She picks up what I assume to be my chart off the table and studies it carefully.

"Do you think this is going to work?" she asks, turning to Dr. Franken. "I can't afford any more failed experiments."

"Wait—what experiments? What are you trying to do?" I demand awkwardly from my strapped-down position.

"If my calculations are correct, the fey cells will work to stabilize the vampiric ones," Dr. Franken replies, ignoring me. "So they won't oxidize and mutate before we can inject them into our test subjects."

"Excellent," Headmistress Roberta says, rubbing her hands together gleefully. "And, as a bonus, these vamshee hybrids will be even more powerful than just plain vampires would have been." She looks down at me. "I really owe you a big thank you, Rayne. Without you, none of this would be possible."

"None of what? What are you talking about? Why the hell would you want to make vampire fairies?"

"Why, so we can take over the world, of course," she replies, sounding surprised I didn't already know.

Take over the . . . ? I stare at her in disbelief. "But you're part of Slayer Inc.! The good guys! You're supposed to be protecting people from people taking over the world!"

"Please. You think we should be content to live out our entire existence as a police force?" she asks in a haughty voice. "Content to serve and protect all the ungrateful vampires and self-serving fairies out there?" She shakes her head in disgust. "We're done with that. And once we create our master army of vamshees, we'll be on the top of the food chain. For the first time ever, we'll be calling the shots."

This is so not good. I need to warn the Vampire Consortium—not to mention the American arm of Slayer Inc.—before it's too late. But how? I mean, let's be honest here. They've told me their evil plan, which, more than likely, means they're not about to let me walk out of here alive.

Okay, sure, in the movies, that's usually the bad guys' big mistake: spilling their whole evil plan, only to have their captive pull a last-minute James Bond–type move and manage to get away just in time. But sadly I'm far from James Bond. And I have no idea how I'd pull off some thrilling movie-esque escape.

I decide it's best to just keep them talking. At least until I can figure out what I can possibly do. "So this is what Slay School is really about?" I ask, my voice full of disgust. "All these kids training here are just fronts for your . . . experiments?" The word makes me shudder.

"Of course not," Headmistress Roberta replies, looking slightly offended. "Riverdale really does train normal human slayers and has been doing so since before you were born." She shrugs, then continues. "Most of our Slayers in Training will graduate and be sent on regular assignments, none the wiser to any of this building's activities. But a chosen few—the best and the brightest—will continue their studies after graduation, becoming part of our Night School program."

I gasp. Night School. The Alphas. *Corbin.*

"So let me get this straight," I say. "You tell all the Alphas they're entering some kind of top-secret, kick-ass grad school program that will turn them into slayer secret agents with a license to stake. But instead, you plan to turn them into monsters—and use them as pawns in your Slayer Inc. revolution?"

Headmistress Roberta narrows her eyes. "Soldiers, not pawns. And it's a great honor to be chosen," she snarls. "These Alphas will be responsible for shaping the future of our world."

I open my mouth to try to say something noble, like, "You'll never get away with this!" but since I'm not so confident that's true and I can't manage to lie, I'm unable to spit it out. So instead I content myself with saying, "My parents will be back for me!" instead. "They'll figure out you're up to no good!" Which could very well be true. Though I'm not sure their timing is going to match up with what I need in order to stay alive.

"Will they?" Roberta asks innocently. "Or will they simply accept the sad, tragic fact that you were slain by an evil fairy, on a mission to kidnap your sister and bring her back to fairyland?"

I let out a frustrated breath, realizing she's got me there. I mean, sure I'd love to be all like, "No way! My parents will totally see through your evil lies and realize you stole their daughter to aid you in your sinister plot to take over the world!" But really, that doesn't seem all that realistic.

Hopelessness wells up inside of me. Is this really the end? After all I've been through—evil vampires, werewolves, fairies—will my last moments really be spent lying on this uncomfortable bed as my blood is harvested to create a supernatural army of über slayers?

I totally take back what I said about wanting an original, creative demise . . .

Suddenly a commotion by the door interrupts my thoughts of death. I turn to see what's going on. Two attendants are wheeling in a second bed. I gasp as I catch sight of a shock of black hair.

It couldn't be. Could it?

"Corbin?" I whisper, my voice hoarse with horror.

He moans fitfully and I realize he's unconscious and bound in the same magical ropes that knocked me down earlier. I turn my head to locate Headmistress Roberta, my eyes wide. "What have you done to him?" I whisper.

"Don't worry," the headmistress says, thanking the orderlies who wheeled him in. "He'll wake shortly. Though I imagine he's going to be a tad testy with you, now that we've confirmed you were the one who bit him . . ."

Testy doesn't even begin to describe how Corbin must feel. Knowing that I mercilessly sucked the blood from his veins without asking permission.

"Let him go!" I beg. "You've got me. I'm who you wanted. He's innocent."

"My dear, I don't think you understand," Headmistress Roberta coos, walking over to Corbin and brushing a lock of hair from his eyes. "We need him for the experiment."

I swallow hard, praying she doesn't mean what I think she means. But of course she does.

"Once we've analyzed your DNA and mixed up a little blood cocktail, we're going to give your boy here a transfusion." She looks down at Corbin with a proud smile. "He will become our Adam. First in the line of an all-new, all-powerful vamshee race able to slay any otherworld creatures who dare get in their way." She looks up, her face fierce with pride. "No one will ever laugh at Slayer Inc. again."

"But . . . but . . ." I can barely find the words. "Can't you experiment on someone besides Corbin? He hates vampires. His parents were killed by one!"

"My dear, why do you think we chose him?" Headmistress Roberta asks, shooting me a patronizing look. "The anger and rage inside of him will make for an excellent vamshee. And if he has the sudden undying urge to kill vampires once we've turned him? Well, that's kind of the whole point of a slayer, isn't it?"

I imagine poor Corbin, waking up and discovering he's been turned into the one thing he hates more than anything in the world. It'll kill him, for sure.

"You're a monster!" I cry, my voice choked with tears.

Headmistress Roberta rolls her eyes. "Monster?" she repeats with a chuckle. "Please. Have you looked in the mirror lately?" She turns to Dr. Franken. "How long before you'll have a clean sample?"

He looks up from his microscope. "It's going to have to congeal awhile before we can start working with it. Come back tomorrow morning and we should be ready for the injection."

"Very well," she says. "I will be back." She looks down at me and smiles her sick grin. "'Til we meet again, my little vamshee."

Ugh. I really wish people would stop using that term.

19

After she leaves, Dr. Franken injects me with some kind of sedative and I'm knocked out almost instantly. When I awake, I find myself in some kind of windowless room. I'm on the ground, my back against a cold stone wall, and my arms and legs are bound with silver shackles, which have burned ugly red circles around my wrists and ankles.

My stomach heaves and I turn my head just in time to escape throwing up in my lap. Whatever they injected me with is doing a number on my insides; I feel nauseous and hungry and really weak from all the blood loss. So not good.

I blink a few times, trying to adjust my vampire eyes to the darkness. They fall upon a dark mass at the opposite end of the room. I take a tentative sniff and my nose recognizes the familiar hint of vanilla and sandalwood.

"Corbin?" I query. "Is that you?"

I hear an affirming groan and watch the mass shift—head rising, eyes opening, face recognizing.

"Rayne?" he cries, his voice filled with panic.

I nod. "Yeah, it's me."

"Where am I?" he asks. His wrists strain against his bindings, his arm muscles contracting. "Why am I chained up?"

I swallow hard. Here goes nothing. "Well, the best that I can figure is we're in the Night School building," I tell him hesitantly. "As for why, well it's probably best you don't know." I pray they haven't injected him with my blood yet. That it's not already too late.

I can see him shaking his head, trying to remember. Then he looks up, his eyes filled with horror. I can just tell he's reliving that moment in the library when he first felt my wings "You drank from me," he whispers hoarsely. "It was you all along."

"Yes," I say. What good would it be to deny it now, even if I could? "Look, Corbin—"

"Oh God." He slams his head against the concrete wall. "I can't believe this is happening." He looks over at me with sick revulsion on his face. "How could you do this to me? After all we shared—after what I told you about my parents . . ."

I cringe, feeling the ravaging guilt trying to swallow me whole. "I know. And I'm sorry. I know that probably sounds totally lame, but I am seriously really freaking sorry. Believe me, it was the last thing I ever wanted to do. And if it wasn't a life-or-death situation . . . well . . ." I hang my head. "I know, it doesn't matter. I still should have asked." I give him a brief play-by-play on the night the fairies attacked in the woods.

"I didn't want to do it," I conclude. "Not to you. Not to anyone. In fact, before that night, I'd never even drunk human blood.

I'm a freaking vegetarian after all. But when Sunny and I were dumped here to hide out from the fairy army, there was no Blood Synthetic on campus. So it was basically drink human or die." I make a face, disgusted with myself even now. "And you just happened to win the vampire victim lottery."

Corbin is silent for a moment, digesting my story. "How do I know you're not lying to me now?" he says at last, in a tired voice.

"Evidently fairies can't lie," I admit. "It's one of our more annoying traits."

"Yeah. I can see how that might cramp a vampire's style," Corbin snarls sarcastically.

I let out a frustrated sigh. "Look, I don't expect you to forgive me. Hell, I don't even forgive myself at this point. I'm going to have to live with what I did to you 'til the day I die." I pause, then add, "Which will likely be very soon unless we figure out a way to get out of here."

"We?" Corbin repeats bitterly. "There's no 'we' in this scenario."

Right. Of course he'd feel that way. I'd feel that way if I were him. But in this case, it's counterproductive. I draw in a breath, trying to keep my patience. "Look, Corbin, I don't think you understand how much trouble we're in here."

"You almost killed me twice this week. How much worse could this be?"

I hang my head, not blaming him one bit for his anger. He feels betrayed and confused—and deserves to feel all that and more. But, at the same time, all this emotion is wasted energy. We have to work together to get out of here. For his own good as well as mine. How can I convince him of that?

Of course I could just re-glamour the guy. Make him fall in

love with me again and do whatever I say. That'd be the easy way out. But looking at his angry, hurt face, I just can't bring myself to do that. To trick him again.

No, I have to be more honorable if possible. Only do that as a last resort.

"Corbin, listen to me," I say, trying another tact. "I've wronged you. Badly, horribly, unforgivably wronged you. I know that. And I will pay for it, one way or another. But right now, this isn't about me. It's about getting you out of Night School. Because tomorrow morning they plan to inject you with my blood. To make you into the same kind of monster I've become."

"I don't believe you," he snarls back at me. "They wouldn't do that."

"They've *been* doing it," I insist, gritting my teeth. "I heard them talking about failed experiments. And if we stay here, you're going to become one of them."

"No," Corbin says stubbornly. There's a hysterical edge to his voice. "You don't understand. I'm an Alpha. I'm going to Night School!"

I swallow hard. "Corbin, we're in Night School now. Does this look anything like what they promised you?"

He shakes his head miserably. Gone is all the cocky arrogance. He's just a confused little boy who's had the rug pulled out from under him.

I take a deep breath. "Look, Corbin, I know this is a lot to deal with. But we have to figure out a way to escape, okay? Then we can deal with the rest of it."

He nods slowly. Good. "But how?" he asks.

I think for a moment. "What about the other Alphas? Would they help?"

"If they knew we were here, probably," Corbin says with a

shrug. "But they don't. I was alone when they captured me. And we can't exactly text them our location now."

Right. Of course. I bite at my lower lip, thinking. My vampire strength has already dwindled and I don't think—even if I could reach him—Corbin's going to let me bite him again, even if it means regaining my vampire strength for a quick escape. "If only there were other vampires on campus," I muse.

"Why?"

"I have, like, one vampire power," I explain. "I can submit psychic cries for help that can be heard by other vampires."

He snorts. "That's a power? I think I would have held out for a kung fu grip or something."

I give him a half smile. At least he's making jokes.

"Well, it's not like I got to choose," I tell him. "But at times it is useful."

"Well, give it a try then. Maybe there's a wandering vamp out there in the woods. You never know."

"Okay." I'm not optimistic about that, but what the hell. We've got nothing better. I close my eyes and lean my head back against the wall. Concentrating, I push my mental message as hard as I can.

Corbin and Rayne. Trapped in Night School. In danger. Need rescuing!

I open my eyes.

"Any luck?" Corbin asks, his voice betraying his eagerness. "Any vampires respond?"

"Um," I say sheepishly, "I don't actually know."

"What do you mean?"

"Well, I can send. But I can't receive. So I don't exactly get an answer back."

"Now I'm positive I would have held out for a kung fu grip."

"Well, you may get your chance if we don't get out of here," I remind him, which sobers the mood. We fall into an uneasy silence, each listening to the still air, straining to hear a sound of rescue. For about a half hour we hear nothing. Then . . .

The door creaks open. I look over in shock, my eyes widening as none other than Lilli herself steps through the entrance. She grins widely, showing off her fangs. "The vampire cavalry is here," she announces. "Prepare for rescue."

20

"Lilli?" I cry in shock. "You're a vampire?" I can't believe it. Nor can I believe her outfit. I almost don't even recognize her. Gone is her cute little Catholic schoolgirl skirt and Little Orphan Annie hair, which I now realize must have been a wig. In its place is Goth Barbie's dream outfit, complete with black corset top, vinyl miniskirt, fishnet stockings, and platform boots, her long black hair pulled back into a ponytail.

She pulls out a pair of black leather gloves from her messenger bag and slips them on before attempting to break my silver chains. "My name's not actually Lilli," she says. "I'm Rachel."

"Rachel?" I repeat in shock. I *knew* she looked familiar. "Like, Rachel and Charity? Magnus's blood donors?"

"*Former* blood donors," she corrects, grabbing a pair of pliers out of her bag and cutting my chains. "We got infected by the blood virus, remember? So they turned us into vampires to save our lives, much like Jareth did with you. And just like you, we can go out in the sun."

"But why have I never heard of this? I thought Jareth and I were the only ones."

"Because we're working undercover, still living in the human world and pretending to be normal, mortal teenage girls. We can gain access to a lot of places that vampires can't, but at the same time, we're stronger than humans so we can get ourselves out of trouble." The chains snap and fall to the ground. I rub my wrists gratefully and she starts working on my feet. "I was assigned here six months ago. The Vampire Consortium believed some high-up Slayer Inc. operatives had broken off from the main agency and were working to stage a coup." She looks up at me ruefully as the chains clatter to the ground. "Which, of course, seems to be true."

"Didn't you recognize us? Why didn't you tell us who you were?"

"I'm not supposed to break cover," she says. "No matter what. I did try to give you some hints. I even tried to share my stash of synthetic with you. But you kept refusing it."

I suddenly remember all her offers of getting me lunch. The gifts of red Kool-Aid that I never drank. Could I have prevented all of this, just by taking a sip?

"Oh man," I moan. "I'm such an idiot." I stagger to my feet, gripping the wall for support. My body's weak from all that blood they took and my toes have fallen asleep. Is this what Corbin felt like after I nearly drained him dry? I look over at him guiltily. At least if we get out of here he'll never have to go through something like that again.

"And then when I heard Corbin over there had been bit, it was pretty easy to put two and two together. So I contacted the Blood Coven and told them we were going to have to spring you, even if it meant breaking cover and aborting the mission. But by the time Magnus gave me permission, your sister had already turned you in."

"Not my sister," I correct. "A changeling pretending to be her."

Rachel nods. "Well, all I can say is thank the Goth gods you sent me that cry for help. Without it, I'd never have known where they'd taken you."

I throw Corbin a smirk. "Kung fu grip my ass," I quip.

Corbin just rolls his eyes. Rachel approaches, kneeling in front of him and examining his chains. She grabs his arm and he grunts in pain.

"Sorry," she says. "Sometimes I forget how fragile you humans are."

He scowls at her, his muscles contracting as he tries to break his own chains. "I don't need your help, vampire," he snarls.

"Oh relax, Mortal One." Rachel smiles sweetly at him. "I don't bite." Then she laughs. "Well, okay, that's not exactly true, but in your case, I promise to make an exception."

"Come on, Corbin," I beg. "We need to get out of here. Rachel's the only hope we have."

He lets out a long breath. "Fine," he says through gritted teeth. "Do what you have to do."

"Such gratitude," she muses out loud. "No wonder you guys remain at the bottom of the food chain." She cuts through the shackles and they clatter to the ground. "Now, try not to stake me while I continue to save your life, okay?"

"I don't make promises to vampires," Corbin mutters as he staggers to his feet.

"Come on, you two," I cry. "Less bickering, more getting the hell out of here." I make a dash for the open door.

"Wait! You've got to—!" Rachel cries out after me. I stop, turning to question . . .

. . . and an alarm starts blaring through the building.

Uh-oh. Did I do that?

"You've got to watch for the infrareds," Rachel says with a sigh. "Or, you know, not."

"Too late now," Corbin cries. "We need to get out of here, fast!" He runs out the door and down the darkened hallway, which flashes with red lights, pulsing in time with the siren. We reach a set of double doors and push them open, bursting into the same laboratory I woke up in. At the end of the room, a large, bright exit sign is illuminated. We rush toward it, but Corbin stops short, forcing Rachel and I to slam into him. A few beakers fall from the table and shatter with a loud sound. Corbin puts a finger to his lips.

We listen. From below we can hear shouts, footsteps pounding on the stairs, doors slamming. "We can't go this way," Corbin says. "We'll run right into them. Go back the way we came!"

So we head back through the double doors and into the red flashing hallway. This time we take a left and shoot down another dark corridor.

"In here," Rachel says, pointing to an unmarked door. We push through, entering a large, high-ceilinged room, filled with . . . beds?

"What the . . . ?" Corbin looks down in horror at the bed nearest him, his face whitening and his mouth opening into a scream. Rachel catches it just in time, covering his mouth with her hand.

"Shhh!" she commands him. "Don't give us away."

He manages to close his mouth and Rachel removes her hand.

He points at the bed with a shaky finger. I look down at the figure lying upon it. A boy, probably about eighteen. Blond hair, pale skin, eyes closed. He looks almost dead, but I can see the slow pulse at his neck. Coma, perhaps?

"Parker . . . ?" Corbin whispers hoarsely, staggering backward. Rachel catches him and holds him up until he can regain his balance.

"Who's Parker?" I ask curiously, grabbing the chart off the end of the bed. Sure enough the paperwork identifies him as Parker Anderson. "Injected with nine milliliters of vampire blood," I read. "Current condition: comatose."

Corbin shakes his head in horror. "No . . ." he whispers.

"This is what I've been trying to tell you," I say gently, believing he's finally ready to hear the truth. "The Alpha program? They're trying to turn you all into vampires—so you can fight as soldiers in their war to take over the world. But evidently they haven't gotten their formula quite right yet." Thank goodness, too, or we'd be in even more trouble than we are already.

"Trinity, Taylor, Conner, Julian—all of Riverdale's former Alphas are here," Corbin says, going from bed to bed. "I thought . . . I thought they were . . ."

"James Bonding out there in the otherworld?" Rachel says wryly. "Yeah, not so much."

Before anyone can answer, we hear a door open and what sounds like a hundred footsteps clomping just outside. Rachel dives for the door, locking it behind us. "We need to get up to the roof," she says. "To the helicopter."

"Um, can anyone here actually fly a helicopter?" I venture as we run through the room and to the back door. Behind us, I can hear them banging on the door, trying to break it open.

"I can," Corbin says, his distraught face thankfully morphing into a determined one.

Rachel looks at him skeptically. "A real one, or are you talking video game simulation?"

He scowls. "Well, unless you've got your pilot's license, honey, I'm the best chance we've got."

"Less fighting, more running," I call breathlessly up at them.

I lose track of floors as we run up flight after flight. After what seems a million years, we finally reach a door at the top. I wrap my fingers around it and turn.

Locked.

"Great. Now what?" Corbin asks angrily. "You vampires have advanced lock-picking powers, maybe?"

"Nope, but I've got super strength," Rachel says with a smile. She slams her body against the door. The wood creaks and moans, but doesn't give way.

"Might want to turn up the 'super' a little," Corbin suggests, unhelpfully.

Below, the voices are getting louder. "Up here! They've gone to the roof!"

"After them!"

"Come on, Rachel!" I urge. "You can do it!"

Rachel slams the door again. And again.

"Hang on," Corbin says after her fourth attempt. "Allow me." He backs up and charges the door, throwing his full weight upon it. The wood gives way and Corbin crashes through.

He grins mockingly at Rachel. "After you, vampire."

Rachel gives him a grudging nod of respect, then dashes through the hole that used to be the door. I follow directly behind, out onto the roof. It's nighttime and the wind whips through my hair as we make a mad run for the small chopper sitting on the helipad. Corbin takes the driver's seat and starts fumbling with the controls. The propellers begin to slowly whirl and a moment later we're hovering a few feet off the ground.

"Let's go!" I cry.

"Hang on," Corbin says, madly working the gears. "This is supposed to just be a two-person helicopter," he says. "We need to throw some stuff off." He grabs a parachute case and tosses it to the ground.

"No, wait! You barely know how to fly this thing. You're going to need those," Rachel reminds him, jumping off to throw the case back in, then boosting herself back up.

"I know, but . . ." Corbin looks around frantically for other possible discards. At that moment, the rooftop swarms with guardians spilling through the shattered doorway, armed with stakes and crossbows.

"Get off the helicopter," one of them commands into a megaphone. "You're under arrest."

The three of us look at one another. Then Rachel shoves an unfolded map in my hands. "The Blood Coven is waiting for you here," she says, pointing to an X on the map. "Good luck!"

"Wait, what are you—?" I start to say, but before I can get out the words, she's jumped off the 'copter and is running toward the slayers. "Come and get me, bitches!" she cries.

"Rachel, no!" Corbin and I cry in unison.

But it's too late. The guardians turn on her and let loose their crossbows. As the stakes pierce her body, she instantly poofs into nothingness—as if she were never there at all.

"Corbin, go!" I cry, bloody tears flooding my face. "Go now!"

Corbin slams the gear and the helicopter jerks upward, rising over the guardians. They try to shoot, but the wooden stakes bounce harmlessly off the bottom of the 'copter and rain back on the ground below.

I lean my head against the side of the helicopter, trying to catch my breath. "She didn't have to do that," I moan, mostly to myself.

"Actually, she did," Corbin says simply, staring out the front window, steering the 'copter toward our destination. "It just surprised me that she did it."

21

"Rayne!"

I whirl around, my heart leaping to my throat as my eyes fall on Jareth—beautiful, sweet, adoring, wonderful, boyfriend Jareth—pushing through the cafe door and running toward me with all abandon. A moment later, I'm in his cool, vampiric embrace, his arms wrapped around me, squeezing me tight. I bury my face in his shoulder, bloody tears of relief raining down on his *Batman* T-shirt.

"Oh, Rayne," he murmurs. "I thought you were dead. I thought you were dead and I didn't know what to—"

"Shh," I comfort, looking up at him. He's got bloody tears in his eyes, too, and the love that radiates from them scorches me down to my core. I've missed him so much. More than I even realized. Because this is love. Real, honest, deep love between two people who trust each other more than anything in the world.

Not some cheap, dirty lust brought on by a craving for blood. He lowers his head to brush his lips against my own and—

Corbin clears his throat. Ugh. Speaking of . . .

I reluctantly break free from Jareth's hug and turn back to see the Alpha has come up behind me. Guilt slashes through me as I catch sight of his agonized face. I guess all residue of the vampire scent has not deteriorated as I'd hoped. He hates me and yet he can't help but love me. He's fighting it, but it's a brutal battle. And it's all my fault.

"I'm Jareth," my boyfriend greets, stepping up to Corbin and putting out his hand. "Thank you for helping Rayne escape from Riverdale. I am forever in your debt."

Corbin scowls, refusing to take Jareth's hand. He turns to me. "I just came to tell you that they brought over your Bloody Mary. Though sadly for you, I don't think they used real blood," he snarks bitterly.

I give him an apologetic look. After Rachel sacrificed her vampire life for us, we used her map, along with the helicopter's onboard GPS, to find the nearest town and started heading in that direction. Luckily, Corbin's virtual experience made him a pretty good real-life flyer, with the exception of a rather bumpy landing I'm sure I got bruises from. (But considering the alternative, I'll take them!) From there, I purchased a pre-paid phone card and called Jareth on his cell to let him know we'd arrived.

Corbin slinks back over to the table, his shoulders hunched miserably. Jareth turns to look at me with questions in his eyes.

"Uh, sorry," I say. "Let's just say Corbin here isn't the biggest fan of vampires."

"I see." Jareth watches him for a moment. "Rayne, can I speak to you alone?" he says suddenly.

"Um . . . sure." I follow Jareth out of the little town cafe and onto the cobblestone street. There aren't many people out and about in this predawn hour, but he pulls me into a dark corner anyway. Then he turns to me, accusation in his eyes.

"You've drunk from him."

My eyes widen in surprise and the familiar feeling of guilt slams through me once again. "Uh, how can you tell?"

"Because, my dear, it's painfully obvious," he replies, running a hand through his blond hair. "It's also, I might add, going to be a painful problem."

I cringe at his disapproval. This is so not how I wanted our reunion to go. "I couldn't help it!" I protest. "There was no Blood Synthetic on campus. At least none that I knew of at the time. And I was dying of thirst."

"You should have drunk from your sister then."

"I couldn't. She's got this Holy Grail crap in her bloodstream," I remind him. "It's like vampire poison."

"Well, then what about an animal?"

"I tried to eat a few extra-rare hamburgers. I just threw them up." I screw up my face, remembering. "Anyway, I don't get it. What's the big freaking deal? You drink human blood every day."

"Yes, from donors who are contracted and well-paid for their services," Jareth clarifies. "In this day and age no one goes and glamours an unwilling victim, stealing their blood without permission. That's completely against the consortium's rules. You could be kicked out of the coven if anyone finds out what you did. After all, you're still on thin ice from that incident back in England."

I scowl. Those stupid idiot English vampires who flipped their lids when I pulled out my stake. "It wasn't like I was *actually* going to slay them," I protest. "I was just trying to scare them a little for being such jerks."

Jareth suddenly puts a finger to his lips and I turn to see Magnus, on approach. All talk of Rayne's bad behavior must cease in front of the master. "Rayne!" he cries, his face wild and frightened and his long brown hair tousled as he hurries toward me. "Are you okay?" He grabs me and pulls me into a big hug. Which is awkward, considering, on the whole, I don't think he likes me all that much. I'm too much of a troublemaker for a law-abiding vampire like him.

"Magnus, you're crushing me," I mention.

He releases me, looking sheepish. After all, this is no way for the master of one of the largest covens on the Eastern Seaboard to behave. "Tell me everything you know," he demands.

I do. I tell him about our parents' shocking news. About being brought to Riverdale. About Sunny being stolen away by the fairies and replaced by an evil changeling. About me being brought to Night School and Slayer Inc.'s evil plan to take over the otherworld.

I don't, however, mention the little Corbin detail. There'll be time for Rayne to get in trouble later. Or never. I'd be okay with never, too.

Magnus swears under his breath. "This is terrible news," he says. "I knew something was up there—that's why I sent Rachel in the first place—but I had no idea it was such a large-scale operation. And now that they've got your blood . . ."

"We must launch an all-out attack against them," Jareth declares. Now that he's co-master of the Blood Coven with Magnus, he gets a say in these kinds of things. "They have to be stopped before they can perfect their formula and start creating these vampiric Sidhe."

"Indeed," Magnus says, nodding his head distractedly. "But first things first: We must rescue Sunny from the fairies." At Jareth's disapproving glance, he adds, "I made a promise to her in Vegas that she would always come first. And I intend to keep that promise."

I look at him with sudden admiration. If only Sunny were here to hear him say those words. The girl would be over the moon.

"That said," Magnus adds, "you're welcome to start gathering your troops. As soon as we free Sunny, we'll make Slayer Inc. our number one priority."

This seems to appease my boyfriend a bit. "Very well," he says. "But breaking into fairyland is going to be no easy task," he reminds Magnus. "They live at the edges of the world in another dimension beyond our own. To even get there, we'd need fairy magic to part the curtains between the worlds."

Magnus scratches his head. "Do we know any fairies?" he asks.

"Hello?" I wave my hands in their faces. "I'm a fairy, remember?"

The two of them turn and look at me doubtfully. "So, how do you break into fairyland then?" Magnus asks.

"Well . . . I don't know," I admit. "But I'm sure I can—"

"It's not something you can just go and Google, Rayne. These secrets have been kept by the fey folk for thousands of years."

"But I'm fairy royalty. Surely if I knock they'll open the door!" I suggest, knowing my answer sounds weak, even to my own ears. But still, I have to try. I mean, it's my sister that we're talking about here. I can't let her languish in fairyland, away from her true love.

"Well, then what about this?" I ask. "What if we at least head to Ireland—to the town closest to where Tír na nÓg is supposed to be? And then we can see about finding a fairy guide at the very least, if I, myself, can't figure out a way to do it."

He seems to consider this for a moment, then grunts a grudging assent. "Fine," he says. "I guess we have no other choice but to try. Let's head out to the airport. There's no time to waste."

"Um, what about Corbin?" I ask, motioning back to the cafe where he's eating his predawn breakfast. "We can't just leave him here. Slayer Inc. might find him."

Magnus frowns. "I don't know," he replies. "I don't like the idea of having someone trained by this subset of Slayer Inc. tagging along with us. Especially when we're away from home and without proper security. What makes you think he won't get a call from his bosses instructing him to sneak into our hotel rooms and stake us in our sleep?"

"Because those *bosses* tried to kill him," I remind the vampire. "And they destroyed the lives of his friends. There's no way he'd go back to them now, knowing what they're capable of." But even as I'm defending him, I wonder. I remember the hatred in his eyes when he talked about the vampires who killed his parents . . .

But still. He deserves a chance to make good—especially after what I put him through.

"Look," I plead to Magnus. "He saved my life. Without him, I'd be stuck at Night School and Sunny would be stuck in fairyland and you guys wouldn't have a clue as to what happened to us. Because of him, I made it out, Sunny will be okay, and you have a fighting chance to defeat this subset of Slayer Inc. before they take over the world."

"Fine," Magnus relents, still not sounding like he's going to be signing up for the Corbin fan club anytime soon. "He can come. But technically he'll be our prisoner until we can figure out what to do with him. One false move and we will take him out. No questions asked."

"No problem," I say, relief washing through me. "You won't have to do anything, I promise. He'll be so well-behaved you won't even notice him."

"Well, then," Jareth says. "If that's settled, what are we waiting for? Let's get to fairyland and rescue your sister!"

22

"Wake up, sleepyhead. We're going to land in a few minutes."

I yawn and stretch my arms over my head, reluctantly opening my eyes. I smile as they fall on Jareth, who's kneeling above me on the private plane's cushy, velvet-covered bed (I so don't sleep in coffins!), looking down at me with his beautiful, loving eyes.

"Are you okay?" he asks, handing me a squeeze bottle of Blood Synthetic. "You slept like the dead."

"Stands to figure, since I'm a vampire and all," I tease.

He grins. "That's my Rayne."

He lies down beside me and takes me into his arms, pulling me into a comfortable embrace, his body pressed against mine. I deeply breathe in his rich, dark scent. I've missed him so much. My heart feels as if it might literally explode with love.

He strokes my back, his gentle hands running over my feathery wings, which have grown almost to full size. Luckily they also tuck in very well and with my shirt on, you can't really notice them.

"I was so worried," he whispers, his mouth brushing up against my ear. His toes intertwine with mine. He nuzzles my cheek, as if he's still checking to see if I'm really here, in the flesh. "When Rachel called and said you were in danger, I almost died."

"It's a good thing I'm such a kick-ass, don't-need-a-guy-to-rescue-me type of girl, huh?" I tease, but at the same time I can feel the tears well up into my eyes. The fact that he put everything on pause, just for me, is beyond wonderful. For all our past fights and difficulties, he loves me. More than anything in the world. And I need to appreciate that with all my heart.

Because I feel the same way about him.

The moments spent with Corbin now seem a pale imitation, a parody of romance on the weakest level. A mere lusty need, not a deep, mature love like I have with Jareth. The thought now of Corbin's lips on mine only serves to make me sick. I wish I had never touched the guy. I wish I could forget it ever happened. I wish I had never drunk anything but the synthetic as long as I lived. Then I wouldn't know how the other stuff can be.

I let out an involuntary sob.

"Don't worry, my dearest," Jareth murmurs, misunderstanding my tears and wiping them away with a gentle thumb. "We'll find Sunny. And she'll be fine. She's their queen, after all. Hell, she's probably being treated like royalty right about now. All the nectar she can drink."

"But she doesn't want that," I remind him, grateful to switch topics. "Sunny just wants to be human."

"I know," Jareth says, planting a fond kiss on my forehead. "And that's why we're going to get her back. We'll bring her back to the Blood Coven and all four of us can live happily ever after."

"Mmm," I say dreamily. "That sounds amazing." I tangle myself deeper into his arms. "Happily ever after for everyone," I murmur as I plant my lips on Jareth's and we begin to kiss.

"Ahem."

The sound of a clearing throat causes us to break away. I look up. Corbin's standing at the door, looking really uncomfortable. He shifts from foot to foot. Instinctively, I put a little space between Jareth and myself. "What's up?" I ask.

"Sorry," he stammers. "Magnus told me to tell you to buckle up for landing. We'll be on the ground in six minutes." He turns quickly and walks away.

I glance guiltily over at Jareth, who's looking at me with worried eyes. "I'm really not sure it was the best decision to bring him along," he says in a low voice. "He has much anger inside of him. And for good reason, too."

I hang my head and grab the blood substitute, taking a swig. Yuck. This stuff is disgusting. How have I been drinking it for so long?

"I know," I say. "I feel terrible about what I did to him."

"He's also got a lot of power and training," Jareth adds. "He could be dangerous."

"No." I shake my head stubbornly. "He's a good guy. I swear. He's just hurt because of the whole blood thing. He thinks he's in love with me."

"Oh Rayne," Jareth says with a deep sigh. "How do you always manage to get yourself into these kinds of situations?"

I shrug, grinning impishly at him. "Just lucky, I guess. Just like you're lucky to have me!"

He laughs and grabs me, playfully wrestling me into submission. "Am I?" he asks, tickling my ribs. I squeal and giggle in protest. "Am I lucky to have you?"

"YES!" I cry. "Now stop! We've got to follow FAA regulations and buckle up for safety. Seatbacks and tray tables and all that."

He snorts and stops tickling me. "Oh fine," he says in a mock huff. "Be that way!" Jumping off the bed, we head into the main cabin to take our seats for landing. As we descend, I glance out the window at the expanse of green below me.

"Don't worry, Sunny," I whisper, dragging a finger down the glass. "We're coming. We're going to save you. No matter what."

We land at a small airport, outside a little town called Donegal, which is complete with requisite ancient castle, lively pubs, and quaint shops. Because the sun is just coming over the horizon, we're forced to stop for the day at a little bed-and-breakfast in the center of town so the vampires can get their sleep on. Even Jareth, who technically can go out in the sun, decides to take a little nap. He's been trying to get back on schedule with his fellow vamps now that he's co-master of the coven.

I, however, having slept on the plane, am restless. Pacing the room until Jareth finally suggests I go out and explore, so he can get some sleep. I acquiesce and head out to the local pub to see if I can find out some information about Tír na nÓg, the fairy land my parents came from.

I decide to try a place called the Olde Castle Bar, which is predictably across from the castle itself. The place looks ancient from the outside, with rough stone walls right out of medieval times, but inside it's cozy and cheery, with simple furniture and wall hangings. I pull up to the bar and order a pint, giving the young bartender, who can't be more than my age, a wide smile.

"You here on holiday, are you?" he asks in an endearing, thick Northern Irish accent as he hands me a frothy pint glass in exchange for my coins.

"Not exactly," I say, taking a sip. Ugh. I forgot they serve ale at room temperature in these parts. "Actually, it's more like a quest."

"A quest, eh?" he repeats with a laugh. "You've come to see the fairies, then?"

I raise my eyebrows. "You know about fairies?"

"Sure I do," he says with an amused gleam in his eye. "Ireland's a magical place after all. And we have our fair share of the fair folk, for good or ill. Every night we leave milk and honey out for them, so they don't cause mischief." He glances around at the older patrons in the bar. "We've got mischief to spare as it is at the Olde Castle Bar."

I slump in my seat, suddenly realizing he's just teasing me. What was I thinking? "Have you heard of the island of Tír na nÓg?" I ask, changing tactics. "We're trying to get there."

This time the bartender just breaks out into a loud guffaw. "You'll be trying a long time, lass," he says. "Seeing as it doesn't exist."

I do a double take. "Wait, what?"

He shakes his head patronizingly. "It is an isle of legends, but appears on no map you'll find. And you'll only get lost if you try searching the sea." He offers me a sympathetic smile. "Why not give up your quest for fairies?" he suggests. "There's a lot more to see in Donegal, after all. We've got fabulous views from the craggy cliffs, and castle tours start daily at ten." He grins. "Of course, you're always welcome to while your hours away here at the pub. The fairies know we need the coin to keep them in their milk and honey."

I scowl and am about to thank him for his time and leave when an old woman interjects into the conversation. "Now, now, Collin," she scolds. "You'll be talking a girl's ear off if she gives you half a chance." I turn to my right to see the craggy-faced, white-haired little woman who has sidled up beside me at the bar. She smiles at me and I realize she's missing more than a few of her teeth. "Come sit beside me, dear, and drink your pint," she urges, "I get lonely taking tea by meself and I promise I won't blather on like Collin about our local tourist attractions."

At first, I'm not sure, but something about her hopeful smile compels me to nod in agreement. I follow her to a booth at the very back of the pub, away from all of the other diners, and settle down onto a hard wooden bench.

I turn to the woman and am surprised to see that suddenly her whole manner has changed. Her once-smiling eyes are now piercing and her mouth is set into a firm, scolding line. "Now, how about you tell me," she says in a steely voice that's suddenly not even the slightest bit crackly, "why a mischievous Sidhe like yourself would try to trick a simple bartender?"

I stare at her, wide-eyed. "Wh-what?" I ask, shocked beyond belief. How does she know I'm Sidhe? Is she a fairy herself? I suddenly realize I'm shaking with fear.

"I can assure you, Collin is a very sweet boy. And he does his duty well. I'll not have you try to trick him into breaking the rules, just to test his will."

"But . . . I wasn't . . . I'm not . . . I wouldn't trick him," I stammer. "I really am trying to find Tír na nÓg. I've never been there before and I'm desperate to reach it as soon as possible."

The woman looks at me incredulously. "But how can you say

that?" she demands. "I've seen you there myself. On the throne, on your coronation day."

My mouth drops open. Of course! "You mean, you saw . . . oh my God." I swallow hard, my whole body buzzing with excitement. "You saw Sunny!"

"Yes, Sunny," the woman agrees. "But you are Sunny! You think I wouldn't recognize you, just because you colored your hair? Give me a little credit here!"

"No, no—you don't understand! I'm her sister. Her twin sister. And I've been trying desperately to find her. Please," I say, entreating the woman with my best pleading gaze. "Can you help me? Can you help my friends and me find Tír na nÓg?"

"Well, of course I can!" The woman smiles a big toothless grin. "I wouldn't be a very good fairy godmother if I couldn't, now would I?"

23

"Fairy godmother?" I repeat in disbelief. "You're a freaking fairy godmother?"

"Of course," she says, looking a bit offended. "Don't you recognize one when you see them? We're the only Sidhe who look like old ladies, after all."

I shrug. "I've never seen a real Sidhe of any sort. I mean, besides my own family, I guess, and we just look plain old human. What do normal Sidhe look like?"

"Young, beautiful, thin, tall, blond, perfect figures." She sighs miserably. "You know, your typical Disney princess type plus wings. It really is completely unfair."

"Wow. So how come Sunny and I aren't like that?"

"Probably because you didn't grow up in fairyland. After all, they don't call it Tír na nÓg for nothing, you know."

"Oh yeah. That's right." I remember reading that in my studies somewhere. Tír na nÓg means "place of eternal youth and beauty" or something like that.

"Once you step foot in Tír na nÓg, you'll never grow old," she says in a sing-songy voice. "Well, unless you're destined to become a fairy godmother, that is." She scowls. "Thank you very much, Walt Disney."

"Wait, what?"

She shakes her head in disgust. "Once upon a time, we fairy godmothers were just as young and beautiful as the other Sidhe," she informs me. "But then Disney comes along and creates movies like *Cinderella*. Now everyone expects their fairy godmother to be a plump old lady with no fashion sense. It's ridiculous." She sighs. "Our union tried to lobby the powers-that-be for a while. We even launched a full-on PR campaign to prove to people that fairy godmothers can come in all shapes and sizes. But no one bought it."

"No?"

"Let's be realistic here. You descend down into someone's bedroom window as a fat old lady with a magic wand offering to make that person's wish come true, you're a welcomed guest. You show up as a young, hot debutante in slinky silk Armani and they're on the phone with the coppers before you can say *bippity boppity boo*."

"Yeah, I guess I can see that."

"So eventually we had to have Glinda, the Good Witch, take us down the Yellow Brick Road to see the Wizard and have him age us up so we'd better appeal to the masses."

"The Wizard?" I repeat. This story is getting crazier and crazier. "But I thought he was a fake."

"That's what we wanted Dorothy to believe . . ." the fairy godmother replies with an exaggerated wink.

I lean back in my seat, not knowing where to start.

"Anyway, if you can get past the old crone thing, it's really not that bad a gig," she continues. "We get to travel a ton, helping our godchildren with things like designer clothes, tickets to the hottest balls, elegant transportation . . ."

"Oh, like a carriage made out of a pumpkin!" I exclaim.

She gives me an amused look. "Yeah, if we were in the Middle Ages!" she says sarcastically. "Today, it's more like a Mercedes made of melons, thank you very much."

Of course it is.

"So then can you help me?" I ask hopefully. "Can I be your Cinderella? I have to get to Tír na nÓg and find my sister."

She glances at her watch. A Rolex, in case you were wondering. "I have a flight to catch in an hour," she muses. "Some servant girl in Slovenia is hoping to hook up with the prime minister at the royal meet-and-greet tonight." She taps a finger to her chin. "I guess I could give you directions at least. And how about a Lamborghini made of lemons?" She pauses, then adds, "Just make sure you have it back by midnight or there could be some . . . complications of a decidedly sticky sort."

I make a face. "It's okay," I tell her. "I'll just take the directions, if you don't mind."

She grabs a napkin and a MAC lipstick out of her Chanel purse and draws a small little map. "Most people think Tír na nÓg is an island," she says. "But actually it's here on the mainland. Just a different 'here.' "

"Right. And there's some secret way to part the curtains of the world?"

She looks up. "Your parents didn't teach you anything, did they?"

I shake my head.

"It's okay. After all, if it weren't for absentee parents, I'd be out of a job." She waves her hands and mutters something under her breath and a moment later a small piece of parchment paper flutters to the table. I pick it up eagerly.

"Are these directions?" I squint at the paper.

"No, no. I don't have time to conjure up a full-on poem on the fly. It's just the URL for the fairyland cheat codes. Print out the magic words and then head here." She presses a finger to the map. "The rest will be obvious, you being Sidhe and all." She looks up and smiles at me. "You sure you don't want the lemon Lamborghini? Or maybe a frankfurter Ferrari?"

I'm tempted, but I shake my head. "That's okay," I say. "Thank you. You've been very helpful."

"Good luck," she says. "Tell your sister I said hello." She rises from her seat.

"Wait. You've met Sunny?" I ask. "In Tír na nÓg?"

"Met her?" The fairy godmother laughs. "I conjured up her wedding gown."

And with that, she pulls a wand out of her purse and waves it twice, disappearing into a cloud of glitter. I look around the pub, but no one seems to have noticed anything except me.

I sink into the booth. Fairy godmother. Who would have thought? And what was that she said about Sunny . . . ?

Oh my God. She said wedding gown! That means . . .

I grab the napkin map and run for the door. We need to get to Tír na nÓg now! Before it's too late!

24

I run back to the hotel, but realize once I get there that I neglected to take my key. I pound on the hotel room door where Jareth and I are staying, but there's no answer. Vampires, probably not so surprisingly, sleep like the dead during the day and it's nearly impossible to wake them up. I thought perhaps Jareth would be an exception, seeing as he no longer has that pesky sun allergy, but I guess not so much.

Frustrated, I pound again. Louder this time. From the next room over, another door opens and Corbin peeks his head out.

"You okay?" he asks.

"Yeah, just trying to wake the undead," I say, giving up and walking down the hall toward him. "How are you doing?"

He shrugs, but widens the door so I can step inside his room. Part of me thinks this could be a bad idea—being alone with him and all—but at this point I'm stuffed full of Blood Synthetic and not in a snacking mood. I figure if I start feeling the urge to splurge, I'll check out quick.

So I enter the room and sit down on an old-fashioned cushioned armchair by the window. He sits down on the double bed, which, I note, has not been slept in. "I can't tell you how weird this all is," he confesses. "Hanging out with a coven of vampires and all. I never would have thought in a million years."

"Yeah, but you've got to admit, the Blood Coven's pretty cool, right?" I ask. "I mean, they're all civilized and law-abiding and stuff."

He nods. "I had a long talk with Magnus on the plane ride over here," he says. "He's a pretty smart guy. He told me all about the consortium's current politics and how the Blood Coven has been working to develop peaceable solutions when it comes to vampire/human relations."

My shoulders relax a bit; I'm glad Magnus was able to talk some sense into him. "Yeah, most vampires I've met are pretty upstanding citizens. And the ones that aren't? Well, I stake those." I give him a grin.

"So you really are a slayer then?" Corbin marvels. "For some reason I just assumed that was a front so you could hide out at Riverdale. Like Lilli—er, Rachel—was."

"Yup. I'm the real deal. And I've had two major vampire slays to my name, not to mention a whole crazy werewolf cheerleader thing I won't get into."

"So you're a fairy, a vampire, and a vampire slayer . . ." He ticks off my roles on his fingers. "All rolled into one. That's a lot to keep track of."

"You're telling me."

He grows silent for a moment, then adds, "And now you've been reunited with your true love." He stares down at his hands and I notice his fingernails are bitten to the quick. "I guess congratulations are in order."

I sigh. "About that, Corbin. I never meant—"

He waves me off. "It's okay. I get it. You don't have to explain again. You needed blood. Mine was available. You seduced me and I let you take it."

"It's really not that simple . . ." I say, feeling that guilt all over again.

He looks up, questioningly.

"It's not like you were just some random person I drank from. You're the *only* person I've drunk from. My first." I pause, then add, "And as they say, you never forget your first."

"Is that supposed to make me feel better or something?"

I gnaw at my lower lip. "Look, Corbin, I like you. You're a great guy. You're passionate, strong, interesting to talk to . . ."

"Let me guess, it's not me, it's you," he interrupts. "And you'd love to stay friends."

I let out a frustrated breath. "I've got a boyfriend."

"So you say."

"And I love him. As blood mates, we share a very deep bond. Not something easily broken up."

"Right. You've made that very clear."

"But that doesn't mean . . ."

"We can't be friends?" He snorts. "Yes, it does, Rayne. It definitely does."

My eyes well up with tears at the anger I can hear in his voice. "Why not?" I demand. "Why does it have to be all or nothing?"

Corbin rakes a hand through his hair. "Because I don't feel very friendly toward you," he admits. "I love you, but I also hate you. I'm torn between kissing you . . ." He pauses, then looks up with bloodshot eyes. "And killing you."

I swallow hard. "Maybe I should go." I start to rise from my seat.

"You should," Corbin says slowly. "But you won't."

Quick as lightning, he leaps from the bed and grabs something from under the mattress. I gasp.

It's a stake.

"Corbin, what are you—" I back up and hit the glass window. Crap. Nowhere to go and Corbin's blocking the door.

"If I can't have you," he snarls, "then I'm going to make sure *no one* can."

"Corbin, listen," I plead, trying desperately to keep my voice calm while my mind races for an escape plan. "You're just feeling the aftereffects of my vampire scent. You actually hate me, remember? You think I'm a pathetic home-schooled slayer vamp. Don't throw everything away on a feeling that's not even real."

His face turns purple with rage. "Vampire scent?" he repeats. Uh-oh. Maybe I shouldn't have gone there, now that I think about it. "I should have known! All this anguish I feel inside . . . all this agony and pain . . . it's been your evil pheromones this whole time, hasn't it?"

I nod weakly. This is so not good.

"I should have never trusted you," he growls, brandishing his stake as he takes a step closer. "You're just like the rest of them. A sick, twisted, disgusting bloodsucking beast. And just like the rest of them, you don't deserve to live."

He flies at me so fast I barely have time to react. I manage to duck a split second before his stake makes contact with my heart. Instead, he crashes into the window, the impact shattering the glass and cutting his hand. Blood drips from the wound and I can feel my fangs elongate in eagerness.

I head for the door, but he's too quick, diving at me and managing to latch on to my ankle. I lose my balance and slam to the ground. As he yanks me back toward him, I claw at the carpet, but can't seem to get a handhold. So I kick backward with my free foot, my steel-toed Doc Marten boot connecting with his nose. I hear a crack, followed by a scream of pain, and my ankle is now free.

I flip myself over and leap to my feet, grabbing him by the shoulders and smashing him against the wall. His head slams with a thud and he slumps to the ground, unconscious, as blood fountains from his nose, hands, and head. The smell and sight of it all overwhelms my senses, and the next moment I find myself on top of him, fangs buried deep into his neck, and there's nothing I can do about it.

I can feel his feeble thrashes beneath me as he regains consciousness, but he has all the strength of a premature baby. I taste his anger, his pain, his agony—each sip more delicious than the last and I find I can barely form a conscious thought over the ever-flowing ecstasy. His heart thuds beneath me, strong at first, then weakening as I gulp mouthful after mouthful of his spicy, hot blood.

Soon his protests stop and his body grows limp, his pulse slows and the blood gets even more delicious, if that's possible. I'm drinking his essence now, I dimly realize, his very soul and life are draining into me. And it's so, so good.

No! I can't do this. I can't hurt him any more than I already have. If I do, I'll be proving to him what he believed all along. That vampires are evil. And I'm not evil. I just . . .

I just need help!

It takes every ounce of my strength, but I force myself to pull away. I look down at him, horrified, praying I wasn't too late. That I didn't take a life. Corbin's life, of all people. To hurt him—after he saved me from Slayer Inc. back at Night School . . .

I really would be a monster.

My eyes catch a slight rise and fall from his chest. He's alive, but maybe barely. And maybe not for long. I summon up everything inside me in a psychic scream, begging Jareth to wake up and help me as I try to press a towel to the wound to stop the flow of blood.

He bursts into the room a moment later, his eyes wide and horrified when he sees what I've done. "Please," I beg. "Please help him. I didn't mean to . . ."

"Move aside," he instructs and I comply, whimpering in a mixture of horror and fear as I crawl into the corner of the room, pulling my knees to my chest and hugging them tightly. Blood—Corbin's blood—drips onto my skirt, staining it crimson, and I want to throw up.

Jareth was right all along: I need help. And if I get out of this mess—if Corbin lives—I swear I will suck up my pride and ask for it. I will accept any help I can get. Counseling, blood rehab, whatever it takes. I admit it—I can't do it alone. The monster inside is too strong.

I watch as Jareth checks Corbin's pulse, then puts his ear to his mouth to feel for any breath. *Please, please be okay!* I bite my lower lip, forgetting my fangs are still out, and my own blood fills my mouth, mixing with my victim's.

"Oh, Rayne," Jareth says hoarsely, rising from Corbin's limp body and turning to look at me. "What have you done?"

"Jareth, please save him," I beg. "I didn't mean to . . ."

But Jareth isn't listening to my reply. His attention is back on Corbin, his movements frantic as he tries to perform CPR. My stomach swims with nausea. "Listen to me, Corbin," I vaguely hear Jareth saying, over my own troubled thoughts. "You've lost a lot of blood. I need you to make a decision for me."

Horror slams into my gut as I realize exactly what Jareth is going to ask him. "No!" I cry, stumbling blindly to my feet. "He doesn't want that! Anything but that!" After all, Corbin hates vampires. They killed his parents. He'd rather die than become one of us monsters.

Which, it appears, thanks to me, is his only other option.

"Rayne, leave the room. Now!" Jareth growls at me, baring his fangs. I shrink back in horror, my beautiful boyfriend morphing into a menacing beast. Is that what I looked like to Corbin? No wonder he tried to kill me.

I back out of the room, closing the door behind me. I collapse onto the hall floor, not sure where to go or what to do. Inside, I can hear noises. Jareth murmuring to Corbin in a voice too low to understand. Corbin, evidently having regained consciousness, murmuring back. I try to swallow, but the lump in my throat is too big. What will he decide? And is he really capable of making this important decision in his current state?

After what seems an eternity, Jareth steps outside the room. He nods his head at me and I scramble to my feet to follow him down the hall and into our hotel room. If only I hadn't forgotten my key. None of this would have happened.

"Is he okay?" I ask.

"Depends on your definition of okay."

"Is he . . . dead?"

"Technically he will be soon. He's lost way too much blood to live."

"Technically?" Fear wells up inside of me. "So you mean . . . ?"

Jareth slumps down on the bed. He looks exhausted. It's then I see a swath of bloody cloth tied to his wrist and I know exactly what he's done.

"But Corbin never wanted to be a vampire," I protest, the horror growing inside of me at a mind-numbing rate. "He hates vampires more than anything. He wants to slay the entire race."

"He may feel differently once he turns into one," Jareth says wearily, reaching down to grab a blood bag he'd stored in the minibar. Evidently he needs a refill.

I draw in a breath. "But I thought vampires were only supposed to turn one person in their lives. Their blood mate. And you've already done that with me."

Jareth nods. "According to the consortium's rules, yes, one offspring per vampire. But in some situations the rules must be . . . bent. And as co-master of the Blood Coven, I have the authority to make that call."

I fall backward into an armchair, guilt ripping through me, so sharp I feel like I'm going to be sick.

"I couldn't stop myself," I say at last. "It was scary. I . . . I think I need help."

Jareth turns to me, his eyes full of an emotion I can't explain. "Yes," he says simply. "You do. Are you finally ready to accept it?"

I swallow hard, feeling embarrassed and stupid and weak. "Yes. Yes, I am."

He smiles sadly at me, then pulls me toward him. I collapse into his arms. "I'm such an idiot!" I wail. "I should have taken a donor from the start. I should have listened to you when I wrecked my car back in October, after that fight with David and my mom. But I was too ashamed to admit I couldn't handle it. That I wasn't cut out to be a vampire."

Jareth strokes my head lovingly, shushing me in my ear. "Being a young vampire is tough in the best of circumstances," he soothes. "And your transition hasn't been easy from the start." He takes my head in his hands, tilting it up so he can meet my eyes with his own deep ones. "You're not Supervamp, Rayne McDonald. And admitting that is the first step."

I nod, giving him a rueful smile. "I admit it," I say, swallowing hard. "I admit it from the bottom of my no-longer-beating heart."

He smiles and leans down, pressing his cool lips against mine, and I can feel the blood tears drip from my eyes at his tenderness. What would I do without my Jareth?

"Don't be scared," he murmurs. "We'll put you in a program—get you the help you need. And everything will be okay. I'll be there every step of the way. I'll never leave your side."

"But what about Corbin?" I can't help but ask. "I think he's going to need more than a twelve-step program to come to terms with his new undead status."

Jareth looks weary. "I got him to sign an agreement saying he willingly gives his life over to the Blood Coven. So he can't sue us or anything if he changes his mind once he turns. And I'll assign a few of my men to bring him back to headquarters, once he's completed his death and transformation, which will take about seven days. There, he'll be assigned a trainer and he'll learn how to become a vampire." He shrugs. "He's very strong. I'm sure he'll be okay, once he accepts his fate."

Okay isn't the word I'd use. And I doubt very much Corbin will ever be able to completely accept his fate. And I'll have to live with that guilt for the rest of my life.

"What if he tells everyone I'm the one who did it to him?"

"He won't. I'm going to have the doctors back at the coven erase his memory," Jareth says. "After that, he won't know anything about you. In fact, he'll never even remember meeting you. So don't go all confessional on him when you do see him again, okay?"

"Okay," I manage to squeak out. Poor Corbin. Poor, poor Corbin. I gave my life to become a vampire. But his was stolen from him, along with his identity. It wasn't fair.

"And as for you," Jareth adds, "you're going back as well. Straight to rehab to start getting the help you need."

I look at him, confused. I can't go now! "Jareth," I say, trying to keep my trembling voice calm. "I promise to go to rehab. But before I do, I have to save my sister."

"Rayne—"

"She's in fairyland and I'm the only one here who can break into their dimension. I have the location now and even the URL with the magic words. I'm her only hope." Tears well up in my eyes again. "Please, Jareth, I'm begging you. I'll get help when I get back. But right now my sister needs me."

"Rayne, I thought you were serious about getting help."

"I am. I swear I am, Jareth. But this is my sister we're talking about here. And our one chance to save her!"

He lets out a frustrated breath, then glances at his watch. "Lord Magnus should wake up in an hour. I'll see what he says we should do."

I grimace, realizing he's going to have to tell Magnus—who's not exactly a Rayne cheerleader to begin with—what happened with Corbin as well. "Well, maybe you could say . . . Corbin, um, just woke up with an undeniable urge to become a member of the Blood Coven and you hooked him up?"

Jareth narrows his eyes at me. Okay, maybe not.

"I'll speak to him on your behalf," he promises. "As co-master, I have a say in things. But you have to promise, whatever is decided, you won't argue. You'll respect the master, at the very least. That's part of being a vampire 101."

I'm about to protest, then remember I'm reformed Rayne from here on out. The girl who actually follows the rules. Or at least attempts to. "Okay," I say instead, squaring my shoulders. "I'll do whatever Magnus says."

I just pray he'll let me help my sister. Before it's too late.

25

A few hours later, we're standing at the craggy shores of the raging sea. X marks the spot on my fairy godmother's map. Foamy waves crash against the rocks twenty feet below us and the wind whips through my hair. Our group has now been pared down to Jareth, Magnus, Francis (the former doorman from the Blood Bar, now Magnus's personal bodyguard), and two other vampires I don't know. The rest of the crew departed at sunset, transporting Corbin to a safe house to help him with his transformation.

Magnus was furious about the whole thing, of course. Rayne breaking the rules once again. Like Jareth, he wanted to send me directly to rehab. But I reminded him of Sunny and the fact that I'm the best chance they've got to rescue her and he quickly changed his tune. After all, he wants my sister back just as much as I do, and he did make that promise about always putting her first. That said, he made it very clear I'm going to vampire rehab the second Sunny's back in his arms. No passing Go, no collecting $200. (Man, no one ever pays me for anything around here.)

But I'll worry about that later. Right now I have a more daunting task. Opening the doors between two dimensions, like the host of the *Twilight Zone*, and escorting five vampires into fairyland to kidnap their queen.

All in a day's work, for Rayne McDonald: fairy vampire–vampire slayer girl extraordinaire. (That's becoming quite a mouthful, huh?)

Before we left, I headed down to the bed-and-breakfast's business center to look up the website my fairy godmother had given me. It took forever to pull it up on the ancient, still-using-dial-up computer, but eventually I was able to download a copy of *Fairyland for Dummies* to the hard drive. After a quick skim (with Magnus impatiently beeping the horn outside the whole time!), I located and printed what appeared to be the relevant chapters and joined the other vampires in the awaiting rent-a-car. (A tiny Mini Cooper that made me wish I had taken my fairy godmother up on the whole lemon Lamborghini thing.)

And now, after an hour's drive down bumpy country roads winding around emerald green fields dotted with white fluffy sheep and cozy little cottages, we're here and I'm preparing myself for my task. I'm more than a little nervous, as you may imagine, that this whole thing isn't going to work. Mainly because 1) I got it from some old lady professing to be a fairy godmother, which, let's be honest, is always a bit suspect, and 2) we don't have a Plan B. Sunny's life is literally in my hands.

I read over the instructions once again, just to be sure I've got them. They seem so simple. Almost too simple . . .

"What are you waiting for, Goth Girl? Halloween?" Magnus asks, interrupting my worried thoughts. "Let's do this already."

I turn around to grump at him, but then decide to cut him some slack. He's worried about Sunny, too. And he hates that feeling of not being in control of things. Or trusting a girl who has screwed up so many times before. He probably doesn't think I can really do this.

Well, I'm ready to prove him wrong. Setting down my cheat sheets, I stand on the cliff's edge, raising my hands over the sea. Here goes nothing:

"Star Light, Star Bright. First star I see tonight.
I wish I may, I wish I might. Have the wish I wish tonight."

Yup, that's the poem. The secret words that should open a doorway to fairyland if recited by someone of fey blood. Funny, I used to say them all the time as a little kid. I wonder if I was constantly opening and closing doors without even realizing it.

I open my eyes and look around. Hm. No portal. No glittery, sparkly path leading the way to an alternate dimension has magically appeared. In fact, to be honest, everything around me looks exactly the same as it did before I spoke that stupid nursery rhyme. I glance back at the vampires, who are standing there, looking at me impatiently.

"Well?" Magnus asks, his voice gritty and tense.

"Um, I don't know. That should have worked." Disappointment whirls through me as I look around for my cheat sheets. Did I do something wrong? "Where are my papers?" I ask, not seeing where I left them.

"These?" Francis asks, holding up a few sheets. "They almost blew away in the wind, so I grabbed them." He hands them over to me and I scan them again, letting out a frustrated breath. It seems so simple on paper. *Stand on the cliff's edge, raise your hands, recite the poem and . . .*

Oh crap.

"Was there . . . one more piece of paper?" I ask Francis in a low voice, mostly so Magnus won't overhear. He's going to kill me. Seriously kill me.

"Um." Francis looks around. "I don't think so. Unless it blew away before I grabbed the stack?"

Or I left it on the printer back at the B&B. Either way, I'm missing a page. Probably a very important page . . .

"Try it again," Jareth urges, unaware of my distress.

So I do. I mean, why not, right? I stand at the cliff's edge, I raise my hands, I say the whole stupid poem. But, of course, nothing happens. Whatever that final step is, the door isn't going to open without it. And we're an hour outside of town. That means two more hours of wasted time if we have to return to the B&B and come back. Two hours for Sunny to go and get married to someone else.

Did I mention Magnus is going to kill me?

"Was there anything else you're supposed to do?" Jareth asks, trying to be helpful. Once again I wish I had real vampire telepathy with the guy to tell him what's really going on without alerting the master. "Another step?"

"Maybe you're supposed to make some kind of hand movements or something?" Magnus suggests, not so helpfully. "Or do a little fairy dance?"

"I don't know, okay?" I cry, exasperated, feeling the bloody tears well up in my eyes. Why wasn't I more careful? Why didn't I look through the notes more thoroughly before I left? I'm such a careless idiot. And now Sunny's going to be stuck in fairyland forever and it's all my fault. "I wish I knew what I was supposed to do. But—"

Suddenly a flash of light bursts from the heavens. I look up, startled. A bright, twinkling star, hanging high in the sky, seems to wink at me, then goes dark again.

And suddenly, I get my wish.

I know exactly how to open the portal to fairyland.

I walk over to the edge of the cliff and step off.

"Rayne! What are you—?"

But Jareth's words are cut off by a loud scraping sound—like that of a skate on a sheet of ice. Mist rolls in over the coastline, climbing the cliff until it reaches the spot where I'm hovering, forming a cloud staircase under my feet.

Sweet.

I glance back at the vampires, who are, I note smugly, mouth-open in disbelief.

"How did you . . . ?" Magnus starts to ask.

"Easy. I just wished upon a star," I reply, taking a step up the cloud staircase. It's soft and a little sticky, like marshmallow, but solid enough, and I'm sure it'll be able to hold all our weight. "Like, literally. This is fairyland, remember?" I add. "From now on, all fairytale rules apply."

The vampires shake their heads in amazement, but after a few tentative steps, they follow me up the staircase. At the top, we come to a door, which opens into a long, dark, dusty hallway. Evidently this entrance isn't used too much. We step inside and walk down the corridor until we arrive at a huge pair of double doors, complete with brass knockers. I consider using them to knock, then decide to see if the doors will open by themselves first. I grab the handles and pull the doors open, revealing fairyland at long last. And it's . . .

. . . Disney World?

26

I do a double take. Sure enough, it appears we're not in Ireland anymore, but rather a good reproduction of Orlando, Florida, standing outside the entrance to the Magic Kingdom itself. Same Mickey Mouse–shaped flower garden on the hillside, same old-fashioned elevated train station above. Same three billion tourists meandering about.

Except many of these particular tourists seem to be sporting wings along with their mouse ears.

"Wow." Jareth whistles under his breath. "I've heard people say fairy tales have become way too Disneyfied these days. But this is a little ridiculous."

The other vampires nod their heads in agreement, all pretty much as speechless as I am. That weirdly handsome fairy army that attacked us suddenly makes a lot more sense.

"Well, at least we'll know our way around," I point out. "I've been to Disney twelve times. We used to go every summer, when visiting Grandma." I stop, sobered as I remember suddenly that the sweet old lady in Florida isn't my real grandmother at all, but rather an actress my parents hired to play the part. Our real grandmother, a woman we never met, was assassinated in this very magic kingdom, not too long ago.

I shiver, suddenly a little creeped out.

"Is it safe to go out there?" Francis asks worriedly. "It looks pretty sunny." It's then that I realize all the vampires besides Jareth and I are pressed against the hallway wall, avoiding the beams of sunlight streaming in from outside.

Magnus sticks his hand through the door experimentally and instantly his palm catches fire. He pulls it back quickly, blowing out the flame. "Damn it," he swears, shaking it off.

"I guess they're in a different time zone than we are," Jareth concludes. "The sun looks pretty high in the sky—I'd say it's about three o'clock in fairyland."

Magnus scowls and attempts to try again. Francis grabs him and yanks him back, a split second before he willfully flambés himself for my sister. "You can't go out there, master," the bodyguard tells him gently.

"But Sunny—" Magnus says, a distraught look on his face.

"You'll be no good to her dead."

Magnus squeezes his hands into frustrated fists. "Hell, sometimes I hate being a vampire."

"Don't worry, m'lord," Jareth interjects. "We'll go." He glances over at me and I nod in agreement. I may not have a kung fu grip, but being able to go out in the sunshine definitely has its advantages. "We'll find her and bring her back safe."

Magnus doesn't look too pleased by this—obviously he envisioned himself being Sunny's big, heroic rescuer—but eventually he nods his head in agreement. "Very well," he says. "But if you're not back by nightfall, we're coming in after you."

"Sure, whatever you gotta do," I say impatiently. "Now let's go. Sunny's waiting."

"One moment, please." Magnus gestures for one of the other vampires to hand him his brown leather satchel. "Before you go," he says, "you need to suit up." He rummages through the bag and finally manages to pull out a pair of fluorescent pink marabou wings. He tries to hand them to me.

"No way, dude. I've got my own built-ins," I remind him, reaching back and ripping my shirt so I can let my freak flags fly. My wings have gotten a lot larger in the last twenty-four hours—perhaps due to my closer proximity to fairyland—and it's started becoming painful trying to keep them under wraps. I wiggle my back as they unfurl to their full glory. It feels good to let them free.

Magnus nods, then turns to my boyfriend, holding out the hideous fake wings to him instead. What, did he steal them off a Vegas stripper or something?

"Oh no," my Gothy but manly boyfriend protests, holding up his hands. "Definitely not."

"You're going into fairyland," Magnus reminds him. "Look outside. Everyone here has some sort of wings. Do you want to stick out like a bloody thumb and get caught before you can rescue my girlfriend?" His question leaves no room for argument.

"Fine," Jareth grumbles, grabbing the wings and reluctantly affixing them to his back. He looks so miserable and ridiculous I burst out laughing and fumble for my phone.

"Hold still! I need a photo!" I cry, grabbing my new cell phone and clicking a photo before he can cover the lens with his hand. I look down at the view screen. "Aw, how pwwetty you look!"

"If you dare post that on the Blood Coven forums—"

"Oh, so *now* you're concerned with your image?" I tease. "Just yesterday you were wearing that dirty old *Batman* shirt again!"

"I'll have you know that's a very rare vintage tee—"

"Enough, you two," Magnus cries in a commanding voice, effectively shutting us up. "Stop wasting time and go get Sunny!"

So we say our good-byes and step out the door and into the sunshine. It feels warm and tingly against my skin and I suddenly feel bad for the other vampires who can't abide it. I can't believe I almost willingly gave up the ability to go out during the day. Sometimes things have a way of working out in a manner you don't expect.

"You look kind of sexy with wings," Jareth says, giving me a wink.

"I'd love to say the same . . ." I tease. He groans. I poke him playfully.

"Okay, so which way should we go, oh Disney expert?" he asks.

"There's only one way in," I say, pointing to the entrance. "Suck in your fangs, vamp boy. Let's go rescue Sunny."

We head toward the entrance of the park, but are stopped by a gated turnstile. A burly dwarf dressed in a rather silly Robin Hood-esque green suit mans the gate. I guess not only fairies live in fairyland. "Tickets?" he asks as we approach.

I glance at Jareth. Fairyland charges admission?

"How much are tickets?" Jareth asks, reaching for his wallet.

"Three hundred drops of nectar," the dwarf replies. "After all, it's a special day."

Great. Jareth drops his hand. "Do you have a currency exchange on the premises?"

The dwarf shakes his head.

"Will you take human cash? American Express?"

Another shake. "Sorry, man," he says apologetically. "The bosses are pretty strict about all that."

I exchange worried looks with Jareth, then turn back to the dwarf. "What's so special about today?" I query.

He looks at us incredulously. "Don't you know?" he asks. "I assumed that's why you came." He grins. "It's a special day in fairyland today. Our new queen is getting married at midnight."

Ugh. I was afraid he was going to say that. Though at least that means we're not too late. *If* we can get in . . .

Suddenly, I realize just what I have to do.

"Of *course* we've heard," I say in my most authoritative voice. "Seeing as I am . . ."

I stop, unable to continue. Damn it, I forgot I still can't lie. This is going to be more difficult than I thought. I stamp on Jareth's foot to get his attention. Maybe he can lie for me . . .

"Ow," he says instead. "What did you do that for?"

"What I'm saying is . . ." I turn back to the dwarf. "*I* am the one who is . . ." I shoot Jareth a pleading look. For a thousand-year-old vampire, sometimes he's a bit slow.

"Oh! Right!" he cries, recognition flashing over his face at last. "She's the one who's getting married. Have you not met our beautiful queen? Sunny McDonald?"

The guard narrows his eyes suspiciously. "If you're our queen," he says in a wary voice, "why are you out here and not in the castle? And, did you dye your hair or something? I thought you were supposed to be a blonde."

"Ugh, I know! We had a total hair emergency this morning! Utterly ghastly!" Jareth cries, suddenly completely into the ruse. "But it's all settled now. She's beautiful, isn't she? I mean, just look at the difference a little color makes!" He points to a banner flying above our heads, which has a very good likeness of Sunny's face emblazoned on it. Which, of course, is also, very conveniently, my face.

The guard looks at the banner, then back at me, then at the banner again. His eyes widen and suddenly he's on his knees, hands clasped in front of him. "I'm so sorry, Your Majesty," he blubbers. "Please don't put me in the stocks, I beg of you. I have three little dwarfettes at home and I was only trying to do my job!"

I smile magnanimously. Seriously, I would make the best queen ever if given the chance. "You're forgiven," I tell him. "Like you said, you're only doing your job." I pull him to his feet and kiss the top of his bald head. "But let us through now. We must hurry to get to the . . ." I glance up, looking for a landmark. ". . . the castle," I conclude.

"Yes, yes, of course!" The dwarf steps aside and allows us to go through the turnstiles. "Bless you, m'lady. You're a good soul. Fairyland is honored to have you as their new leader."

I give him a little bow, then hustle Jareth under the elevated train tracks and around the circle, down the replica of Disney's Main Street USA. Cinderella's castle—or I guess Sunny's castle in this case—lies directly in front of us now, shining with a sparkling brilliance you don't see in the real Orlando. Also different? No grumpy, lumpy tourists and crying kids; these streets are packed with fairies—all tall, blond, and beautiful. No wonder my fairy godmother wasn't happy about her ensemble. The grandma look isn't very big in fairyland.

A couple of brightly dressed fairies point to Jareth and giggle at his wings. He turns bright red. "I'm going to kill Magnus for this," he growls.

"Oh come on," I scold, grabbing his hand. "Enough with the vanity already. We've got a rescue to perform."

But before we can take another step, a set of trumpets sounds. The crowd scurries to clear off the street and we're jostled to the side. Dwarves, dressed in green like the guy at the entrance, walk the street, carrying red velvet ropes to section off the sidewalk.

"What's going on?" Jareth hisses at me.

"I think it might be the three o'clock parade," I reply, as I try to avoid being poked by a fairy wing. Crowds are really tough when you have such large appendages to deal with.

A moment later, the crowd bursts into applause. Sure enough, a fairy marching band heads down the street, playing bright, happy music. They're followed by a set of scantily-clad fairy dancers, prancing down the street merrily.

"This is a waste of time," growls Jareth.

I shrug. We're stuck in the middle of a pack of fairies and there's nothing we can do about it. I watch as three little pigs, accompanied by a snarly wolf, march proudly down the street, followed by a cat wearing boots and a goose laying golden eggs every few feet. Children scurry to grab the eggs and I realize they've got chocolate inside.

Fairy tales come to life. I gotta admit, this is pretty cool.

After a few more fairy-tale favorites, the crowd's roar rises to a nearly deafening level. I strain to see over the throng and finally catch sight of what appears to be Cinderella's crystal carriage heading down the street, drawn by six white horses. I draw in an impressed breath. It's gorgeous.

Then I see who sits inside. Not Cinderella at all.

My sister.

Sunny's dressed in a shimmery ball gown that looks both pure silver and a kaleidoscope of colors, all at the same time. Her hair has been lightened to a platinum blond shade and her large eyes shine with the emerald green color she always wished she'd been born with. Her hands are clasped in her lap, heavy with silver jewelry, and on her back she sports the most gorgeous pair of airy gossamer wings I've ever seen. They sparkle so much they're practically blinding to look at.

"Sunny!" I cry. "Sunny, it's Rayne!" I try to make my way through the crowd, but Jareth grabs me by a wing and yanks me backward.

"Let me go!" I cry. "I need to get to my sister." I turn back to the street. "Sunny! Sunny, it's me!" I call out, desperate to get her attention.

Sunny turns her head slightly, as if she hears me, glancing blankly out into the crowd. Then she gives out a small, Miss America–type wave before folding her hands back in her lap and turning to face front again.

"What's wrong with her?" I cry, turning back to Jareth. "She looked at me as if she didn't recognize me. My own sister!" I swallow back the huge lump that's formed at the back of my throat and wipe the bloody tears that would give me away as a vampire.

Jareth squeezes my shoulder comfortingly. "She's obviously undergone some kind of brainwashing," he says. "Which is why we need to exercise caution. Grab her now and she'll think she's being kidnapped rather than rescued."

"Brainwashed and turned into a fairy against her will. My poor sister." I lean against a nearby post. "My poor, poor sister."

I remember her words back at Riverdale. How she just wanted to be a human girl. And now, yet again, fate has worked against her. My heart breaks as I watch her continue down the street, just a shell of her former sweet, passionate self. If only I hadn't been so self-involved. I would have noticed she was gone earlier. And maybe I could have rescued her before they transformed her . . .

"Stop it, Rayne!" I can dimly feel Jareth shaking me by the shoulders. "Beating yourself up about things is not going to help us here. What's done is done. But it's not too late to save her."

"But how?" I ask, wandering over to an empty alley away from the colorful parade. "There's only two of us. And there's a billion of them. I mean, look at that castle," I add, gesturing to the building. "There's got to be a thousand guards and they've all got very large guns."

Jareth looks over in the direction I'm pointing, then frowns. "Tooth fairy snipers," he says with a scowl. "I was afraid of that."

"Wait, what?"

"Deadly assassins with black-market munitions. They travel the world, buying their bullets off young children who've lost their teeth."

Oh-kay then.

Jareth runs a hand through his blond hair. "Maybe we should consider coming back later," he says. "I'm guessing the reason this place is so well-guarded is because of today's wedding. Maybe once it's over—"

"No! We can't let her get married to some fairy!" I protest. "She's gone through enough already." I scrunch my face up, thinking. "We have to figure out a way into the castle."

"But how? Your switcheroo trick isn't going to work, now that everyone's seen the real Sunny," Jareth reminds me. "You may look a lot alike, but your hair is completely different. Not to mention your wings." He gestures to my definitely inferior, stubby-feathered wings.

"Well, at least they're not made of marabou," I grouch as I scan the area, trying to remember if I know any good shortcuts from visiting the real Disney. My eyes fall on a small service door, tucked away into a dark corner. "I've got it!" I exclaim. "We'll go underground."

Jareth looks at me. "Underground?"

"Yes," I reply impatiently, dragging Jareth over to the door. "How do you think employees get from one end of this place to another fast? Dodging tourists? I don't think so. If this place is an exact replica of the Orlando park, which it seems to be, then there are underground tunnels under the whole thing linking all the various sections together."

"That's genius!" Jareth says, looking impressed. "There will certainly be fewer people down there. And we can take out any guards without worrying about tooth fire."

We make sure no one's looking, then quietly slip open the service door and step inside. Sure enough, a set of stairs leads down into the darkness. Luckily, as vampires, we can see well enough in the dark not to need a flashlight.

"Let's go," I say, taking the first step.

We head down into a twisty labyrinth of spider-webbed, dusty passages. Evidently the fairies don't use these tunnels as much as the employees of Orlando Disney do. Following various signs posted at each intersection, we make our way toward the castle. We're just about to turn the last corner, when Jareth grabs my arm, his face pale and worried.

"I hear something," he whispers. "Kind of like bells—"

Suddenly, a brilliant white light flashes through the passageway and in steps a beautiful blond fairy with a perfect hourglass figure: big breasts, tiny waist, and a sparkly green tutu riding low on her perfect hips. My eyes widen as she puts one hand on her hip, her little red mouth set in a deep pout, and she shakes her head no.

I glance over at Jareth, who's staring at the newcomer with shock and recognition in his eyes. "Is that . . . ?" he starts.

The fairy opens her mouth. But instead of words, all that comes out is the sound of tiny, tinkling bells.

Jareth nods grimly. "Tinkerbell," he affirms.

I stare at the fairy. Tinkerbell? Are you kidding me? Man, this place gets weirder and weirder by the second. My mind races, trying to remember what I know about this legendary fairy from the movies, but I come up blank. All I know is she's supposed to be pint-size—not six feet tall.

I step forward. "Please, Miss Bell," I try to appeal to her. "We need to get to the castle. My sister's getting married there today."

Unfortunately, Tink doesn't seem to care too much about Sunny's impending matrimony or my mission to get to the church on time. She gestures for us to back up, scolding us again in her weird bell language.

"Aw, come on, Tink," I try again. "Have a heart, please."

She rolls her eyes and lets out an annoyed huff, then reaches into a little green satchel tied to her tiny waist and pulls out a handful of something sparkly.

"Pixie dust," Jareth whispers hoarsely. "Rayne, we've got to run."

But before we can even turn around, Tinker*bitch* brings the dust to her lips and blows it in our direction. My lungs seize up, filled with sparkles, and I start choking uncontrollably. Beside me, Jareth falls clumsily to the ground, incapacitated.

"The dust," he moans. "Paralyzing . . ."

Tinkerbell calmly walks over and grabs his fake wings, yanking them off of his back. She giggles in satisfaction, then turns to me. Behind her, Jareth moans in pain, completely paralyzed.

But I'm not. And now that I've survived the initial dose, I'm perfectly fine. Guess the stuff doesn't work too well on real fairies.

Tinkerbell looks at me, her head cocked in question, probably wondering why I'm not paralyzed, too. She reaches for my wing. I slap her hand away.

"They're real," I inform her. "Unlike your breasts."

Without any more warning, I lunge, slamming my hands into her chest. She tries to take flight, but the tunnel ceilings don't give her enough air space to take off. Stumbling backward, she flails to maintain her balance, but I charge again, ready to take her down for good this time.

No one paralyzes my boyfriend. Especially not some nasty pixie.

But just as I'm about to knock her down, she snaps her fingers and suddenly she's the pint-size Tinkerbell from the movies again. Damn it! Flitting around me, she nips at my skin with tiny, sharp teeth.

"Ow!" I cry, swatting at her like a fly. But she's too quick—buzzing at my back and grabbing a handful of hair. She's strong for someone so little and manages to jerk me backward. I lose my balance, careening to the ground, slamming my head against the concrete. Tinkerbitch laughs and floats up toward the ceiling, then dive-bombs down at me, armed with a tiny knife.

The knife, which feels like only a pinprick due to its diminutive size, gets lodged in my stomach. Tink lands on me, trying to pull her knife free to stab me again, but I close my fingers around her little body before she can fly off.

"Got you!" I cry, pinching her now *really* tiny waist. She

squirms angrily in my grasp, but I hold on tight. I could easily squash her like a bug, but that seems kind of awful. I mean, killing Tinkerbell?

Unfortunately, my good-hearted hesitation gives her the opportunity to poof back to human size and I'm forced to let go. She's now straddling me, knife back in her hand (which, luckily for me, is still pint-size).

Before I can react, she leaps to her feet, giving me a sound kick to the side of the head. The pain reverberates through me as I struggle to keep conscious. But it's not working. I quickly swim into blackness.

Yes, I'm afraid it's true. I, Rayne McDonald, fairy, vampire, vampire-slayer extraordinaire, have just gotten my ass kicked by Tinkerbell.

27

I wake up on a creaky cot, my back aching and my head pounding like a mother. Sitting up, I look around, trying to take in my surroundings. I appear to be in some kind of dark, dingy jail cell that smells a lot like a septic tank. In the opposite corner, there's a small, dirty sink and a broken toilet filled with brown water. A *Saw* movie come to life.

I suck in a shaky breath. Okay. I'm alive. That's something at least. Damn Tinkerbell. If I ever get my hands on that pixie, I'll . . .

A deep, familiar groan interrupts my thoughts of revenge. Diving out of bed, I dash to the front of my cell, my fingers brushing the bars. Pain reverberates through me at the touch of metal—a sick burning feeling—and I quickly step back. They must be made of iron—poison to fairies.

Jareth is in the cell across from me, lying prostrate on the ground, bare-chested. Smoke rises from his pure white skin, which has been draped with silver chains. Guess the fairies wanted to make double sure he didn't use his powers to escape, seeing as vampires aren't allergic to iron like fairies are. Thank goodness they must have assumed I was just one of them, due to my wingspan and immunity to pixie dust. Though the iron bar thing is going to make it very tough to escape.

"Jareth!" I hiss, trying to wake him.

He tosses his head from side to side, still groaning in his sleep, clearly in agony. I bite my lower lip in worry; if he doesn't regain consciousness and remove his chains soon, the silver will kill him.

"Jareth!" I try again, louder this time. "Wake up!"

"Hey, we're trying to sleep over here!" a man cries from the cell directly to my right. I turn to yell back at him, but the words die in my throat as my eyes fall upon two people—a man and a woman—huddled under ratty blankets in the next cell.

"Mom?" I cry, my voice cracking in a mixture of excitement and horror. "Dad?"

The two look up, their faces white with shock. A split second later, they're on their feet and in front of the adjoining cell wall, careful not to touch the bars. Mom reaches through, clasping my hand in hers and squeezing me so tightly at first I wonder if she's going to break bone. But I don't really mind the pain. It's so good to see her again. To see both of them. I hadn't realized how much I missed them until now. My mom's soft scent of honeysuckle. My dad's favorite Old Spice aftershave. I don't know how it's possible they smell so good down here in this dirty fairy jail cell, but somehow they do all the same.

"What are you doing here?" Mom demands. "I thought Heather relocated you somewhere safe."

"Safe isn't exactly the word I'd use to describe Riverdale," I tell them. "And besides, the fairies came and kidnapped Sunny. I had to come rescue her."

Mom's face crumbles and her hands drop to her sides in defeat. "So they did get her after all," she says sorrowfully. "We weren't sure. We were taken prisoner from your dad's condo and have been down here in this cell ever since, begging for an audience with the prime minister."

I stare at her in shock. And here I was complaining about the isolation of Riverdale. Mom and Dad had it a billion times worse.

"I'm so sorry," I cry. "I had no idea . . ."

"The prime minister didn't appreciate the fact that we fought back when his soldiers came to collect you two the first time," Dad explains. "We never got a chance to negotiate as we had planned to."

Horror sweeps through me as I remember the fight. How I stabbed Apple Butter. How everyone freaked out about it. "It's my fault!" I realize, guilt stabbing me like a sharp stake to the heart. "It's my fault you're here."

"No, no!" Mom cries, shaking her head vehemently. "Rayne, don't blame yourself for one second. We were the ones who ran away from fairyland to begin with. We put you in this position. You only did what you thought was right to protect your family. And you should never, ever be ashamed of that."

I don't know if I can completely accept this, but I decide to move on anyway. I've learned the hard way that guilt is just way too unproductive in these kinds of scenarios. "What about Heather?" I ask. "I thought she was going to go help you with negotiations."

Mom and Dad glance at one another and I catch the worry

in their faces. "We haven't seen or heard from her since that night at the condo," Dad says at last. "We sort of figured she stayed with you two."

I shake my head. "I hope she's okay . . ."

"Rayne McDonald!" Mom says suddenly, her voice sharp. "You have wings!"

My face heats. "Oh yeah," I say, positive I'm blushing deep red. "I . . . um . . . well, it's a long story, really."

Mom opens her mouth—probably to lecture me some more—but at that moment, Jareth lets out another loud groan. I whirl around, praying he's at least regained consciousness. Happy family reunion or not, I have to get him out of those chains.

"Jareth!" I cry.

"Is that your boyfriend, Rayne?" Mom asks, squinting her eyes at the unconscious vampire. "He looks familiar."

I nod miserably. "Yeah, that's Jareth."

"What is he doing here? Rayne, we told you not to mix up any mortals in this," Dad rebukes me sternly. "It's too dangerous."

I draw in a breath. Here goes nothing. "He's not mortal, Dad. Look at those silver chains burning his skin."

Dad's eyes widen in realization. "He's not a . . . ?"

"Vampire? Yes. He is."

Both my parents shriek in unison and shrink back in their cells.

"You're dating a vampire?" Mom cries. "Oh, Rayne! How could you? First you turn yourself into a fairy after I specifically told you not to, and then you tell me you're dating a vile, disgusting creature of the—"

"Mom, stop it!" I interrupt, more than a little annoyed at their reactions. "You can yell at me all you want later. Ground me—whatever. But right now, we need to focus on getting out of here so we can save Sunny." I mean, they're both freaking fairies, for goodness' sake! How can they be so prejudiced against vampires? And what would they do if they knew yours truly was also one of these so-called disgusting creatures of the night?

Mom falls silent, but she doesn't look too happy. Geez, even trapped in a fairy jail, I manage to get the parental units mad at me. I have such a knack.

I turn to my dad, realizing he's shaking his head. "Honey, there's no way out of here," he informs me, his voice filled with sorrow. "We've tried, believe me. Since the day we got here."

I frown, refusing to accept his words. I've been in tight situations before and I've always managed to come through. Even at Night School, where I was sure we were doomed. I just called for help and . . .

That's it! I can try to channel Magnus. Let him know where we are. I wonder if it's dark yet. I don't think Jareth can hold off much longer. I close my eyes and picture the coven leader in my mind, then push my cry for help, just in case.

I open my eyes. Guess we'll just have to wait and see. I could really use Corbin's whole kung fu grip thing right about now. I wonder if he'll have normal vampire powers or be gimped like me, since he was bitten by Jareth. Poor Corbin. If only I hadn't vampire scented him to begin with . . .

That's it!

"Hey!" I start screaming at the top of my lungs. I take off my shoe and bang it against the cell bars. "Guard! I need some water. Come here and give me some water!"

Mom and Dad look at one another, then at me. "What are you doing?" Dad hisses.

"Trust me," I mouth, then bang some more. "Hey, jailkeeper dude! Get your ass over here. Now!"

It takes about five minutes, but finally a grumpy-looking dwarf (maybe Grumpy himself?) waddles up to the cell, peering at me with an annoyed look on his pockmarked face. "Cut the racket, Fairy!" he snarls. "I'm trying to read." He holds up a brand-new copy of *Snow White*.

"The prince kisses her awake and they live happily ever after," I say. "Now focus. I need you to let me out of this cell."

He rolls his eyes. "And why should I do that?" he demands.

Here goes nothing. I turn on the vampire scent full blast and get down on my knees so I'm eye level to him. "Please, my height-challenged friend," I say. "I would be oh so appreciative." I bat my eyelashes at him seductively.

"Do you have something in your eye?" he asks gruffly, not even remotely taking the bait. Damn it. It must not work on dwarves. Just my luck.

I grab him by the shirt collar, pulling him against the cell bars, careful not to touch them myself. "Let me out!" I cry.

But sadly, I don't have a kung fu grip. Especially not after Grumpy calmly reaches to his side and pulls out an electric baton, zapping me in the shoulder. "Ow!" I cry, letting go and rubbing my burnt skin angrily.

"That's for grabbing me!" he snarls. Then he turns up the heat and strikes me again. This time, I'm thrown to the back of the cell from the force of the electric charge. My hand lands in the toilet. Ew.

"And that's for spoiling my book!" he adds.

Defeated, I watch as he stomps angrily back down the hall.

"Rayne, are you okay?" Mom asks worriedly.

"Yeah," I mutter, scrambling to my feet. Of course I can't tell her that as a vampire, I heal quickly. Not after the reaction she had to Jareth being one. Coming out of the coffin to her someday is definitely not going to be easy. "I'll be fine. I'm just mad my plan didn't work."

"Actually, it worked perfectly!"

I look up, my eyes widening as I see Francis step into the corridor. He has Grumpy by the neck, in what appears to be a perfect kung fu grip. Behind him are Magnus and the other vampires.

"Was someone in need of a fairy-tale rescue?" he asks with a grin.

28

"Magnus! Francis!" I cry happily. "Thank God you're here. You have to help Jareth!" I point to my boyfriend's cell. He's writhing in pain now, almost convulsing, with white foam sputtering from his mouth. He doesn't look good and I pray they're not too late.

Francis hands off the angry dwarf to one of the other vampires, then hurries to Jareth's cell. He grips the iron bars in both hands and effortlessly pulls them apart, allowing an opening for Magnus to get through. The coven leader dons thick, black gloves, preparing to remove the silver chains from my boyfriend's body.

I plop down on the lumpy cot, relieved beyond belief. "Thank goodness," I say. "My cry for help actually came in handy for once."

"Actually," Francis says, looking over at me apologetically, "we have a GPS tracker on Jareth. As co-master of the Blood Coven, we need to keep track of him."

Oh. Well, whatever. Maybe in another life I'll get the kung fu grip.

"Once the sun went down, the place really cleared out," Francis continues, tossing one of the chains to the side of the cell. "We were able to jump the turnstiles and follow your trail pretty easily, though we had to take it slow, so as to not draw attention to our presence."

I watch as Magnus slices his wrist with a knife and drips blood into Jareth's open mouth. "Is he going to be okay?" I ask anxiously.

Magnus thankfully nods. "My blood will purify his poisoned blood."

Mom stares at Magnus, then at me. "You and Sunny are *both* dating vampires?" she cries. "How did I not know this? I must be the worst mom ever."

"How long have we been here?" I ask Francis, ignoring my mother. "What time is it now?"

Francis glances at his watch. "I fixed it to fairy time," he informs me. "It's about eleven-thirty, give or take."

I swallow hard.

"We have to hurry," I tell them. "Sunny's getting married at midnight."

Magnus looks over at me, horror clear on his face. "Are you serious?" he asks.

"Fairy," I remind him, "can't lie."

He rises from the floor, wrapping a swath of cloth around his still-bleeding wrist. "We can't let that happen!" he cries. "We have to find her." He paces the jail cell floor as Francis goes and rips open my cell. "Where would they hold a wedding in this godforsaken place?"

"In the castle," my dad interjects. Mom kicks him and he turns to her. "What?" he asks.

"Bob, they're vampires, remember?" she hisses.

"Honey, these vampires can help us," Dad chides. "Just because they're different than us . . ."

Magnus approaches my parents' cell, bowing low to my mom. "Mrs. McDonald," he says. "I love your daughter. More than anything in this world. I made a promise to keep her safe, no matter what. And I intend to keep that promise."

Mom still doesn't look too happy, but at last she reluctantly nods her head. My dad pulls her into a comforting embrace. "Don't worry," I can hear him whisper. "We'll get her. I promise." It's then I realize that I need to cut Mom some slack. Like the rest of us, she's just scared and worried about Sunny.

I step gingerly through the now-open jail cell bars, careful not to touch them. Magnus cocks his head in question.

"The bars are made of iron," I inform him. "Iron's poison to fairies. Like silver is to vampires." I show him my still slightly burned fingertips.

His face lights up. "That's perfect!" he cries. Then he turns to the other vampires, who are still guarding Grumpy. "See if the dwarf has any tools in his office," he commands. "Some kind of saw or something. We'll turn these iron bars into weapons." He grins widely. "The fairies won't know what hit them!"

The other vampires hasten to obey orders. Dad turns to Mom, helping her step out of the cell. "See?" he says. "Isn't it good to have them on our side?"

I rush over to Mom and give her a huge hug. The kind I

couldn't give her behind bars. "Don't worry, Mom," I murmur as I take in her soft body and warm scent. "Sunny's going to be okay."

She kisses me on the head. "I know, dear," she says. "Now go ahead and check on your boyfriend."

I flash her a thankful grin, then sprint to Jareth's side. The vampires have moved him to the cot and he's lying there weakly, his face still really white. "How are you feeling, baby?" I ask.

"Like I've been run over by a truck," he mutters.

"He'll heal," Magnus says, looking over. "But it may take a while. I'm going to have Tanner take him out of here and back to Donegal."

"I want to help you rescue Sunny," Jareth protests weakly.

"You won't be any help in your condition," Magnus says. "I'm sorry."

"We got it, baby," I murmur, holding him close and kissing him about a hundred times in a row. "You just concentrate on getting well."

About ten minutes later, we're ready to go. Francis and his friends have cut three long lengths of iron and sharpened them into metal spears. If only I was able to wield one. "Okay, let's do this," Magnus says, taking weapon in hand. "Tanner, you take Rayne's parents and Jareth back to Donegal. We'll meet you there when we're done. Francis, Stilton, and Rayne, let's head out."

"Wait a second!" Mom interrupts. "We're not going anywhere with them."

Magnus turns to look at her in question. "What?" he asks.

Dad steps up to face him, his expression fierce. "That's my daughter they've got up there. And we're not leaving fairyland without her."

Magnus frowns and a silence comes over the jail. For a

moment, I think he's going to refuse them—force them to head back with Tanner and Jareth anyway.

"Please," Mom begs. "After all, you're not the only one who pledged to keep Sunny safe."

Magnus turns to her, his expression softening. He thankfully nods his head. "Very well," he says. "Lead the way, fairies. Let's go rescue your daughter."

29

Mom, having grown up in fairyland, knows all the shortcuts. And all the ways to avoid the guards, too, for that matter. She says she and my dad used to sneak down in these tunnels late at night when they were lovesick teens, forbidden to see one another. They'd wander, hand in hand, through the darkness, talking about everything and anything and making big plans for their futures.

"Your father would take me to some very-out-of-the-way spot, deep within the labyrinth, and surprise me with lighted candles and nectar picnics," Mom remembers dreamily. "He was so romantic back then."

I steal a glance at Dad, who's looking at Mom with fondness in his eyes. It seems their time together in jail has rekindled their friendship. I love that. Almost as much as I love knowing Dad didn't abandon us like we always thought he did. And now if only we can get my sister back—we can actually have a chance at living happily ever after.

"So what's the deal with the Light Court of fairyland looking exactly like Disney World?" I ask curiously as we head down a long corridor.

Mom glances at Dad. "I was wondering when you'd ask that," she says. "Do you remember the story of Peter Pan, when Tinkerbell is going to drink poison because not enough humans believe fairies exist?"

"Yeah . . ." I remember our Mom reading us the story when we were little. We had to clap our hands to prove we believed in fairies to save Tink's life. Of course, now that I know what a bitch she is, I totally regret doing it.

"Well, twenty years ago, fairyland was literally dying just like that—people on Earth stopped believing in us and we started fading away. We were in danger of losing our entire kingdom. So Tatiana, your grandmother, had to figure out what people *did* still believe in. And that turned out to be the Disney happily ever after. It's practically guaranteed . . ." She smiles. "So she did a major remodel of the fairyland Light Court and it's looked like this ever since."

"Wow," I reply, shaking my head in disbelief. "That's quite . . . quite a story."

"And you might have noticed, the new fairyland's not just for fairies either," Mom continues. "Your grandmother wanted it to be a safe haven—a refuge—for all fairy-tale creatures from all over the world." She smiles. "It's really amazing if you think about it. A kingdom for endangered creatures that most people believe are imaginary. Pretty crazy, huh?"

Crazy doesn't even begin to explain it. But if we survive all of this, I'm so going to hit Space Mountain before we leave. Think they have Fast Passes here?

"And what about the Dark Court? Do they look like Disney, too?"

Mom shakes her head. "More like Universal Studios."

We stop short at an intersection and Mom looks from left to right. Then she turns back to us. "We're almost there," she announces. "The castle entrance is just through this—"

"Not so fast!" commands a familiar-sounding voice. We whirl around and my eyes widen as they fall on none other than our old friend Apple Crisp. Evidently he survived my staking him back at Dad's condo. I don't know whether to be disappointed or relieved. Behind him stand about twenty fairy warriors, armed with flaming swords and looking pretty darn bloodthirsty to boot. So perhaps "disappointed" is the way to go here.

"You're under arrest," Apple Butter informs us, unnecessarily. "For trespassing on fairyland grounds." He shoots a glare in my parents' direction, shaking his head. "Bringing vampires into fairyland. You two ought to be ashamed of yourselves."

But Mom doesn't look too ashamed as she steps forward, her eyes flashing fire. "It's you who should be ashamed of yourself, Apple Blossom," she says in a scolding voice. The kind she usually saves to use on me. "Abducting an innocent girl, turning her into a fairy against her will. Leaving us to rot in jail without a fair trial. In my day, soldiers of the Light Court followed proper protocol. They were the good guys. Now, it seems, you're no better than the Dark Court's agents themselves."

Apple Blossom looks a little taken aback, but recovers quickly. "In your day," he sneers. "Please. You left fairyland and by doing so, you relinquished your right to make these kinds of judgments.

We had no choice but to recruit your daughter into service. She's one of only two royal fairies left, thanks to you abandoning your duty. If anyone's to blame for Sunshine's current predicament, it would be you."

Mom's face falls, guilt assaulting her hard and fast. She takes a shaky step backward and I have to grab her arm to keep her upright. "Don't listen to him, Mom," I say. "He's just trying to bait you."

"But he's right," she whispers hoarsely. "This is my fault. All of it."

I can't bear to see her so upset. Turning back to Apple Pancakes, I open my mouth to tell him off. But it seems my dad is already one step ahead of me.

"How dare you upset Princess Violet like that?" he snarls at the fairy. "What, are you still jealous because she chose me over you? It's not like you ever loved her. You just wanted the power that came with the Light Court throne."

Apple Blossom's face twists and turns purple with rage. At first I think he's going to deny it all, but instead he simply raises his sword. "And now I will have it," he says. "Once your pathetic little girl marries my son." He glances at his watch. "Which will be any minute now. Then I will, in all but name, become the ruler of fairyland."

My mom stiffens and lets out a small cry. I squeeze her arm as comfortingly as I can. We have to get away from these guys. We're running out of time. But can we fight them all?

My dad turns to the vampires behind us. "What are you waiting for?" he asks. "Get 'em, boys!"

The vampires need no further invitation. Raising their iron weapons, they charge forward and the fight ensues. Vampires versus fairies. Fairies versus fairies. And one vampire–vampire slayer–fairy cheerleader joining in to boot.

After ducking his sword and then head-butting one fairy, I manage to trip another, then dive onto a third and wrestle him to the ground, knocking his sword from his hand. Beside me, Magnus, Francis, and Stilton attack with iron weapons, bashing heads and bruising ribs. The iron bars were a brilliant idea. They burn on contact and the fairies are instantly sickened, weakening their attack and forcing them to drop their swords, which immediately extinguish when they leave their hands. Most of them can only take one touch of iron before falling uselessly to the ground. I grab a sword from one of the fallen and drive it through the stomach of one still standing. Yank the sword free, then repeat. Killing fairies is pretty gross and bloody, but what can you do?

I'm feeling pretty good about our chances until suddenly I'm grabbed from behind and yanked into the air, my surprise causing my sword to fall from my hands. The ceiling's higher here than in other parts of the tunnels and I'm at least twenty feet up before I can really process what's going on. Twisting my head, I realize it's none other than Apple Crumble himself who's abducted me. And the look on his face tells me he's still not over that whole me staking him thing.

"I bet you're sorry now that you didn't kill me when you had the chance," he sneers, flying me face-first into a nearby wall. My head slams into the concrete and I see stars. "I can tell you now," he adds, backing up for another round, "I will not make that same mistake."

SLAM! Again into the wall, this time splitting my lip and bursting my nose. Blood fills my mouth as I kick my feet uselessly, struggling to free myself from his hold. Without traction from the ground, it's pretty much an impossible task. But I do eventually manage to get one arm free and I use it to elbow him in the stomach, hard.

The fairy bellows and loosens his grip for a split second, causing me to fall from his arms, careening to the ground. I realize dimly that this might not have been my smartest move. I'm falling hard, fast, and the floor is looking closer and closer. . . .

"Rayne!" My mom's call breaks through my panic. "FLY!"

Oh yeah. Duh. A very good reason to have those ugly wings of mine. I squeeze my eyes shut and manage some kind of flapping, seconds before I crash down onto the hard stone floor.

"Oh my God! I'm flying!" I cry. "I'm actually flying!"

My flight is short lived, however, as Apple Cinnamon dives at me, slamming me into the stone wall again, this time back first. My fragile wing bones shatter on impact and I cry out in pain. He grabs me by the neck and I can't catch my breath. I try to kick at him, but can't make contact. The lack of oxygen, accompanied by the searing pain in my wings, is starting to make everything black and fuzzy.

"And now, slayer," he spits out, "let's see how *you* like to be staked." He reaches into my pocket with his free hand and pulls out my stake, raising it up to my heart. He pulls his hand back and I realize dimly this could very well be the end.

"I'm sorry, Sunny," I murmur weakly. "I tried . . ."

Suddenly, Apple Fritter's eyes widen in shock, his mouth dropping open. A moment later, he releases my neck and the two of us fall to the ground. He's heavier and hits first, cracking his skull against the stone. But I'm right behind him, and my broken wings won't save me now. Dive-bombing head first into the—

—arms of Francis and his kung fu grip. He looks down at me and grins.

"Thanks!" I cry, relieved, as he sets me gently on the ground. Everything hurts, but I'm still alive. "I really thought I was done for there."

"Thank your father," Magnus says, walking over to me. The fight is over. The fairies either are dead or have run away. "He grabbed the iron bar from me and harpooned it right into that fairy's back."

Awesome. I turn to my dad, my eyes shining with gratitude. "Thanks, Dad!" I say. "You got there right on time."

"Yeah, well, I've been keeping you waiting far too long," he says with a small smile. Then he lets out a cry of pain and collapses onto the ground. Horrified, I rush to his side.

"Dad? What's wrong?"

It's then that I notice his right hand is bright blue, with blue streaks racing up his arm.

"What's wrong with him?" I cry.

Mom joins me at his side, tears streaming down her cheeks. She turns to me. "Iron poisoning," she pronounces. "From taking that iron bar and using it against Apple Blossom. He's always been especially allergic to the metal—even for a fairy."

I watch in horror as my dad starts convulsing. His face goes white and he's soon foaming at the mouth. What should I do? Stop him from biting his tongue? Give him CPR?

"Dad!" I sob. This can't be happening. "Dad, please! Stay with us!" I can't lose him now. Not after hating him for all the wrong reasons for so many years. We're supposed to have a happily ever after. Like the Disney movies! "Someone do something!" I cry to the vampires, not ready to give up. "We've got to help him somehow!"

His eyes focus on me. "Rayne, my darling," he whispers. "I'm so sorry for not being there for you. I've been a lousy dad. But I love you and your sister so much. I always have. You've got to believe me. I only tried to do what I thought was best." He reaches up and brushes a lock of hair from my eyes. "Don't let this all be in vain," he whispers, then closes his eyes. I watch in horror as his body convulses one final time, then goes still.

"No!" I moan. "Dad! You can't die!" Bloody tears rain from my eyes, splashing onto my dad's body. But it doesn't matter. He's gone. This time for good.

I can feel Francis coming up behind me and gently but firmly pulling me away. I try to fight him, but, of course, he's got that kung fu grip. A moment later, Mom pulls me into a big bear hug, crushing me against her. "Raynie," she murmurs. "I'm so sorry."

I squirm out of her embrace, sadness mixed with anger swirling inside of me. "We have to bring him back," I say. "Magnus, can't you turn him into a vampire or something? Like Jareth did to Corbin?"

"No," he says softly. "Not with the poison in his bloodstream. It's too late. I'm sorry."

The final ounce of strength ebbs away and I collapse to the ground, feeling like I'm going to die myself from the magnitude of pain. My father. The one I hated for so long. The one who always let me down. And now, he sacrificed his very life to save me. And I never got the chance to say I'm sorry. I whisper the words now, just in case somehow he can hear me beyond the grave.

"I'm so sorry, Dad. I love you."

"Come on," Magnus commands. "Don't fall apart on me, Rayne," he says. "We still have to save your sister."

I can feel Mom come up behind me, placing a hand on my back. "Rayne, sweetie," she pleads. "Your father would want us to go on. To finish our mission. You know he would."

I nod slowly, my dad's final words echoing in my brain, giving me the strength to rise to my feet.

Don't let this all be in vain.

"I won't, Dad," I whisper, as I turn to the remaining group. "I promise I won't." My legs still feel wobbly, but at least my wings seem to be healing. "What are we waiting for?" I ask. "Let's go get Sunny."

30

We race up the windy castle stairs, Mom leading the way. It's two minutes 'til midnight now and we've got to get to the church on time.

"Hurry!" I cry, though I know everyone's going as fast as they can.

"It's just beyond this door," Mom says, stopping before an ornate, stained-glass entryway. She leans over, hands on her knees, attempting to catch her breath. Magnus pushes past her and steps through the doors without hesitation. Francis and I are right behind him.

I draw in a breath as my eyes become accustomed to the bright lights after being underground so long. To say the chapel is gorgeous would be like saying the *Mona Lisa* is a pretty decent painting or that *Buffy the Vampire Slayer* was kind of a cool show. The place is a living, breathing work of art, with huge stained-glass windows, depicting well-known fairy tales, cut into gold-plated walls. Pews of rich, dark wood and crimson velvet cushions line the main aisle. The altar on stage is bedecked with sparkling jewels and crystal chandeliers hanging from high ceilings flood the room with light.

Toto, I don't think we're in Disney anymore . . .

But it's the attendees that give me the most pause. Fairy-tale creatures from my childhood, come to life in the pews, just like Mom was talking about. I see Cinderella with a large pumpkin in her lap. (Her ride home, perhaps?) Hansel and Gretel, snacking on a bag full of candy. Rapunzel sitting alone, her long blond braids taking up an entire row. Rumpelstiltskin with straw sticking out of his clothes. You name a fairy-tale creature, it's probably here, in the room, eyes fixed to the front, where the not-so-happily-ever-after wedding is taking place.

I pull my eyes away from the guests and focus on the stage at the front of the room. An impeccably dressed fairy priest stands above two fairy figures—a man and a woman—who are kneeling in front of him. I can only see their backs, but I immediately recognize the sparkly, luminous wings belonging to my sister. She's wearing a simple but elegant medieval-style white tunic, and her blond hair falls past her shoulders in thick, glossy ringlets. On any other occasion, I'd be super jealous that she looks so good.

I grab Magnus's arm and point with a shaky finger. He nods.

"If anyone here has any reason why these two should not be wed," the fairy priest is saying.

"I do!" Magnus cries in a loud, choked voice. "I object!"

The audience lets out a collective gasp and suddenly all of fairyland's eyes are on us. A big, bad wolf snarls from the groom's side of the church, and at least six dwarves give us the stink eye. (Sleepy's eyes remain closed.) Chicken Little even starts running up and down the aisle, insisting the sky is falling, until he's tripped by one of the three Billy Goats Gruff.

Amidst the chaos, a tall, dark-suited fairy rises from his front row seat and turns to address us. The room falls silent as he opens his mouth to speak. Obviously some sort of VIP.

"On what terms, may I ask, do you object?" he demands.

Magnus steps forward, his chin high and his face fierce. "Because this young lady belongs to me. And I will take her home today. By force if necessary." He raises his iron bar and the wedding party gasps in horror.

"Now, now," the black-suited fairy says in a calm voice. He steps into the aisle, approaching Magnus cautiously, as if dealing with a dangerous beast. Which, in a way, I guess, he is. "There's no need to threaten violence, now is there?" He shakes his head. "We are a peaceful people. And would never think to take what is not ours." He turns to my sister, who's watching us with frightened eyes. "If Princess Sunshine agrees that she is yours, then, by all means, she should go with you. But I think you may be mistaken."

I swallow hard. If Sunny's still under that fairy spell, she may not know who she is, never mind what she wants. Which, of course, is probably what this guy is counting on to begin with.

"Sunshine, Princess?" the man says, addressing my sister. "This man here says you belong to him. Is that true?"

Sunny takes a step back, huddling against her prospective groom. Apple Blossom's son, I guess—I see a smarmy resemblance. He grips her arm protectively and whispers something in her ear and she cuddles closer to him.

"Sunny!" Magnus cries, his voice no longer sounding as sure. "I've come to save you, baby."

"Wh-who are you?" she asks in a squeaky, shaky voice. "And why would you interrupt my happy day?"

Magnus staggers backward, as if he's been punched in the face. "Don't you know me?" he cries. "It's me. Magnus. Your boyfriend. I've come to rescue you."

"But why would I need rescuing?" Sunny asks, her overly made-up face crinkling with confusion. "I belong here. In fairyland. The people need me."

Magnus looks back at me, his face distraught. Behind him, I can see Apple Blossom Junior hiding a small smile.

"I think she's under some kind of spell," I hiss.

My sister turns to entreat the suited man. "Prime Minister," she says pleadingly. "Please, can't you get these horrible creatures out of our sacred chapel? They are destroying my happy day!"

The prime minister nods. "Of course, my darling," he says. Then he turns to Magnus. "I'm sorry," he says. "But as you have heard, our princess has spoken. We must, by all rights, do as she commands." He waves to the guards at the front of the room. They step forward. The vampires grip their iron bars, not ready to give up without a fight.

"What are we going to do?" Francis asks hoarsely. "There's too many of them. Not to mention we're weakened from being in a holy church setting."

"There's got to be a way to break the spell," I whisper back. I wrack my brain, trying to remember something—anything—about my fairy research that could be helpful. Some kind of weakness or some kind of rule . . .

That's it! Just like wishing upon a star, here, fairy-tale rules apply. And since Sunny's a princess, under an evil spell, there's only one way to save her.

"You've got to kiss her!" I cry to Magnus. "It'll break the spell!"

Magnus doesn't need to be told twice. He takes off down the

aisle, pushing the prime minister out of the way and waking Sleeping Beauty in the process. The whole chapel erupts in chaos, but no one seems to know quite what to do. Magnus drops his weapon and grabs Sunny, pulling her into his arms and giving her a sound kiss on the lips. One that would make any fairy-tale prince proud.

"No!" The prime minister cries, rushing toward Magnus, but he trips over Rapunzel's long blond braid and goes crashing to the ground instead. "Stop!" he cries as tries to scramble to his feet.

Magnus pulls back and studies Sunny's face, his eyes filled with bloody tears. The crowd goes so silent you could hear a pin drop. (Which, actually, we do, thanks to the Brave Little Tailor at the back of the room.) It's as if everyone's holding their breath, waiting to see what my sister will do.

Sunny looks up at Magnus, her cloudy eyes clearing and her face lighting up in recognition. Yes! "Magnus?" she cries. Then she scans the room, her eyes widening in shock. "Where am I? What's going on here?" She scrunches her face in confusion. "The last thing I remember is being out in the woods, attacked by . . ." She trails off, catching sight of all the wings in the room. "Oh my God!" she cries. "Are we in fairyland?"

"Baby, it's okay," Magnus assures her, squeezing her tight. "You're back and I've got you and everything's going to be okay."

"What is the meaning of this?" demands the prime minister, who's recovered from his fall and is approaching the altar, an angry look on his face. He turns to the groom, his face stormy. "Apple Junior? Do you care to explain?"

The bridegroom shrugs his shoulders, looking more than a little guilty. "I'm sure I have no idea," he says sulkily.

"Well, I do."

Everyone gasps as they turn to see my mother walking into the room, shoulders back and head held high.

"Princess Shrinking Violet!" the prime minister exclaims. "Where did you come from?"

"Your prison," she replies smoothly. "Where I and my husband have been held captive by Apple Blossom and his men for nearly a month."

The prime minister's face reveals genuine shock. I guess he's not the one who ordered her imprisonment after all. "What?" he cries. "Why would he do something like that? And why wasn't I informed?"

"Simple," Mom says. "Apple Blossom had been hungering over the court's power for years. He thought he had a chance to become king by marrying me, but I chose to run away instead, leaving him stuck in the military without any real power. Now that his son is of marrying age, he thought he'd try again. Marry him to my daughter and install him as a puppet king, while keeping all the power to himself, of course."

"Actually, it's even worse than that!" interrupts a familiar voice at the back of the room. We turn to look and my eyes widen as none other than our stepmom, Heather, herself enters the chapel. Where the hell has she been? I hope she's not mixed up in the bad Slayer Inc. stuff . . .

She approaches the stage, bowing low to the prime minister before speaking. "I've journeyed to the Dark Court and back," she says. "And I have proof they were not involved at all in Queen Tatiana's murder."

"What?" the Prime Minister cries. "But if not them, then who?"

"Apple Blossom," Heather pronounces, looking scornfully at the groom. "He had her killed and blamed the Dark Court. That way, he could not only gain the power he sought through his son becoming king, but also gain support for the fairy war he's been itching to start for years."

The prime minister stares at Heather in horror. "This can't be!" he cries. He turns to Apple Seed. "Is this true?" he demands. "Did your father do all of this?"

"You should know your father is dead," Mom adds. "So don't go thinking he's going to save you from any of this."

Baby Apple hangs his head in shame. "I didn't want to go along with it." He sniffles. "But my dad . . . he's really strict. And he doesn't exactly take no for an answer." He sounds so dejected I almost feel bad for the kid.

"Guards, take him away!" the prime minister commands, evidently having heard enough. Two burly fairy guards approach and grab the boy's arms, dragging him offstage. The prime minister watches him go, shaking his head sorrowfully. Then he turns back to us.

"Princess Violet," he says, bowing low to my mother. "Please forgive me. I had no idea any of this was going on. They told me that your daughter had willingly come to fairyland. I didn't know she was under a spell." He lets out a slow breath. "And your mother. Nectar help us, we loved her so. It's such a tragic loss—especially to know it was by the hands of our own people . . ."

Mom lays a hand on his arm. "It's okay," she says. "We've all made our mistakes. Mine was running from fairyland to begin with. If I hadn't, none of this would have happened."

"And now we have no queen at all," the prime minister says dejectedly. "I don't know what will become of us."

Mom gives him a slow smile. "Actually, that's not true," she says.

He looks up in surprise. "Are you saying you'll let Sunshine stay?"

"I'm saying I will stay myself."

I stare at her in disbelief. Wait, what? Did she just say—

"Technically, I am still next in line for the throne, am I not?" she asks. "And I was hand trained by my mother from birth so I'm more than qualified to wear the crown. Of course, I hope it's okay I don't have my wings anymore . . ."

The prime minister's face brightens and he smiles widely. "Of course! We'll make you a pair of prosthetic ones—not a problem at all! This is such great news! The crown is yours. As it always should have been." He turns to the crowd. "Ladies and Gentlemen, I give you Queen Shrinking Violet!" he cries. The crowd cheers.

Except for me. "Mom!" I cry, horrified. "You can't—"

She turns to me, her eyes filled with affection. "Sweetie, I don't have a choice," she says. "These people need me and it is my duty to help them. I can do good here—much more so than back home. I can bring peace to the courts, end the corruption, punish those who betray us—all the things I should have done a long time ago, instead of running away." She reaches over and touches my arm with her hand. "I'm sorry. I wish there was another way."

"But you'll live here?" Sunny cries, looking as upset as I feel. "Not with us?"

She nods. "Heather will take care of you until you're eighteen and go off to college. It's something we talked about a while ago and she's agreed to help."

"You planned this all along," I realize. "Before the fairies even showed up."

Mom nods. "When your father came to Massachusetts and told me what had been going on, I realized what had to be done. We'd started making the arrangements, but were interrupted by Apple Blossom's attack."

"Wow. I had no idea . . ." I'm pretty much blown away at this point. My life and Sunny's—completely turned upside down.

"In any case, that doesn't mean I won't be around. We can Skype every night and you can come visit me every summer. And I want copies of all your report cards faxed directly to me. No slacking off just 'cause I'm not around to ground you." She looks at us, tears in her eyes. "I know it's hard. And I feel terrible for having to leave you. But I hope you understand this is for a greater good. It's my destiny. And I've learned you can't run away from your destiny."

Looking at her, standing tall and proud and noble, I realize she's right. These people need her and I can't be selfish. Just like Sunny and I want to live our lives the way we do, Mom should have the same right.

"Oh, Mom," I cry, throwing myself in her arms. "I'm going to miss you so much."

"No more than I'll miss you. My girls." She squeezes me back. "My precious, lovely girls."

We hug for what seems an eternity and then finally break free. Sunny steps forward, pulling the golden crown from her head and placing it reverentially on my mother's. I draw in a breath. She looks so beautiful. Like a real fairy queen. A swirl of pride sweeps through me as she turns to the people of fairyland. They all get on their knees, bowing respectfully. Then they rise and let out a great cheer.

And I find myself cheering right along with them.

Epilogue

Sunny

Rayne looks a little healthier than usual as she greets me at the cemetery the evening after our father's funeral a week later. She's on leave for the night from the Bloody Ford Clinic, the Vegas-based vampire rehab she's been staying at. She's still pale skinned, of course—what else would you expect from a Gothy vampire like her?—but there's a slight rose blooming on her cheeks all the same. Probably from all the regular blood she's been drinking. No more starving herself or drinking the synthetic—she's a full-fledged vampire now. And when she gets out in a few months, she'll be assigned a donor, just like the rest of the coven.

"I still can't believe he's gone," she says, staring mournfully at the mound of dirt that covers the remains of our father. Mom shipped them here from fairyland so Heather could give her husband a proper burial. "I feel like I've wasted all these years hating him. And now I can't even make up for lost time."

I reach over and grab her hand, giving her a comforting squeeze. "At least you got to say good-bye," I murmur, feeling tears well into my own eyes. "I hate that I never got a chance to see him one last time. He was a much better father than we gave him credit for."

Rayne kicks the ground with the toe of her boot. "It's weird, you know? Trying to let go of all that anger I held inside all those years? All that misplaced hatred took up a lot of room. I feel . . . I don't know. A little empty, to be honest."

I give her a rueful smile. "Well, are you talking about it? In rehab, I mean."

She nods. "I'm trying to. It's tough to open up. But I think it'll be worth it."

"I know it will be," I reply, reaching over to give her a big hug. "I love you, sis. Thanks for saving my life."

"Again," she teases.

"Yeah, yeah. Whatevs."

She pulls away from the hug and we start walking back to the parking lot. "So speaking of, what's going on with the whole evil Slayer Inc. thing?"

I frown. "Well, when I brought Jareth and his army back to Riverdale, the whole place was abandoned. Teachers, students—all gone. And it appeared they left in a hurry."

"With my blood," my sister adds, scowling. "What about Night School? Were the failed experiments there?"

"Yeah, they left all their comatose victims in that room you told us about. But with the electricity out, there was nothing to keep them alive." I shake my head as I recall the horror of that room. The smell. "Many of them died. A handful survived, but they're starved and stuck in deep comas. Teifert is putting his best people on them, though. If we can bring them back to consciousness, we might get some useful information."

Rayne shakes her head. "Wow," she says. "Well, I guess it's good Teifert and Heather aren't part of the evil faction. I'd hate to have to slay my mentor or stepmom."

"No kidding," I reply. "And the best part is—now everyone's working together. The vampires, Slayer Inc., and even the fairies. We'll totally get your DNA back before the evil part of Slayer Inc. discovers the secret formula."

"And Mom? Have you talked to her lately?"

"For about an hour last night. She's doing great. She sounds really happy. David even came for a visit last week. Sounds like they're going to try to make the long-distance relationship work."

Rayne nods approvingly. "I'm glad for her. I miss her, but I know she's doing what she has to do." She looks at me curiously. "What did you decide about your wings?" she asks.

I can feel my face turn a bit red. "I decided to keep them," I confess. "I had them trimmed down so I can fold them neatly under my clothes. But to be honest, I'm not comfortable with having them amputated just yet. I mean, what if something happens to Mom someday and they need me to take over?" I shrug.

"I thought you were determined to stay human at all costs," my sister reminds me with a small smile.

"I was," I admit. "But seeing Mom up there, facing her responsibilities head-on, well, that was pretty inspiring. So I've decided to keep my options open. Take things one day at a time. Besides," I add, after a pause, "Magnus thinks they're hot."

Rayne grins knowingly at me and we break out into giggles.

"What about you?" I ask.

"Amputated," she replies. "I decided being a vampire–vampire slayer was enough to be without adding fairy wings to boot. I guess I'm still technically a fairy. But no one has to know. Especially since I won't be caught dead wearing pink."

I smile ruefully, realizing how much I've missed her. "Oh, Rayne," I say. "Never change."

We're about to step into the limo to go back to Heather's condo when suddenly a black Jaguar screeches into the parking lot. Rayne looks at me and I shrug. A moment later, Magnus and Jareth burst from the car.

"What's wrong?" I ask, catching Magnus's white, worried face, my heart suddenly pounding in my chest.

"It's Corbin," Jareth replies.

Now Rayne's face drains of its color. "What about him?"

"He murdered the doctor doing the memory erase. And then he ransacked the coven headquarters, breaking into our safe and stealing some very top-secret documents."

"Oh God!" Rayne cries. "Do you think he . . . ?"

Jareth nods grimly. "I think he's gone back to his friends at Slayer Inc.," he says. "With information that could compromise our entire operation."

"Oh no," my sister says, leaning against a gravestone for support. "This is all my fault. If only . . ." she trails off, looking ashamed and miserable.

But I grab her and pull her to her feet, feeling my fairy powers surge inside of me. I may not be a vampire, but I'm no longer a helpless mortal girl anymore either.

"Well, then," I say, giving Magnus a confident smile, "let's go track them down. I think it's time to teach Slayer Inc. a lesson."

After all, no one messes with the Blood Coven. Not on my watch, anyway.

~ TO BE CONTINUED ~

The sixth book in the Blood Coven Vampire series
by Mari Mancusi

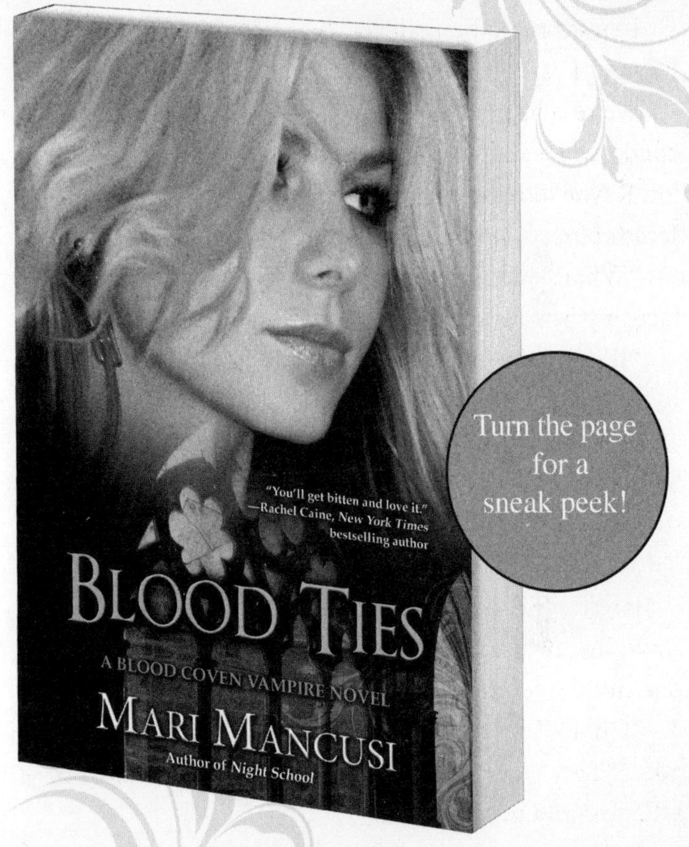

Coming Summer 2011

"The Blood Coven series is like vampire candy. Readers will devour every bite!" —Heather Brewer, *New York Times* bestselling author

www.bloodcovenvampires.com

penguin.com

"Hey, Sunny, over here!"

I look up from stuffing my field hockey stick into my bag, my eyes widening with horror as they fall upon a long, black stretch limousine, pulling up curbside to my new high school, behind the waiting school bus. The window slides down and from inside I can see Magnus, still shadowed in the darkness, beckoning for me to come over. I try to pretend I don't hear him. Don't even know him. So of course that makes him shout even louder.

"Oi! Sunny! I'm right here!"

"Whoa, who's the hottie?" whistles Kierra, the field hockey center and one of the only potential friends I've managed to score my first week here at Las Vegas High School. In other words, the last person on Earth I want to introduce to the master of the Blood Coven—one of the largest vampire groups on the Eastern Seaboard—aka my current boyfriend, Magnus. Who, I might add, may soon become my *former* boyfriend Magnus if he doesn't pull away from my high school parking lot in the next five seconds.

Kierra squints to get a better glimpse into the luxurious limo. I mean, really, Magnus? A freaking limo? Could we get any more *My Super Sweet Sixteen* if we tried? These girls are so going to get the wrong idea about me.

"Wow, Sunny," chimes in Hana, the goalie. "You've been holding out on us!"

Magnus grins, tossing the girls a friendly wave. My only saving grace is the knowledge that he'll literally catch on fire if he tries to step out of the car and into the sweltering Vegas sunshine.

"Is he your boyfriend?" Taylar, the midfielder, queries.

I try to send Magnus mental signals to vacate the premises. If only I had vampire telepathy like Rayne does with Jareth. Then again, I think she only has the ability to summon her boyfriend *to* her, not away. Which, evidently, I don't need special superpowers to do.

I realize the three girls are staring at me questioningly. "Oh, him?" I stammer. "He's just . . . some guy I know."

"Yeah. Some guy in a *limo*!" Taylar adds. "It's like, seriously so Chuck Bass in *Gossip Girl*!" She pretends to swoon.

"Yeah! And you're like Blair!" gushes Kierra. "Except, you know, without the designer wardrobe." The three girls study my tank top and jeans ensemble from Old Navy with critical eyes. I am so going to kill Magnus. What is he even doing awake this time of day, anyway?

"Hi, Chuck Bass!" coos Hana, running over to the limo and sticking her head in. She's quickly joined by Taylar and Kierra. "Buy any hotels lately?"

Magnus cocks his head in question. "I'm sorry?"

"Um, he doesn't get out much. I mean, stay in much," I interject, running to the car and pushing them aside. "I mean, he doesn't watch a lot of TV."

"Actually, I do quite enjoy *The Vampire Diaries*," Magnus interjects with a sly smile.

Oh. My. God.

The field hockey players squee in unison, squeezing past me, their heads all trying to fit through the limo window at once.

"Want to come hang with us?" Hana asks.

"We're going to crash the Mandalay pool to catch some rays," adds Kierra.

"And no offense, man, but you sure look like you can use some," teases Taylar playfully.

"I appreciate your offer, ladies," Magnus says grandly. "But I must regretfully decline. Perhaps another day, or night, I mean, after the sun goes down."

Okay, that's it. I'm done. I push through the blockade of girls and yank open the limo door. "Sorry, they're busy," I reply, before any of them can answer. I dive into the limo and slam the door shut behind me. "See you guys tomorrow!" I cry, stabbing at the window button, praying it will move faster the more times I press it.

"Can we, like, go?" I bite at the chauffeur as I watch my new friends try to squint through the one-way glass. Luckily the guy obliges and we pull out of the school parking lot at long last. Excellent. Now I can at least die of embarrassment off of school property.

"Sunny?" I realize Magnus is staring at me questioningly.

I turn to him. "What the hell was that, Magnus?" I demand.

"What was what?" he asks innocently. "I just thought you'd like a ride home."

"Yeah. In a school bus. Or a normal car. Not a stretch limo.

Do you know what they're going to think of me now?" I can just imagine them texting their friends as we speak. Three days at my new school and I'm already going to be limo girl with the bad wardrobe.

"I'm sorry, Sunny," Magnus replies, sounding slightly amused. "But limos are just easier for me to get around in during the day." He pauses, then adds. "Next time I'll bring the Jag."

Argh. I flop back in my seat, so giving up.

"What's wrong?"

"What's wrong?" I repeat. "Hmm, I don't know, Magnus. How about the fact that I'm starting a new school and I'm trying to make friends and fit in. That's not easy to do when my vampire boyfriend shows up with a limo and starts talking all weird to my friends."

"Come on," he cajoles. "I thought vampires were all the rage with high school girls these days."

I glower at him. "Only if they sparkle."

Magnus starts laughing at this. I try to frown, to keep being mad, but I have to admit, it is kind of funny. And soon I find myself giggling alongside of him.

"Am I forgiven then?" he asks fondly, looking at me with his beautiful emerald eyes.

I grunt. "Oh, I suppose." I curl into his cool body, rejoicing at the feel of his long, lean frame pressed up against me. After all those lonely nights at Riverdale Slay School, I can't resist a little cuddle from the guy every now and then. Even if he does refuse to follow orders to stay away from my high school.

"Sorry," I say sheepishly. "I know you meant well. It's just . . . I'm in a weird situation, you know? Going to a new school, trying to get people to like me . . ."

"Who wouldn't like you?" Magnus asks, planting a kiss on my freckled nose. "You're perfect."

"*You're* prejudiced."

"Maybe so." He tosses his head arrogantly. "But I've also had a thousand years' experience to draw from. These girls you're trying to impress? They've got seventeen, eighteen, tops."

I can't help but giggle. "So you're saying in a thousand years of searching, you've never found a girl as perfect as me."

"Vampire's honor," he says, holding his fingers up in a Boy Scout pose. Then he grabs me and pulls me close to him, kissing me hungrily on the mouth. I kiss him back, enjoying the feel of his soft lips moving against my own. It's so good to have him back in my arms. I just pray he doesn't have to leave again.

"So I may have to leave again," he announces suddenly, pulling away from the kiss.

"What? Why?"

He slumps back in his seat. "The consortium may have found a lead as to where the Slayer Inc. fringe group is hiding out. They want me to go investigate it."

"Isn't that more like Jareth's job? You know, the hands-on kind of stuff? No offense, baby, but you're more politician than warrior."

He scowls. "Um, former knight in shining armor, remember?" he says, patting his chest. "And in any case, Jareth's coming along, too. In fact, the majority of consortium leaders are mobilizing for this. It's just too big a risk to be taken lightly. Especially now that Corbin's stolen some valuable information from the Blood Coven that can be used against us."

Corbin. The vampire slayer my sister almost killed by drinking his blood. Jareth saved his life by turning him into a vampire.

But let's just say the guy wasn't so grateful for the favor. Now he's on the loose and probably hell-bent on revenge against the entire coven. Not to mention my sister.

"Okay, then," I say, gearing up for the challenge. I guess normal high school life will have to be put on hold again. "Let's swing by the house and I'll pack a bag."

Magnus frowns.

"What?" I ask.

"Sunny, you're not coming."

"Um, excuse me?" Is he for real?

"It's going to be war," Magnus reminds me. "It's too dangerous for you."

"Hello, Magnus!" I wave to him. "Fairy princess, remember? No longer the fragile human girl you need to protect from harm. I want to help."

But my boyfriend just shakes his head. "I don't think it's a good idea, Sunny. If anything were to happen to you, I'd never forgive myself. Not to mention, just having you there would be . . . a distraction."

I stare at him, mouth agape. I can't believe it. Once again I'm being shut out.

"Look, Sun, I'm not trying to be a jerk here . . ."

"Well, then you're failing miserably," I retort. "Driver, stop the car. I'm going to walk the rest of the way." The driver slows down.

"No!" Magnus cries. "Keep going." The driver sighs, then speeds up again.

As if that's going to stop me. "Fine, have it your way." I press the button to open the skylight, then push my head through. I can hear Magnus protesting below as I crawl out the window, unfurl my wings out the sides of my tank top, and flutter off the moving vehicle and down onto the nearby sidewalk, leaving my sun-allergic boyfriend stuck in the car, trying desperately to close the skylight.

"Sunny!" he cries furiously, banging on the window. But I ignore him, stuffing my wings back under my shirt. (It's better not to risk walking around as a fairy in daylight, though in Vegas, technically anything goes.) Then I storm off down the street heading toward my family's high-rise condo just off the Strip.

"Stay at home, Sunny," I mutter under my breath. "It's way too dangerous, Sunny." I'm so sick of everyone thinking I'm the weak one. After all, no one ever says stuff like that to Rayne. In fact, she's actually assigned death-defying adventures for a living. But as for me, I might as well be made of freaking glass, according to Magnus and the rest of the sorry vampire race.

It's so freaking unfair.

I walk down an alley through a shortcut off the Strip. About halfway through, I wonder if I've made a wise choice. The shadows in the dark seem to claw at me menacingly and I keep hearing strange catlike mews echoing through the air. I wrap my hands around my arms and pick up the pace.

Suddenly a loud clattering sound makes me practically jump out of my skin. I whirl around, my eyes catching movement in the darkness. A shadow that can only be human.

"Who's there?" I demand. "Stay back! I've got Mace and I know how to use it." I don't really, of course. But I do have some fairy powers to unfurl if push comes to shove.

"S-S-Sunny?" a weak but familiar voice cries. "Is that really you?"

"Jayden?" I exclaim, rushing toward the shadow. "I've been looking all—"

I stop short as my eyes fall upon the figure on the ground.

While it's definitely Jayden—my best Vegas friend and maybe something more—at the same time he looks . . . wrong somehow. Scarily skinny, all bones and sinew, his eyes are black and hollow-looking and his mouth is bloodstained. I realize in horror he's holding something furry and dead and half-eaten in his hands.

"Oh my God!" I cry. "What happened to you?"

He looks up with pitiful, scared eyes. "Sunny," he whimpers. "You've got to help me. I think . . . I think I might have been turned into a vampire."

The Blood Coven Vampire Novels
by Mari Mancusi

Boys That Bite

Stake That

Girls That Growl

Bad Blood

Night School

"Delightful, surprising, and engaging—you'll get bitten, and love it."
—Rachel Caine, *New York Times* bestselling author

Don't miss *Blood Ties*, the next book in the Blood Coven Vampire series, coming Summer 2011 from Berkley!

www.bloodcovenvampires.com

penguin.com

T126.1010